ROWAN WOOD LEGENDS

OLIVIA WILDENSTEIN

ROWAN WOOD LEGENDS
BOOK 2 OF THE LOST CLAN SERIES

For information contact:
OLIVIA WILDENSTEIN
http://oliviawildenstein.com

Cover art by *Celin Chen*
Under cover art by *Oksana @__alex_oxy__*
Painting of Ace & Cat by *@artbysteffani*
Portraits of Catori and Ace created using *Midjourney*
Editing by *Becky Stephens & Jessica Nelson*
Proofreading by *Josiah Davis & Rachel Theus Cass*

DISCLAIMER

The Gottwas are a fictional tribe inspired by the Ojibwe People. I did not want to cause offense to Native Americans by writing about customs and traditions that aren't mine.

GOTTWA GLOSSARY

aabiti: mate

    abiwoojin: darling

    adsookin: legend

    baseetogan: fae world; Neverra; Isle of Woods

    bazash: half-fae, half-human

    chatwa: darkness

    debwe: truth

    gajeekwe: the king's advisor, like a minister

    gatizogin: I'm sorry

    Gejaiwe: the Great Spirit

    gassen: faerie dust

    gingawi: part-hunter, part-fae

    golwinim: faerie guards (firefly shifters)

    gwe: woman

    ishtu: sweetness

    kwenim: memory

    ley: light

    ma kwenim: my memory

    maahin: come forth

    Makudewa Geezhi: Dark Day

manazi: book
mashka: tough
mawa: mine
meegwe: give me
meekwa: blood
naagangwe: stop her
pahan: faeries
tokwa: favor

FAELI GLOSSARY

alinum: rowan wood
  astium: portal, door
  calidum: lesser fae; *bazash*
  caligo: mist
  caligosubi: one who lives below the mist, aka marsh-dweller
  caligosupra: one who lives above the mist, aka mist-dweller
  calimbor: sky-trees
  captis: magnetize
  clave: portal locksmith
  draca: first guard; *wariff's* protector (dragon shifter)
  enefkum: eunuch
  fae: sky-dwellers; Seelie fae
  forma: underground-dwellers; the Unseelie fae
  gajoï: favor
  hareni: Neverrian grotto
  kalini: fire
  lucionaga: faerie guards
  mallow: an edible plant; faerie weed; doesn't affect humans the
same way it affects faeries and hunters are immune

Massin: Your Highness
Neverra: baseetogan; Isle of Woods

Don't just make a wish...
Make it come true.

I

THE FORK

I stared around our small wooden dinner table at my father and aunt, and swallowed, not for the first time, to displace the throb of fear still pulsing inside my throat. I'd almost lost one of them to an ancient spell; the same spell that had stolen Mom from me.

If I hadn't reached them in time...

If Ace hadn't phoned and Kajika hadn't run...

The throbbing grew so insistent that I clasped my glass of water and chugged down the icy contents. It soothed me, the same way Dad and Aylen's lively chatter about cooking lulled my nerves.

"How about I teach you how to make the fried rice tomorrow, Cat?" my aunt asked.

"I'd love that." I speared a few peas onto my fork and slid them into my mouth.

My enthusiasm enchanted my aunt who went into more details about the proper way to fold eggs into the rice while Dad leaned back with his beer and shot me the slyest eyeroll. He loved Aylen, but my aunt was the human equivalent of a can of Red Bull, which could be slightly exhausting at times. After so much death and dying, though, I was all about vivaciousness.

Between cooking pointers and filling my hollow stomach with sustenance, I began to feel better . . . more human.

Spending the afternoon with Kajika in the tree house had probably helped, too. The hunter was a new comforting presence in the strange world that had become mine after Mom had dug up the rose petal grave that contained our ancestor. One by the name of Gwenelda who acted as though this were still the 1800s and faeries were the most horrid beasts to prowl the Earth.

I did not hold the fae in such contempt. Perhaps because I hadn't lived through the massacre—the Dark Day or *Makudewa Geezhi* as the Gottwas called it. Or perhaps it was because I was *gingawi*—mixed—half-hunter, half-faerie. An atrocity in the eyes of both species.

At least, I'd *been* an abomination until this afternoon in the tree house. Sure, Kajika had been reluctant to accept my offer of friendship, but I suspected that had more to do with my uncanny resemblance to his dead mate, Ishtu—his greatest heartbreak. Unless what had sanded down his revulsion to the fae wasn't me at all, but his fledgling alliance with Cruz and the prince of Fairyland.

Prince... I still couldn't believe Ace Wood was actual royalty, even though he totally had the personality for it. I wondered where he'd flitted off to after my father and Aylen almost resuscitated Elika, Gwen's mother.

Although the circle of rowan trees wasn't visible from our kitchen window, I peered past the crocheted white curtain at the heaps of snow glittering like sprinkled sugar atop the ocean of headstones.

My entire childhood, I'd wanted to live anywhere but in a graveyard, but now, I was glad for where my grandfather had built our house for it allowed me to keep an eye on the nine remaining, undug graves.

I balanced my fork on my index finger as I thought of the hibernating hunters. The utensil teetered like a seesaw until I found its center of gravity somewhere close to its neck. Would I ever find a balance between my two sides?

I imagined the tines were my faerie side, and the butt of the fork was my hunter side. For a while, both remained aligned, but it was a fork, and I wasn't a utensil.

The doorbell rang.

The fork wobbled and fell prong-side down against my plate with a startlingly loud ding.

"Are you expecting company, Cat?" Dad's chair legs squeaked as he pushed away from the table.

"I didn't invite anyone." But when had that ever stopped people from bursting into my home and my life? "I got it, Dad." I tossed my napkin beside my plate and walked to the front door.

A teeny, tiny part of me hoped Kajika was standing behind it. Or Ace, because I had a boatload of questions for him.

I swung the door wide and gaped at our visitor who was neither a hunter nor a prince.

2

THE CORPSE

My best friend's brother was wringing his trooper cap between his fingers as though it was waterlogged, but it was as dry as my throat.

"Hi, Cat. Um . . . is your dad here?" Jimmy asked.

"D-Dad?"

The floorboards creaked as Dad approached. "I'm right here, Jim."

Jimmy's large forehead was pasty and slick with sweat. Since no one sweat in below-freezing weather, my pulse accelerated.

"Sorry to disturb you so late, Derek, but we got a body for you."

Panic shot up my spine. "A body?"

"Whose body?" Dad and I asked at the same time.

Jimmy wiped his forehead with the back of his hand, then set his cap back on top of his head. "Holly."

"Holly?" I whispered. "Holly died?" My breaths surged up fast. Too fast. They made my head spin and quickened my heartbeat.

Black dots flickered on the edge of my eyesight, fragmenting Jimmy's face. I zipped my hand out to grab ahold of something before I keeled over like my fork.

That something was Dad's sleeve. My body swayed, and the

4

next thing I knew, Dad had one arm around my waist and was steering me toward the couch.

He settled me down while Aylen dashed out of the kitchen clutching a glass of water, which she slipped into my shaky fingers.

"How?" I croaked. "*How*?"

"Her great-nephew dropped by the station to report her passing. Now, we're pretty sure it was a natural death, even though she had—" He stopped short.

"What did she have?" I asked.

"I think she might have contracted chicken pox or something."

She was a faerie. Faeries didn't contract human diseases, did they?

"Sheriff Jones would like your father to validate the cause of death."

"That's not—not really my area of expertise." Dad's complexion had become as ashen as the new headstone that graced our land, the one that now marked Blake's grave.

Oh, why did I have to go and think of him? Tears leaked from my eyes and blurred everything around me.

"I know, Derek, but maybe you could give us your thoughts. Could we bring her here?"

"Of course, but—"

Jimmy was already on his phone, so Dad stopped talking.

"EMTs are on their way," Jimmy said after disconnecting.

"Where's her great-nephew?" Dad's gaze warmed the side of my face. Did he think Kajika was behind Holly's death?

"I don't know. He seemed distraught. Which I suppose is normal considering the circumstances. He said he would meet us at the farmhouse, but he never did."

Dad stole another disquieting glance at me. "Did you have time to question him at the station?"

"Like I said, he was distraught. And then, when we asked him for his alibi, he said he'd been with Catori all afternoon."

5

My cheeks smoldered, the only warm spot on my chilled body. Not even the salty dampness could cool them down.

"Her car broke down a couple miles away, so they had to get it back from the towing company." Dad peered beyond Jimmy, squinting into the darkness. "Actually, where is your car, Cat?"

"I, uh . . . it wasn't ready." The lie made my pulse hammer.

I hated deceiving my father, and yet, ever since Mom had passed, ever since I'd found out about faeries and hunters, I'd been feeding him lies almost every day. I called it shielding him from the truth.

Still, lies.

"I thought you ran out of gas," he said.

"There's actually a problem with the fuel gauge." *Liar. Liar. Liar.*

When Ace had called to tell us Aylen and Dad were digging up a hunter grave, I had mere minutes to reach the cemetery. Cars didn't go that fast. But hunters did. So I'd abandoned the car on the side of the road and allowed Kajika to run me home.

Dad's eyebrows peaked.

"They said it would be ready tomorrow," I added.

Tires crunched the gravel, taking the focus off my missing Honda. A whirling red light ignited the night. Even our living room turned red and maroon from the powerful strobes.

"*Did* you spend the afternoon with Kajika, Cat?" Jimmy asked.

"Yes."

"You ain't covering up for him, are you?" he continued.

"No." I finally located a modicum of strength, enough to make me rise from the couch and rise to Kajika's defense. "Kajika wouldn't murder Holly."

Dad placed a gentle hand on my shoulder. "No one said anything about murder, honey."

Neither his hand nor his words soothed me, and when they wheeled Holly in, the emotional rollercoaster I'd ridden all day took yet another treacherous turn.

I approached the stretcher. They'd forgone the body bag.

Instead, they'd wrapped her in the thick comforter Gwen had kept tucked around Holly's deteriorating body.

A vicious rash covered her exposed skin, including her scalp. Pink bumps meshed with her sparse white hair.

I bit back a surge of bile.

"Honey?" Dad lifted my chin with his finger. "Why don't you help Aylen make tea?"

I was pretty sure Aylen could handle boiling water on her own.

I backed up as Dad spearheaded the small cortege and led them down to the morgue.

I didn't follow them.

I also didn't make tea.

I took my phone out of my sweater pocket to dial Kajika but realized he didn't have a phone.

My hands shook.

My heart shook.

The timeliness of Holly's death irked me. Yes, she was ninety-nine years old and ill, but how convenient that she'd died the day the book she'd sent me—*The Wytchen Tree*—the book that held all of her secrets, and now all of mine, had been stolen.

The brand Cruz Vega had burned atop my hand flared, a V-shaped trail of fire. I hated the mark; this magical leash that kept me tethered to a faerie I despised, allowing him to track my every move.

I was still bitter about how he'd weaseled out the location of the book by using the faerie bargain I'd unintentionally struck when I'd asked him to resuscitate Gwenelda. The pain of the claimed *gajoï* was the worst physical pain that existed, akin to being all at once quartered and compressed.

My brand grew warmer, brighter at the abhorrent memory.

I wasn't sure whom I hated more at that moment—Cruz or Stella. Where Cruz had never been a friend, Stella had been almost family.

7

Where Cruz and I had spent a handful of hours of together, I'd known Stella nineteen years.

Where I'd never loved Cruz, I'd loved Stella.

As cupboards clacked and the tea kettle whistled, I strode out my front door, brimming with barely-contained anger. I didn't think fresh air would cool me down, but it beat standing listlessly in the living room, replaying how easily I'd been duped by not one, but two faeries.

I kicked the beam holding up our porch, but that did little to flush the tension from my body.

"What did that poor piece of wood do to you, Kitty Cat?"

I whirled around, heart vaulting into my throat.

Ace was leaning against the railing, arms folded in front of his chest, skin glowing like the moon.

8

3

THE BLAME

The left side of Ace's face was splashed red from the strobe light atop the EMT van, which the responders had left on even though they were all huddled in the morgue downstairs.

"You okay?" Ace's eyes blazed like faceted blue topazes.

"Peachy."

His gaze ran over my face. "You sure?"

"Holly just died," I blurted out.

"I know." His lips barely shifted as he spoke.

"You know?"

"That's one of the reasons why I'm here. I came to collect her."

Goosebumps scattered over my arms. "Collect her?"

"Faeries disintegrate."

"What?" I gasped but then added, "Shh," as I remembered Aylen was in the kitchen, mere feet away.

My aunt was oblivious to the existence of faeries and hunters.

"Cat, unless you want to end up with a pile of gray ash in your basement, I need to take her away."

"How come she hasn't transformed into one already?"

9

He unfolded his arms and stalked toward me. Probably to slip past me and get to Holly.

I whipped up my palm and pressed it against his torso to stop him. "There are lots of people downstairs."

He looked down at my splayed hand, then back up into my face, technicolor irises pulsing with annoyance. He could be annoyed all he wanted by my obstruction, but no way was I letting him through.

"There must still be some fire in her veins. But it will burn out soon."

My fingers tingled with my frenzied pulse, which lit up my stupid brand. Blushing—the Great Spirit only knew why—I yanked my hand away. What was I doing touching this guy?

"How did you even know she was dead?" I crossed my arms.

"Gregor sent me to ask her how to read the book. You know, the one you didn't want to give me because you didn't trust me."

"I didn't want to give it to you because it was *mine*."

"Cat, who are you talking to?" Aylen's voice snuck around my neck, and then she was there, right beside me, because my aunt never passed up a chance to butt into conversations.

The mug she held slipped from her fingers, splashing boiling tea onto my legs. Although I jerked to the side, the warm liquid penetrated into the stretchy leather and singed the side of my right leg.

I gritted my teeth. I'd endured worse pain, but damn, did that sting.

"Oh . . . Great . . . freaking . . . Spirit, you're Ace Wood!" she all but shrieked.

Like when she'd met Lily at Bee's Place, she was transfixed by the sight of the male before her. And she wasn't even aware that he was a magical prince with fire beneath his skin that made him glow like toxic waste.

Though she was *gingawi* like me, Aylen had been spared the sight—one of the hunter gifts bestowed upon me. My other gift was, according to Ace, smelling like decaying flesh to faeries. Did Aylen smell or was she spared that hunter trait as well?

"Aylen, right?" Ace offered my aunt a decorous smile that didn't quite reach his eyes but that made Aylen so weak in the knees that she swayed a little. "Catori's told me so much about you."

Aylen flapped one hand in front of her face while sticking out the other. Oh my God, was my aunt actually *fanning* herself? That was sure to go straight to Ace's head and inflate it some more.

"I'm sorry, but I don't shake hands. It's an old pet peeve of mine." Aylen sulked, so Ace added, "A crazed fan tried to poison me once."

"Was that crazed fan a hunter?" I asked sweetly.

Aylen didn't react to my needling comment, too starstruck. Then again, I hadn't said *faerie* hunter. That would probably have gotten a reaction.

Ace's lips stretched the slightest bit higher. In response to my question or simply for Aylen's sake? "It's truly been a pleasure to meet you, Aylen."

That kindled a vigorous smile onto my aunt's face.

"Now I—"

"It's a pleasure to meet you, too, Mr. Wood. Actually, it's way more than a pleasure. It's an honor!" Out of the corner of her mouth, she stage-whispered, "Cat, why didn't you tell me Ace Wood was your friend?"

"Because we're *not* friends."

Ace hiked up a dark brow that vanished beneath a lock of golden hair. Had he believed we were friends? Not only had our interactions been few, but ninety-nine-point-two percent of the time, they'd been anything but friendly.

"Your niece is a difficult girl to seduce into friendship."

Aylen cooed something unintelligible while I glowered.

Seduce? Really? "I like my friends honorable, and honorable people are hard to find."

Aylen gagged on a shocked breath. "Excuse my niece," she said between coughs. "She's been through a lot."

Ace tipped me a brazen smile, fingers indolently dragging a lock of hair off his forehead. He had really nice fingers, long and solid with blunt nails that seemed to have been polished to a high-shine. "I'm certain I'll win her over, eventually."

That cut my ogling short. What was I doing admiring any part of this male's body in the first place. I snorted a murmured, "When the *baseetogan* freezes over . . ."

That merely cemented Ace's grin.

"Can I ask a teeny tiny question?" Aylen stepped in front of me, fur slippers crunching on the shards of her forgotten mug, and reeled her mascara-laden lashes high. "I read something about you expecting your first child in the fall. Is it true?"

Again, I jerked, but not because of any tea this time. "A baby?"

A muscle leapt in his jaw. And was that a blush that stole across his sharp cheekbones? "*I'm* not. My fiancée is." His tone was blunt and somewhat bitter, definitely not embarrassed.

"So it's true," Aylen exclaimed. "Oh my God, oh my God, oh my God! I need to call my friends." She clapped her hand in front of her mouth, her opal ring flashing red in the revolving strobe light.

I imagined the stone was set in iron, and iron singed faeries, which explained why Ace hadn't shaken her hand. Or maybe, he really did have a thing against being touched.

"Sorry. I should've asked for your permission first. Maybe you don't want anyone knowing the rumors are true."

His jaw ticked again. "It's no secret."

And yet *I* hadn't heard of it. Then again I didn't read gossip columns all that regularly.

"They're going to *flip*." She pulled her cell phone out of her jeans' pocket and started typing a message when her thumbs froze over the screen. "Can I take a picture with you?"

Before Ace could even answer, she'd raised her phone in the air and snapped a selfie. "*Eek!*" Yes, Aylen, my thirty-six-year-old aunt, actually produced that sound as she started typing manically, probably posting the picture all over social media. "Hey, chica, you'll never believe who I just met."

She stepped around the puddle flecked with ceramic shards, too entranced by her piece of gossip to remember the mess.

I knelt down and began collecting the pieces but froze when I spied the word *Mom* in white lettering on a blue chunk. I delicately scooped it up and cradled it in my palm, wishing what little faerie magic I possessed could mend objects, but faerie magic only worked on living—

I craned my neck so fast it cracked. "Can you call Holly's soul back?" True faeries—not a half-breed like myself—could resuscitate the dead.

"It's too late."

"You didn't even try."

"It has to happen in the seconds following a person's death. Besides, do you really want to owe me?"

"This wasn't me striking a bargain, Ace. This was me asking you to be kind. Compassionate."

"Same thing. Different wording."

So Holly was really gone.

Just like Mom.

Just like Blake.

"She was sickly." His timbre gentled, as though he truly regretted that this old woman had died, but my ears were surely playing tricks on me, because Ace Wood had the compassion of a vinyl sticker. "I doubt she would've wanted to come back."

He was probably right, but had it really been her time to die? I stared at the navy shards at my feet. Everything was breaking or falling to pieces around me. With shaky fingers, I started collecting the remnants of the mug I'd bought Mom with my pocket money when I was nine.

Ace crouched in front of me. "Are you crying?"

The scorching heat from his skin blasted my downturned face, heating my stinging eyes. "No."

"Liar."

I inhaled a slow, deep breath in an attempt to calm the whirlpool of emotion spinning inside of me. "I'm just tired."

I didn't confess that what really bothered me was that everything I cared about broke and everyone I cared for died.

Maybe I should just stop caring.

Maybe that was the solution.

"Move your hands, Cat. I got it."

I sat back on my heels and watched his palms hover over the debris.

Blue flames flickered over his skin and then scattered over the thick porcelain, incinerating it before my very eyes. Instead of turning to ash or melting, all traces of the broken mug evaporated into thin air.

I stared wide-eyed at the empty space. "How come the slats didn't catch fire?"

"We focus our fire on what we need burned."

That's how Cruz had made vomit vanish from the hearse the night I met him!

That's how he'd cleaned up the dish that had fallen out of my father's hands and shattered on our kitchen floor!

"Neat party trick," I muttered, still clutching the larger shards which his fire hadn't touched.

"Perhaps I'll teach you someday."

My fingers spasmed, and the shards glided onto the spotless floor. Hunters didn't have fire, which meant Ace was aware of my secret.

4

THE SECRET

I slid my lips against one another, the ceramic shards dancing in the pool of spilled tea. "Have you forgotten that I'm a hunter?"

"But you aren't solely a hunter, now are you, Miss Price?"

I towed my gaze off the cracked mug and held his stare. "How long?"

"How long, what?"

"How long have you known?"

Ace unfurled his long, lean body until he towered over me. It struck me as droll that I'd called him diminutive. The faerie prince was anything but undersized.

Yes, Kajika was taller, but Ace's chest and shoulders strained the white fabric of his button-down, hinting at days devoted to weightlifting or sprite-throwing or whatever sport was popular among the fae.

"Remember when I stopped you from eating the cupcake back at Astra's?"

I tugged my attention off his muscled torso. "You told her I was allergic to beets."

I found out later that they were spiked with mallow, a hallu-

15

cinogenic Neverrian leaf that didn't affect hunters, but which made faeries high and humans overeat.

"I had my suspicions then, but after seeing your dilated pupils that day in the attic, I was sure you had some faerie blood."

I finally stood, clutching the shard painted with the word 'Mom.' "What spurred your suspicions?"

He dipped his chin ever so slightly and regarded me through narrowed eyes. It was a look I imagined an entomologist giving a new specimen of insects. "The way you smelled."

"You mean, like rot and garbage?"

His mouth seemed to tighten as though he was trying to restrain the truth from slipping out.

"Oh my God, you lied. I don't smell like week-old trash!" I should've been relieved, but instead, I was wholly furious. He'd made me feel so freaking self-conscious. "Asshole." The slight passed my lips before I could think better of insulting a man who wielded fire while I did not. When he didn't incinerate me, I asked, "You owe me the truth now. What do I smell like?"

"I don't owe you anything, Miss Price."

"Fine. Whatever. I don't care how I smell to you, even though now I regret my scent isn't noxious. Then maybe it would keep you away."

I started to turn when he said, "Sickly sweet."

"Sickly sweet? *Wow*. Great."

The sharp apple in his throat glided up and down once before settling. "Word on the street is that you can choose. Like your ancestor."

I wondered what 'street.' An earthly one or a Neverrian one? "I can, but I won't."

His eyes scraped down the bridge of my nose, settling on my lips for the briefest of moments. "Why the hell not?"

I rubbed the word I'd gotten inked into my skin—*human*. "Because I'd rather stay exactly the way I am."

"Why?"

Deciding to put an end to this pointless debate, I asked, "So faeries don't know how to read English?"

"Excuse me?"

"You said you came to Rowan to ask Holly how to read the book."

That earned me a snort. "We know how to read English."

"I don't understand then."

"The pages are blank."

My heart jumped. I'd read stories on those pages. I'd seen words. I'd even seen a diagram. Had I imagined everything? No, Aylen had seen things too. "Stella read the book with Aylen."

Ace scrutinized my face. "Stella said Aylen read things out loud to her, so I'm assuming the ink only appears to those who have the sight."

"Except Aylen doesn't . . ."

"So maybe it appears to hunters."

"I'm not a hunter."

"Oh, you know what I mean." He dug something from his pocket and handed it to me. It was a ripped piece of paper.

My gaze skimmed over the words:

The Wytchen Tree
Copyright © 1938

And then there was a little symbol of a tree. I assumed it was supposed to be a rowan wood rendering.

"You see something?" he whispered.

I considered telling him it was blank but chose to go with the truth; if Stella knew Aylen could read it, then it was no secret. And perhaps it would force them to return it to me.

I nodded.

"That's what I thought."

"It's all just a bunch of myths and legends inside, Ace."

"If that was all there was, then why did Holly make her text invisible to faeries?" His attention traveled to the 'V' glowing atop my knuckles. "And why did your pulse just speed up?"

"Because I'm human, and I have a heart. Which beats. You know, to keep me alive? Don't you have one?"

"Me? What would I need a heart for?"

"Right. It would just get in the way. Just like a conscience, huh?"

The metallic clank of the stretcher alerted us to company.

Ace's demeanor sharpened as he peered beyond me into my house. "Please, Cat, what did you see in the book?" His voice was hushed with a dash of agitation.

I studied his profile—the stiffness of his mouth, the tic of his jaw, the incandescent glow of his irises. "Give it back, and I'll tell you."

He rubbed the back of his neck. "It's not mine to give back."

"Well, it wasn't yours to give away in the first place."

"I'm sorry."

"I am too." A realization prodded my chest, slowing my heartbeats. "That day in the attic, you said Gregor ordered you to kill Holly."

He took a step back even though I hadn't taken a step forward. If I had, we'd have been chest to chest. "I can't believe you'd think me capable of murdering an old woman."

"I think you capable of murdering plenty of people."

He levitated and loomed over me.

I was too riled up to be intimidated by his little show of dominance, or whatever the heck had prompted him to float higher. "You're the one who told me Gregor wanted her dead if she didn't cooperate. You said—"

"I know what I said. Just like I know what I did." He flicked his gaze to the living room, at the two approaching EMTs. "This conversation isn't over," he muttered, shooting up into the sky.

Finally, something we could agree on.

A small object glinted in the air, then clinked against my porch. Had a coin escaped Ace's pocket?

I squinted.

It was no quarter.

I shot my gaze in the direction of the hearse.

Next to it sat my Honda.

Had Ace—Had *Ace* brought my car back? Just before the stretcher rolled over them, I swiped them off the floor and squeezed them tight.

My accusation of him being a murderous creature began to taste bitter. Perhaps the prince of Neverra wasn't completely heartless. Heartless people didn't bother collecting a stranger's car from highways or impound lots or wherever my car had ended up.

Unless . . . unless they needed a favor. My palm drifted protectively to my stomach.

Did I owe Ace for bringing back my car?

5

THE VANISHING BODY

After Jimmy and the EMTs left, after my father went to bed without having determined a cause of death, Aylen stayed up with me.

"You know, Mom used to tell me and Nova this *adsookin*—this legend—at bedtime. That the Gottwas used special wood to bury their dead. Rowan wood. Apparently it has magical properties. At least, that's what our tribe thought."

I looked away.

"They also used to wrap their sick in rowan bark and stick them in sweat lodges. Apparently rowan smoke worked wonders on the new diseases the settlers brought with them from Europe."

With my eyes, I traced the cherry pattern on the ceramic bowl I'd painted during Cass's seventh birthday party. It sat in the middle of our wooden coffee table, a gash of vermillion in our navy living room.

Aylen crouched in front of our fireplace, holding a long match to the wad of fluffy lint she'd scraped off our dryer's filter. Fire ignited and consumed the gray fluff before spreading to the logs.

"I'm making a rowan wood fire in honor of Holly. Apparently, the smoke will help guide her to the Great Spirit."

Holly had chosen to become fae. I doubted the Great Spirit wanted anything to do with her. But maybe our Great Spirit was forgiving.

Aylen sat back on her heels and stared at the fire. "It's crazy to think that such a large tribe was entirely decimated. That we're the last. And we're not even pure Gottwa. It almost feels as though we're the last of our kind. Maybe that's how dinosaurs felt."

I smiled at her comparison. But then I thought about her words. "Or you could see it like we're the first of a new kind."

A smile usurped her thoughtful expression. "Look who's become an optimist."

An optimist? Is that what I was? Or was I simply a scientific observer?

Aylen came over to me, kissed my forehead, and told me she was going to bed. After she closed the door to the guest room, I stared off into the fire. The flames made me think of Ace, but thinking about the faerie rattled my nerves, so I blinked away the image pressed into my lids and studied instead my grandmother's copper basin, which Mom had suspended over the hearth.

Each summer, Grandma Woni would make jam in that pot, filling the house with the fragrance of syrup and juice. She'd always mix edible flowers into her stewing fruit. Foraging for the flowers was my job. She'd slip the journal filled with watercolor paintings of comestible plants into my little hands and send me out to Holly's field to pick them.

Sometimes Blake came with me, and we'd imagine we were on a treasure hunt. We'd roam around the field, checking and rechecking the pages, hoping to find exact matches. When we succeeded, we felt as thrilled as if we'd won a prize.

After filling my tote bag with mauve angelica blossoms or marigold petals, we'd lie in the grass and watch tireless bees sip nectar and surf drunkenly through the crackling air.

The fire popped, whisking me away from the buzzing blue field, away from Blake.

A charred log toppled over and hissed, splattering embers onto the rug. I shot up, dragged the fireguard Aylen had forgotten to slide back in place, and swept the ashes off the rug with the chimney brush.

After making sure no more cinders darted over the screen, I padded down to the basement. It took me two attempts to find the cold chamber that contained Holly. They'd unwrapped the blanket from around her body but hadn't stripped off her white cotton nightgown.

Seeing her so frail twisted my insides. I skated the drawer out completely and gazed down at the ancient gardener. I wasn't sure if it was because Ace had told me she would turn to ashes, but her skin seemed almost silver.

"What happened to you, Holly?" I murmured, gaze roving over her unmoving face. "Did you really catch something so human as chicken pox?"

I received no answer. Not that I was expecting one. My gaze tracked down her arms that were covered in the same welts as her face. Even the long scar, which ran from her thumb knuckle to her wrist, was covered in pink bumps.

Oddly, whatever infection she'd contracted hadn't spread to her chest and legs. I was pretty certain varicella was not a localized illness, but perhaps it affected faeries differently than it affected humans.

My mother hadn't taught me much about examining cadavers —mostly because I'd always pressed my palms against my ears and hummed loudly whenever she went all mortician on me—but I'd seen enough CSI shows to identify signs of struggle.

Without daring to touch Holly, just in case it *was* an infectious disease, I checked her neck for bruising. Found none. And no residue clouded the white crescents of her nails. Would she even have had the energy to claw at an attacker?

I looked around me, trying to find gloves to shift her over, when I noticed movement on the stairs. I jerked sideways so fast I

22

slammed into the metal shelving. My pulse rattled as loudly as the surgical utensils behind me, and my marked hand blazed.

"Kajika," I exclaimed, clapping my hand over my heart.

"I did not mean to frighten you." His dark brown eyes were pink with burst blood vessels and his shoes were stained with mud.

I spotted a rip in his sweatshirt sleeve and a dirty scratch on his cheek. "What the hell happened to you?" I pushed away from the shelving. "Did you get into a fight?"

"No." Kajika ran a hand through his cropped hair, his raw knuckles standing out starkly against the black silky strands.

"Then why is your hand bleeding? Why is your sweater torn?"

"She is gone, Catori," he murmured.

I looked up at him. I was tall, but he was taller. *Much* taller. "I know, Kajika."

"You know?"

I frowned and tipped my head toward Holly. "She's here."

He peered around the dimly lit chamber. "Where?"

Couldn't he see Holly? I pointed to her. "Right there."

"I am not talking about Holly. I am talking about Gwenelda. When I returned to the house, Holly was dead, and Gwenelda was gone." His rocky breaths reverberated against the stainless-steel doors. "What if she—"

"Killed Holly?"

"No!" He squared his shoulders. "No. Gwenelda is no murderer. She cared about the old woman. More than she should have."

My mouth went dry. "Why shouldn't she have cared about her?"

Seconds ticked by. I could hear them clicking on the clock Mom had nailed to the wall. She'd so enjoyed spending time with the dead that she often lost track of time. Cadavers soothed her. I'd never understood it. I mean, yes, they were quiet, but they were also empty, malodorous shells.

Instinctively, I sniffed the air. The scent of damp earth mingled with that of cold embers. Either Holly's flesh had absorbed the smoky aroma of her bedroom's fireplace, or her own fire was almost out.

"Why *shouldn't* she have cared about her?" I repeated.

Kajika fixed me with his reddened eyes. "You know why."

"Because they were enemies?" I stayed quiet for a while. So did he. "What does that make me, Kajika? What the hell does that make me?"

He closed his eyes and took a raspy breath. "Please, Catori, I do not want us to argue about this. Not again. You are *different*. You are *not* like them."

"But I'm also not like you."

"Maybe one day you will be."

I turned back toward Holly. I didn't want to fight about my nature, and especially not beside Holly.

Even though she was no longer alive, she deserved respect.

The dead deserved the respect of the living.

"Catori—"

"Are you a hundred percent sure Gwenelda didn't kill her?" I asked, asserting as much control over my vocal cords as humanly possible.

"*Look* at her. She has a rash all over her arms and head. Only *gassen* causes a rash like this one." He was breathing hard. "Ace was at the farmhouse. He flitted away before I could interrogate him but I saw him. If anyone killed her, it was him, Catori."

Frustration swamped my insides, replacing the anger Kajika's spite for the fae had stirred up.

Had Ace asphyxiated Holly with his dust? And if he had, when had he done this? After collecting my car?

I had my back to the hunter, yet I felt him take a step toward me. Felt the air move with his wild, green scent. And then I felt his palms land on my shoulders, his touch solid and yet the slightest bit jittery, as though his heart was pouring chaotic beats into his extremities.

"I know I said I would work with the faeries, but I do not think I can trust them. I do not think *we* can trust them."

Cruz had proved untrustworthy, but Ace . . .? The prince might not have liked the Neverrian governor but he nonetheless did his bidding.

I let my lids slide shut over my tired eyes, Kajika's accusation distressing my ragged mood. "Or she died a natural death." I said this with very little conviction.

Kajika spun me toward him. "At the risk of sounding insensitive, I am more worried about Gwenelda than about Holly and her manner of perishing. Can you help me find Gwen, Catori?"

Sighing, I nodded. "That's what friends are for, after all."

Kajika's lips curved into a grateful smile that did little to brighten his ragged expression.

"Where have you already looked?" I asked.

"In the woods. She left many trails in many directions, as though she was being chased."

The memory of a hiker who'd been mauled by a bear years before crept into my mind. "Were there paw prints?"

The hunter arched a brow. "No other prints than her own, which leads me to believe she was being chased by faeries."

The image of a predatory bear faded, replaced by blazing *golwinim*—the faerie guards who could transform into fireflies. They'd already attacked Gwenelda once. They'd killed her, but Cruz had called her soul back after ridding her body of their venomous dust and brought her back to life.

I'd been so thankful, so awestruck, that I'd succumbed to the charm he'd wielded over me like a bladed weapon. Little had I known how soon and how deeply he'd slip that knife into my back.

The vile memory slammed a horrid thought into my mind: did I owe Ace for bringing back my car?

Was that *why* he'd recovered it?

I rammed my hand through my long, black hair with such force that I strained the follicles. "If they haven't gotten to her, she'll come find you, Kajika. Who else would she run to?"

"But what if they have? What if they have captured her? What if they have already killed her?" His anguish bled into his timbre and across his features.

I didn't want to consider that possibility. Maybe Aylen was right and I was an optimist after all. "If they've captured her, they'll let her go, because I have something they want."

His pupils throbbed against their ochre background.

"I can read Holly's book."

"Holly's book?"

"Holly wrote a book about faerie and hunter legends. *The Wytchen Tree.* That's what Cruz asked for in Boston; what he tortured out of me. I believe he sent Stella to steal it from my house when we were driving back." Or it was pure coincidence that she'd happened on the book before he got there. Whatever the story, they were both on my no-trust list.

"What do the *pahans* want with a book about *adsookins*?"

"I believe they want your tribe's secrets, Kajika."

He flinched. Was it my choice of pronouns that caused the recoil or my theory? Did it matter? We had far more pressing matters than my allegiance to discuss.

"And they want to know where Negongwa is buried." The diagram that had leapt out from the pages reshaped in front of my eyes as though it was hanging in the thin divide between our faces. "They want to raise Negongwa to have the dust regulation annulled without having to awaken the others."

Kajika's nostrils flared. "Because they still believe our leader will pardon their wrong-doings and allow them a limitless supply of dust? *Pahans* should consider themselves lucky to have access to their dust. If it had been up to me, I would have asked the Great Spirit to strip them of the deceitful magic."

"Could he?"

"*She.* The Great Spirit is female."

"I didn't mean the Great Spirit. I meant Negongwa. Did he have that much power?"

"He could converse directly with the Great Spirit, and She is all powerful."

I sucked in my lower lip, wondering if a man could truly possess as much power as a deity.

"You are certain they cannot read the book, Catori?"

I nodded. "Ace told me this himself when he dropped by."

"Dropped by?" he all but growled. "Ace Wood paid you a visit?"

I nodded.

A vein throbbed at Kajika's temple. "When?"

"An hour or so ago."

"Why?"

"He wanted to take Holly's body. He said it would disintegrate once her fire went out."

Almost afraid my words would prompt the phenomenon, I whirled back toward Holly. She was still there, but her skin was now steel-gray, and her hair, which had been matted when she'd been wheeled into my house, had vanished.

I threw caution to the wind—hoping her rash wasn't contagious—and touched her scalp. My fingertip came back caked in leaden dust.

A wave of nausea crested through me. I ran to the sink in the corner and clutched its edges. Cool sweat moistened the nape of my neck as I leaned over the basin and dry-heaved until the nausea abated.

I washed and rewashed my hands with the pink antiseptic soap, and still they didn't feel clean.

"We will need a bag."

Kajika's voice pierced through the sour fog clogging my head. "A bag? For what?"

"To carry her out of the house."

I was still staring into the sink, still feeling queasy. "You mean a body bag?"

27

"Any bag large enough to fit her body will work."

As I imagined Kajika cramming Holly into one of Mom's recyclable fabric totes, bile basted my tongue and palate.

"Forget it. It is too late to move her."

"Too late?" I croaked.

Keeping one hand on the stainless-steel basin, I turned back toward Holly.

The top layer of her body was flaking away, as though inhabited by termites. I shuddered.

No more nose, no more chin, no more breasts, no more toes.

Another layer sloughed off. And then another.

With vile fascination, I watched Holly's flesh turn to ashes that blustered off her rounded form like dry sand sliding off the crenelated edges of a sandcastle.

The erosion took minutes but felt longer, as though time had been suspended to slow down the passing of a life. When it was over, all that remained of Holly were dunes of silver sand.

6

THE SILENT TREATMENT

"How am I going to explain this to my father?" I hissed at Kajika as he carried Holly's remains into the starlit graveyard.

Kajika had swept my relative inside my hand-painted cherry bowl I'd carried from the living room into the morgue, not wanting Holly to be packed into a supermarket tote. It didn't seem right. Even though she was no longer there, the least I could do was honor her with a meaningful vessel.

"Tell your father we cremated her. That is how you say it, correct? *Cremated*?"

"Yes. But we don't do it inside our house. We don't own an incinerator."

"Tell him I took the body with me then. That it had been her dying wish."

I stopped his mad dash through the cemetery with a palm to his taut, muscled forearm. "Here." I pointed to the headstone that read *LEY*.

I'd always imagined Holly's mother's remains sat beneath the earth, tucked inside a casket, but since she'd been fae, no skeleton rested beneath the soil. Was there even a casket? She'd died back in the sixties, long before I was born, and almost a decade before Mom burst into the world.

Kajika started tipping the bowl, but before Holly could flutter out, I seized the ceramic vessel. He frowned as a soft, cool breeze twined around us, swirling the silver motes. They drifted from the bowl like smoke from an extinguished wick.

"I'd like to bury her. Could you get the shovel?" I asked. "I put it in the shed."

Kajika's expression tightened at the idea of honoring a faerie with a burial. Nevertheless, he went to the shed to retrieve the shovel and returned pinching it between two fingers, as though touching it were painful.

Perhaps it was.

And perhaps it was insensitive of me to have sent him to fetch it. After all, he'd used it to bury his adoptive mother after Aylen and my father had dug up her grave. But I'd tasked him with the errand because I didn't trust him with Holly's ashes.

He handed me the shovel. I placed the cherry bowl on the thin crust of snow, took the shovel from him, and began digging.

Although cold, the earth yielded beneath the blade. My shoulder blades ached by the time I'd excavated a deep enough hole.

"What was that funerary song Gwen sang for her mother? How does it go?" I asked Kajika before pouring her out.

"It is a hunter song."

"A hunter song? Or a Gottwa song?"

He stared hard at me. "I will not sing it for Holly because she stopped being Gottwa when she chose to become a faerie." His eyes basked in livid shadows.

Where was the kindness, the gentleness he'd exhibited earlier in the tree house?

Where was the compassion?

"She spoke Gottwa. Collected the stories of your tribe. Have mercy on her spirit, Kajika."

"Mercy?" he sputtered. "You did not live through the *Makudewa Geezhi*." Kajika was wound as tightly as the little ballerina in my music box, but unlike her, he'd break before he emitted a melodious sound.

"I know I didn't, but Holly didn't either. She didn't kill Ishtu. I'm not asking you to sing for Lyoh Vega or Borgo Lief"—the two hateful faeries who'd slain Kajika's mate—"I'm asking you to sing for my grandmother's cousin."

"You are asking for too much." His eyes flashed to my face. "I will remain at your side while you bury her but I will *not* sing."

I bit my lower lip and dragged my gaze down to the bowl. The cherries swam in front of my eyes, clumped and stirring like red blood cells traveling through plasma. Even though his refusal saddened me, I respected it.

As I tipped the bowl over the hole, my heart began to spin in slow revolutions. "Goodbye, Holly."

I was about to shovel the cold earth back on top of the ashes when the gray flecks liquified like molten silver. Particles shimmered as the stream thickened and flowed through the grooves of the upturned earth before sinking in.

I threw my head back in awe. "Did you see that?"

"I did." He stared quietly at the veined earth. "Faeries are poisonous. So is their blood."

"Are you saying I poured poison over Ley's grave?"

"Did grass ever grow in this spot?"

"I don't—I don't know."

The cemetery was vibrant with color in the warm months, so Ley's ashes couldn't have contaminated the entire grounds. Which meant Holly's ashes wouldn't either. *Right?*

"I hope it does not taint your water."

My breath caught. "Maybe ashes don't turn fluid each time. Maybe Holly's were special? What happened to Ace's grandfather when your people killed him?"

"I did not stand near enough to observe his transformation."

I stared at the ground, hoping I hadn't done something foolish. At least, not *too* foolish. It seemed that was the only way I did things these days. I should've probably handed Holly's body to Ace.

I shakily shoveled the dirt over the empty hole, praying to every god out there that I hadn't endangered the cemetery's flora or the town's water. I had a vision of desiccating bushes and yellowing grass; of cracked headstones and crumbling trees; of Rowan residents hacking and graying like Holly had.

I looked around in anguish. The rowan trees still stood, leafless but strong; the gravestones were smooth and upright; the perennial bushes, lush and glossy. Nothing had changed.

Yet.

As I wheeled my gaze back to the smoothed earth above Ley's grave, I caught Kajika's broad figure stalking off into the forest without so much as a goodbye. Was he angry at me, or had he taken off to resume his search of Gwenelda?

Should I have offered to accompany him? My dismal speed would probably have held him back or have gotten in the way.

Besides, I wasn't sure what to think of Gwenelda. Yes, she'd saved my aunt and father earlier—she'd stopped them from reading the spell etched in the casket that brought hunters back to life—but I could tell from the wails that rose out of her afterward that she'd hated every second of it. She would rather have resurrected her mother than saved my father.

Could I blame her?

I returned the shovel to the shed, washed the cherry bowl with hot soapy water until the enameled bottom shone, then crept up to my bedroom, wincing each time a step creaked. Neither Dad nor Aylen stirred though.

I drew the drapes closed and ran myself a hot shower. How I wished I could soak in a scalding bath, but Aylen had the only room in the house with a tub. A shower would have to do.

I'd take a bath tomorrow, after dropping her off at the airport.

And every day after that.

After scouring the night away, I pulled on a purple T-shirt that read *Ooh La La*. I was not in an *Ooh-La-La* mood, but none of my other clothes were clean, and the suitcases I'd packed were still in my car. Unless they'd been stolen. Which was a very real possibility.

Not craving more bad news, I decided to wait until the morning to check and collapsed onto my bed. I tossed and turned, kicking off my too-warm covers, dragging them back over me. Restless, I unplugged my phone and scrolled through my list of contacts.

My finger hovered over Ace's name.

Before I could give it *too* much thought, I typed: **Thank you for returning my car.**

After powering off the device, my mind wandered to Neverra.

Had faeries set up cell towers in the *baseetogan*, or did they only receive calls when they were on Earth? Did they have a magical way of communicating?

Back in Boston, a gold circle slashed by lines had lit up their wrists. I remembered thinking it resembled the suns I'd draw as a kid, the ones Mom would gush about and tack up to our fridge.

When the circle had appeared, Cruz and Ace mentioned they were needed on Neverra. Was that another form of magical brand?

I had so many questions, but was I ready for the answers?

Would they even tell me about their world?

My curiosity was rabid, but nothing new there.

Once upon a time, I'd asked my grandfather how many bricks he'd laid to erect our school cafeteria. He'd said ten thousand. I thought the number too round to be true, and I'd challenged him, so we'd spent an entire summer day counting the bricks. It turned out the correct number was three-thousand-two-hundred and twenty-six bricks.

I wondered if faeries had Internet.

I wondered if they had cemeteries.

I wondered if they had farms.

I wondered if they had hospitals.

At some point, I stopped wondering and finally slept.

I AWOKE with a most frightening hairdo.

Sleeping on wet hair had not been a wise idea. Not only did I sport more volume than Amy Winehouse, but the tangles were out of control.

I wet my hairbrush and smoothed my tresses until I resembled a drowned rat instead of the music phenomenon who'd left our world way too young. I squeezed hydrating drops into my blood-shot eyes then applied a touch of concealer to hide the purple circles.

Feeling a tad less like roadkill, I pattered down to the kitchen in my slippers and opened the fridge. After a long inspection of its contents, I grabbed the carton of eggs, the milk, and the butter.

The heavy door slammed so hard, the glass Tupperwares vibrated inside. I set everything down on the counter, grabbed the flour and baking powder from the pantry cupboard, and snagged a bowl from underneath the sink. I cracked the eggs and mixed them with the milk and dry ingredients until the batter thickened like churned cream.

I thought about Holly, about how she'd decomposed in front of me mere hours before, and shivered.

I whisked harder, attempting to beat the memory out of my mind, but her gaunt face, her soft voice, her graying flesh haunted me.

Wrist smarting, I ladled the mixture into the pan and waited for the doughy disk to froth before flipping it over. The first pancake didn't brown, so I nibbled on it while I cooked the rest of the batter. By the time Aylen emerged from the guest room and Dad came downstairs, I'd plated a dozen pancakes.

From the dark smudges rimming his eyes, I gathered my father had slept as well as I had.

Aylen, as per usual, was wearing too much makeup to tell how her night had been.

"Cruz is coming over this morning." Dad dropped heavily into a chair, making its legs creak.

I jolted at the news, both my knees knocking into the table. "Cruz?"

"Yes. To establish cause of death since I wasn't able to tell what she died of."

"Dad, Holly's not downstairs." I stared at the golden-brown pancakes. "Kajika came to retrieve her body last night. He said she wanted to be cremated, so he took her to a crematorium."

Dad, who was drinking his orange juice, coughed, and juice sputtered from his mouth, dribbling down his chin. He set his glass down so hard I was surprised the glass survived the impact. "And you let him take her?"

"I—"

"We didn't even perform an autopsy!"

I cringed. "I'm sorry. I tried to stop him but—"

"Why didn't you wake me?" he yelled.

Aylen gasped at the severity of my father's tone.

He never raised his voice.

Never.

Mom had been the disciplinarian, not my father.

"I'm really sorry," I mumbled.

For a while, Aylen's chewing was the only noise in the kitchen.

"I'm so disappointed in you, Catori."

"Dad, I said I was sorry," I croaked.

"Well so am I. So am I." He shot up to his feet and walked out of the kitchen before I could ask what he'd meant by that.

That he was sorry he'd been saddled with a daughter like me?

The wood groaned beneath his pounding footfalls.

I pressed the heels of my hands into my tired eyes and inhaled a rough breath.

Aylen seized one of my hands and squeezed. "He'll calm down quickly."

Sighing, I pushed back from the table, carried my plate to the sink, and washed it with too much dish soap. Bubbles filled the entire sink, solidifying to foam. I cleaned the bowl and whisk next, then scrubbed the stainless-steel basin and dried it with a kitchen towel until each side was as reflective as a mirror.

None of it had helped alleviate my gnawing guilt. It took the doorbell pealing to snap me out of my funk.

7

THE VISITOR

My aunt rushed out of the kitchen to answer the door, while I clasped the countertop and stared at the sun-laminated graveyard outside.

Unlike my father's, her footsteps were light and springy, full of excitement at having a visitor. Although I wasn't excited to see the faerie, I was anxious to get answers and hoped he'd provide me with many.

The staircase creaked. Dad paused on the landing, his hands stuffed deep inside his pockets. Before he could walk away from me again, I shuffled forward and hugged him.

He didn't hug me back, but he sighed. "Come on. Let's go tell the medical examiner there's no body to examine."

I released him, and even though I really didn't feel like seeing Cruz, I accompanied Dad to the door.

The faerie stood on the porch with Aylen, deep in conversation. I caught the word Lily a few times, so I assumed they were discussing his fiancée.

"Hi," he said when he saw me, before turning toward my father. "Mr. Price."

"Hi, Cruz." They shook hands while I kept my distance.

Cruz rubbed his neck that had pebbled with welts that were worryingly similar to Holly's. I caught him studying his fingers which had also reddened and roughened.

My arms started prickling. I expected to find a rash, but my skin was smooth. I deduced it was a sympathy pain, like that time back in middle school when Cass had lice and my scalp itched for a week.

"So . . ." Dad expelled a hefty sigh. "We actually won't be needing your services after all."

Cruz tucked his enflamed hands deep into the pockets of his leather jacket. "You . . . won't?"

"Her great-nephew took her body to the crematorium last night. I'm sorry you drove all this way for nothing, Cruz."

Cruz's green gaze sailed my way. "Perhaps I'll pay her great-nephew a visit. He might know what she came down with."

I narrowed my eyes. "You shouldn't bother a grieving man."

Cruz kept his face devoid of emotion. "If an infectious disease is traveling through Rowan, it'd be best we found out, wouldn't you agree?"

"I completely agree." Aylen was nodding energetically, which made her bleached hair flap around her shoulders.

"If it was *that* virulent, we'd all be plague-ridden. Especially Kajika, and he was fine when I last saw him."

"Incubation periods vary."

I mashed my lips together, mentally telegraphing: *Drop the act.*

He didn't. "I'm uncertain where to locate the long-lost nephew."

"I can show you the way." Dad was already snatching the hearse's keys off the hook by the door.

"I doubt he needs an escort. He has a GPS, Dad."

"It's not like I have anything better to do."

I stepped around my father, not wanting him anywhere alone with Cruz, and snatched my own car keys from the row of little hooks nailed to the wall. "Fine. Then I'll go. I wanted to check up on Kajika anyway."

If only I had a way of contacting the hunter to warn him of our visit.

I moved that to the top of my list: *buy a cell phone for my new friend and hope he learns to use it as quickly as he learned to drive a car.*

Dad's warm breath puffed against my temple. "I thought your car was at the impound lot?"

I trailed his gaze to where Cruz's black Maserati was parked beside my beat-up Honda.

In the ensuing chaos of Holly's death, I'd forgotten to update my father on my car's status. "Someone dropped it off yesterday."

"Kajika?" Dad asked.

"No. Someone else."

"Who?"

"Ace Wood stopped by last night," Aylen supplied unhelpfully.

"Ace *Wood* collected your car?" Dad asked.

Aylen poked my arm with one of her acrylic nails. "And you claim you two aren't friends?" Her mouth suddenly rounded. "Oh." Her sooty lashes rose so high that her eyes became as spherical as her lips. "*Oh.*"

A blush stole across my jaw at her awry conclusion, one I prayed neither Dad nor Cruz would draw.

"He owed me for something, so he paid one of his many employees to, um—to get it from"—I twirled a lock of hair—"the impound lot." Could I sound any less ingenuous?

My aunt was still gaping at me. How I wished I could influence her into dropping the subject, but I didn't want to mess with her mind.

A vibration cut through the tautening air that clogged our house's entryway.

Cruz slid his cell phone from his pocket and stole a peek at the screen. "Speak of the devil."

Did he mean Ace?

"Excuse me. I have to take this." Cell phone pinned between his shoulder and ear, he ambled down the porch steps toward his car.

I heard Aylen whisper to my father that Ace Wood was about to become a father, which pinched Dad's already pleated forehead. I'd just grabbed my jacket from the closet and poked my arms through the sleeves when Cruz's gaze blazed my way.

I froze in the doorway, sensing from the faerie's somber expression that something was very wrong. My heart spiked, making the brand flare.

Cruz lowered his glowing palm and pocketed his phone, then drew his car door open. "I'll have to postpone my trip to Kajika's, but I'll be sure to follow up on the reasons for his great-aunt's passing and call you with my findings, Mr. Price."

The long line of questions I had for him jostled inside my brain. "Wait!"

But he'd slipped behind his wheel and revved up his car.

I sprang down the porch steps just as he backed out of the driveway, spraying snow and gravel every which way.

My heart had deserted my rib cage and was now beating inside my throat. Something must have happened, but to whom? Kajika? Ace?

I fumbled to phone Ace. The call went straight to voicemail.

I dialed Cruz next. Same thing happened.

Argh!

I was about to hop into my Honda and tailgate Cruz's fancy car when Dad clasped my shoulder and turned me toward him.

"Cat, what is going on?"

Honesty frothed on my tongue like the pancake dough I'd cooked earlier. Since I refused to involve him, I gritted my teeth until every truthful word deflated. "I just wanted to warn him that Kajika was a bit of a bear and to handle him with care."

Thankfully, Dad ate up my explanation and told me not to worry, reminding me that Cruz was a standup and well-mannered young man.

I kept my lashes pinned to my brow bone to avoid both the

strong urge to roll my eyes and the manic twitching that had seized my lids.

Dad said some more stuff but my mind was back on Cruz's enigmatic phone call and erratic departure.

How delusional I'd been to believe I could stay out of the hunter-faerie quarrel.

There was no escaping.

Not for me.

Not anymore.

8

DAUGHTERS AND MOTHERS

After hauling my duffel bags out of my car and unpacking, I drove to the mall with Aylen to buy Kajika his cell phone. Of course, I didn't tell her that, because it would've spurred a boatload of questions, and I wanted to keep my lying down to an absolute minimum.

On our way back into town, Aylen asked if we could stop by Stella's. "I've called her, like, six times, and she's not picking up. I just want to say bye."

I bit down so hard on my lip I was pretty sure I'd drawn blood. But it beat yelling. Just the mention of Stella's name made me want to scream. I hated her for roping my aunt and father into her little faerie powerplay, for lying to me, for using me, and for the lifelong pretense of friendship.

For the first time in my life, I felt sorry for Faith.

The sky had turned periwinkle by the time we exited the highway toward Rowan. Instead of going left toward the cemetery, I took the road that led past Blake's old place and drove all the way to the cul-de-sac.

Stella's home was a two-story brick and glass construction choked with ivy. It was one of the nicer homes in Rowan, with an infinity pool and an ultra-modern pool house, which had become Faith's when she'd turned fifteen. She threw the best parties in that house—something I'd obviously never admitted to her or to anyone else.

I accompanied Aylen to the front door and rang the bell. No one answered.

"Faith told me her mom wasn't at the bakery." Aylen went around the brick siding where the snow was shallowest, her body brushing the white flakes off the perennial vine. "Stella," she yelled. "Stella!"

I trailed my aunt around the house, past the stone courtyard with the fancy teak furniture and the outdoor chimney. While Aylen peered through the glass doors that gave onto a spacious beige living room, I backed up to scan the second floor. I half-expected a face to look back at me, but empty space stared back.

My bet was that Stella was on Neverra.

With Gregor.

With my book.

As we headed back to the car, Faith arrived in hers. She parked her white SUV next to us, car keys swinging from her clenched fist. Her long amber hair was pulled back in a tight ponytail that made her jaw appear wider. I wondered why this detail of her anatomy surprised me. It wasn't as though I'd never seen her with her hair up, was it?

As she walked toward us, her blue eyes narrowed to slits. "Mom's not home, if that's why you're here." Faith's voice was as tight as her zipped, white puffer coat.

The ill-fitting jacket created several creases across her chest, the fabric squashing her breasts. Either it was a very old jacket or Faith had had a boob job back in New York.

"Do you know where I can find her?" Aylen asked.

"Timbuktu, maybe."

"Timbuktu? Why would she go there?"

"I said Timbuktu like I could have said the Bahamas. She never tells me where she goes. Never invites me along."

I wondered why Stella had kept their heritage a secret from her daughter. Was she worried her daughter, being a purer fae, would be stronger than she was, or was she protecting Faith from learning about this parallel world?

"It's because she's trying to meet a man, honey, and she doesn't think taking her daughter along is very healthy."

"So basically what you're saying is that Mom's a middle-aged sex tourist? That's just great."

"No. That's not . . ."

Faith turned her back and dug out her keys.

Undeterred, my aunt circled her and placed a hand on her shoulder. "Honey, that came out wrong."

Although Faith didn't shrug Aylen's hand away, her back stiffened. "You think?"

"I'll wait in the car." I had enough drama in my life; I didn't need to add any more.

Plus, Faith was a force to be reckoned with if she thought you were eavesdropping or meddling. No matter that I'd saved her life once.

A teeny part of me regretted interfering with Mother Nature. Did that make me an awful human being?

Probably.

More awful than Faith?

Impossible.

Inside the Honda, I popped the sim card into Kajika's new phone and powered it up. A loud ping echoed from the cavernous entrails of Aylen's giant purse. I imagined it was one of her daughters trying to reach her. It pinged again, and again. At the twentieth notification, worry set in. I laid the hunter's phone on my lap and dug Aylen's out.

What if my father was texting my aunt? Or Stella?

A sigh of relief escaped the barricade of my clenched teeth

when I read her best friend's name in the beige bubbles crowding her phone's home screen.

My finger must have grazed one of the bubbles, because I was prompted for Aylen's six-digit passcode. Curious to see how security savvy my aunt was, I punched in her birthday.

Surprise, surprise, it unlocked.

It took me straight to their message thread. I was about to toss the phone back in her bag when I caught sight of the picture she'd taken of herself with Ace.

Oddly enough, I was surprised he showed up in it. *Ace is not a vampire*, I reminded myself. *He's not undead.* He wasn't even dead. I wondered if Kajika would show up in a picture. The thought chilled me down to my very core.

I refocused on the picture. Ace didn't glow. *Note to self: faerie fire doesn't show up on film.*

I glanced through the passenger window. From the tension skewing Aylen's features, I imagined Faith was listing all of Stella's horrid deeds. Again, I felt a twinge of pity for my nemesis. My mother had been everything a mother should be: caring, generous, honest, warm.

Faith's voice rose. She shouted something to my aunt. Something about not understanding anything.

Aylen backed away. I stashed the phone back inside her bag just as she flung the car door wide.

Her cheeks shone as red as Grandma Woni's cherry jam and her eyes as glittery black as polished onyx. "That girl's so . . . so . . ." The descriptor either didn't come to her or she swallowed it back to avoid shocking me. "Stella really doesn't deserve any of the things Faith said about her."

I wasn't certain what exactly had been said, but in my opinion, duplicitous Stella deserved it all.

My aunt's nostrils flared so briskly that I decided to steer her mind off the Sakars. "So what did your friends think about that picture you took with Ace?"

She huffed as she clipped herself in. "They were jealous I got to meet him. He rarely poses for pictures."

I knew her lack of excitement had everything to do with her conversation with Faith and nothing to do with her photo-op with Ace.

She reached into her bag and retrieved her phone as I pulled out of the cul-de-sac. Her breathing evened out as she swiped through her notifications. "I still can't believe you know him."

My fingers clenched around the steering wheel. "I can hardly believe it myself."

"And you're not . . . you know?"

I side-eyed her. "I prefer my men unattached."

She bobbed her head a few times, zooming in on the picture she'd taken with him. "He didn't seem all that excited about becoming a father, now did he?"

So she'd noticed that too . . .

"He's probably just worried. Pregnancies are not always a walk in the park." She swiped to the next picture when her phone pinged with a new message.

Her sigh prompted me to ask, "Everything okay?"

"Saty wants to go to the mall with her friends this weekend, but she doesn't want her sister to come. What am I supposed to do?"

I didn't offer her advice since I doubted she wanted any. Besides, I didn't know the first thing about sibling etiquette. "Did Mom complain about me a lot?"

"Where in the world did that come from?"

I shrugged. "Just thinking about all our verbal spats. I was really hard on her. Especially these last few years."

"You're a spirited teenage girl, Cat. And Nova, well she was quite spirited herself." A fond smile curved Aylen's mouth. "Honestly though, she rarely complained. She loved you to pieces. You were her perfect child."

I knuckled a tear from my eye as we drove home to pick up Aylen's suitcase.

46

Her flight left in two hours, and although part of me ached to see her leave, another part was relieved that she'd be out of harm's way. I almost wanted to suggest that she take Dad with her to Arizona, but my father would never leave Rowan. Especially now that I was home.

During the drive out to the airport, Aylen told me stories of Mom and her as kids. Well, when Aylen was a kid and Mom was a teenager. They'd had a seven-year age gap, so Aylen's earliest memories started when Mom was thirteen.

"Nova was the best sister." She whisked tear after tear off her cheeks. "You know, once she took me to a bonfire party on the beach. She wasn't supposed to bring me, but she was on babysitting duty and didn't want to miss out. Nova must've drank a lot that night, because at some point, she saw Astra locking up the bakery and asked her what she'd put on her skin."

I frowned. "What she'd put on her skin?"

"Nova said she glowed."

I swallowed so fast I choked on my saliva.

"Are you okay?"

I nodded. "What did Astra say?"

"She asked Nova how many beers she'd had." Aylen grinned as I pulled into the kiss-and-fly lane. "Nova was so scared that Astra would tell Mom."

My throat clenched and unclenched, sad that my mother had only found out about magic a few days before her death.

If only she'd heard it from Astra instead of Holly . . .

I pressed away the ifs. The past couldn't be altered so what was the point in listing senseless possibilities? It only did the morale harm.

I grabbed Aylen's suitcase from the trunk and rolled it toward her. A hug and a promise-to-send-news-daily later, and my aunt was gone.

Her angelica blossom and sun-warmed raspberry scent lingered in the car. It smelled like the past, like the jams my grandmother would stir in her big copper basin. I pulled it deep into my lungs as I gripped the gear shift.

I was about to put the Honda in drive when the glow of inhuman skin caught my eye.

An unfamiliar faerie stood by the terminal entrance, gaze fastened to my windshield . . . fastened to *me*.

9

THE SCAR

The faerie glowed so bright I checked around him to see if anyone else was staring. The man was a human inferno; his own star.

Silver hair was parted to the side and combed neatly. I suspected he'd either chosen to live outside of Neverra like Holly, or he was really old—*ancient* considering faerie timelines on Neverra.

Could it be Gregor? Was Gregor in his seventies? Did he have a white scar running the length of his collarbone? What could have created such a ragged, caterpillar-like scar? Not a knife. Or if it was a knife, it'd been outfitted with one *dull* blade.

The faerie shifted, and my gaze darted down to his boots. I expected them to hover. What I didn't expect was for them to be fashioned from brown crocodile hide. It struck me as peculiar, but what did I know of fae fashion?

Lily was always super stylish, and Cruz and Ace both dressed like normal human boys—albeit, wealthy ones—with clothes that fit so perfectly they looked woven from magic.

Maybe they were.

I locked all my doors, as though flimsy locks would save me from a supernatural attack.

The man didn't move, didn't crouch, didn't levitate. He did nothing but stare. I touched my collarbone, wishing my fingers would meet cool metal, but I hadn't put on the opal necklace Gwenelda had given me. Which meant he could sense what I was.

Well, half of what I was.

I'd stopped wearing the necklace because sporting it felt like picking sides. As things stood now, the only person I trusted was Kajika. There were big fat question marks after everyone else's name. Gwen? Ace? Cruz? Lily? Stella?

A car horn blared behind me. I jumped, and my hand exploded with the searing brand at the same time as my heart threatened to derail. How long had I been idling in the kiss-and-fly lane, choking up traffic?

I turned in my seat and raised an open palm to apologize to the driver behind me. When I looked back in the direction of the terminal, the faerie was gone.

I extracted my phone from the cup holder and clumsily scrolled through my contact list. I shouldn't have been typing and driving, especially with as many pedestrians as there were, but I needed to call Aylen. I needed to tell her not to speak with—

How would I phrase it? Watch out for the old man dressed in jeans and alligator boots?

I reasoned that my aunt was wearing her opal ring. He wouldn't know the hunter heritage lurking in her blood. Unless he was intimately acquainted with our family tree.

Our Gottwa ancestry was no secret in the fae world. The only secret was our mixed origin. Apparently, fae sensed we were different, but they attributed that to our diluted hunter magic. They weren't aware that Taeewa, the last hunter, had married the daughter of the *bazash* who'd grown the magical roses that conserved the hibernating hunters' bodies.

My finger hovered over Aylen's name. I dialed it anyway. "Just calling to check that your flight's on time." I sounded edgy, even to myself. I hoped she couldn't tell.

"Yes. Just passed security. They made me take *everything* off. I swear, next time, I'm traveling naked."

I smiled, and it strained my lips, but it also helped bring my heart rate back down. Speaking of, neither Ace nor Cruz had shown up.

Was the old faerie my new keeper? *No.* My hand had glowed *after* he'd shown up, not before.

I drove fast. Too fast. It took me half the time to get back to Rowan that it had taken me to reach the airport.

I plowed straight for Holly's farmhouse, hoping Kajika would be around. The gray pickup truck was parked out front and soft light burned in the living room.

Clutching the gift I'd gotten him, I stepped out of the car and walked over to the front door, rapping on the wood.

"Kajika," I called out.

No answer.

I tried the knob, and the door creaked open. A sign that Kajika didn't fear his enemies or that one had beat me to him?

Skin palpitating with my turbulent pulse, I stepped into the small foyer.

"Kajika?" I went into the quiet living room, which was bathed in the pearlescent glow of burning logs.

Between the lit hearth and the absence of struggle, my heart quieted.

The pitter-patter of footsteps made me whirl. Kajika stood before me, dripping wet, with only a towel knotted around his chiseled waist. I averted my gaze from the trail of dark hairs that started at his navel and disappeared beneath his towel, focusing instead on the cut of his cheekbones that appeared more dramatic in firelight.

Water bled from his black hair onto his muscled shoulders, gliding down carved pecs adorned with swirls of dark ink—seized *gassen.*

As I contemplated the intricate arabesques that contained a misbehaving faerie's dust, I thought I saw them shift, sparkle. "Are the marks moving?"

"Yes. *Gassen* thrives underneath our skin."

One loop went from black to anthracite to silver and then back to black. "How does it not poison you?"

"The Great Spirit made us well."

That's it? That's the reason? That hunters are well made? "There must be a scientific—"

"Science and magic coexist like hunters and faeries, but they do not mix, Catori. At least, they should not mix."

And yet, they had . . . And I was born from that mix.

Since every time we brought up my heritage, we fought, I put an end to the discussion by brandishing the phone. "I got you this. You have unlimited data and national calls."

"You bought me a cellular phone?" The tension in his features slackened, and his lips quirked. Almost a smile, which was a feat for Kajika, who seemed to have forgotten how to smile during his two-century-long slumber.

"I want to be able to reach you when you go out looking for Gwenelda."

His eyes sparked in the silvery glow of the fire, thinning the air in the room. When he took the phone and charging cable from my hand, his fingers grazed mine, lingering a beat too long. I withdrew first, then dug both my palms into the back pockets of my faded jeans.

"You will not come with me?" he asked.

"No. As much as I want to help, I'm afraid of leaving the cemetery unattended."

"The faeries cannot penetrate the circle."

"I know, but they can penetrate our house. I'm worried for my father, Kajika."

He scrutinized my face for a silent moment. "I understand," he said before busying himself with finding an outlet.

At least, he knew how to use my present—thanks to Blake? The fact that Kajika had absorbed my best friend's memories still made my stomach writhe, but what made my gut churn harder was the knowledge that Gwenelda possessed my mother's.

I palmed my abdomen to soothe the thrashing. "Did you find any trace of her?"

When he straightened from his crouch, towel miraculously still in place, he shook his head and a silken lock of hair fell into his molten amber eyes. "Not yet."

"Have you asked Ace or Cruz if they've heard anything?"

His jaw flexed, eliciting a shallow pop. "I have had no contact with the faeries. Have you?"

"No. At least, not with Ace and Cruz."

"But you've had contact with another?"

I shifted, shuffling from one black boot to the other. I slid my hands out of my back pockets and hooked my fingers through the loops of my jeans instead. "I didn't have any contact, per se, unless a staring duel is contact."

"A staring duel?"

"I saw a faerie tonight at the airport. When I dropped off my aunt, there was this old man who glowed really brightly."

"Old?"

"Yeah. He had gray hair and lots of wrinkles."

Kajika went alarmingly still. Even his breathing seemed to halt. "The elders are coming out of the *baseetogan*?"

"The elders?"

"The ancient faeries."

"Holly was ancient," I said.

"Holly was a *bazash*. She glowed faintly. If this creature you saw glowed brightly, then he must be a full-blooded *baseetogan*-dweller."

Maybe that was why I'd never noticed Stella or Holly glowing? Because their blood wasn't pure?

He shoved back the lock of hair obscuring his right eye. "Describe him in detail, Catori."

"Uh. He wore cowboy boots."

Kajika huffed. "How tall was he? Did he have any distinct markings?"

I tried to remember his height. Had he been taller than the travelers passing by him? *No.* "Average height. I'd say he was in his late sixties."

"Catori, give me something I can use," Kajika all but growled.

I stopped fidgeting. "He had a white scar on his collarbone. Like a knife scar, but a badly healed one."

Kajika stilled and his eyes took on a chilling gleam.

"What?"

His nostrils flared as his lids swooped low.

"What?" I repeated, staring at his clasped lids as though his thoughts would magically materialize on them.

"*I* gave the faerie that scar."

10

THE ARROWS

A shocked breath whooshed past my parted lips. "You—you —you . . . ?"

Kajika's eyes were still clamped shut, his dark lashes fanned across his high cheekbones. "Yes, *I* slashed the faerie's throat with an iron blade."

Goosebumps rose and fell in waves across my skin. Even my throat felt coated in them. "Is it—is it Gregor?"

"No." Kajika's lids flew open. "That fae you saw, he is far worse than Gregor." His violent stare pinned me in place like an arrow.

"Who—"

"Have I ever told you about Borgo Lief?"

"The faerie who killed Ishtu?"

Kajika's biceps juddered like plucked twine as he balled his fingers. "Yes. Lyoh Vega's accomplice."

My gaze dropped to his tattoos. I remembered him telling me that one of them contained Borgo's magic. "He doesn't have dust, so he's not too dangerous, right?"

"He has no dust, yet he dares leave the *baseetogan* after I rise?" Kajika let out a mocking snort. "He has either lost his mind or believes he can retrieve his magic."

"How? By fighting you?"

"If faeries played by the rules, I would say yes, but those crea-tures do not abide by any rules. I fear that if he has shown himself to you, he plans on using *you* against *me*."

"Me?" I squeaked.

Kajika stared at the crackling fire. "You resemble Ishtu, Catori."

"So?"

"So he might think I managed to save her, and he has come to finish the job."

"People have heard of me up on Neverra. He can't possibly think I'm Ishtu."

"They are not people."

I swallowed hard. I wasn't on the best of terms with the faeries, but still.

"Burn rowan wood in your chimney, Catori. All night and all day. It will keep them from coming inside."

He walked over to the flowery couch, lifted one of the worn yellow cushions, and retrieved something from underneath. He handed me a rolled-up dishrag. Inside, three little white wooden arrows knocked against each other. No thicker than crayons, they were topped with brown feathers on one end and strung up with a metal tip on the other.

"I do not think you could kill a faerie with them—as your blood is not yet pure iron like mine—but they should immobilize a fae long enough for you to get away."

The metallic tinge of fear coated my palate. I pinched an arrow, lifted, felt its weight, or lack thereof, and twirled it between my fingers. It was smooth and insubstantial, as though made of vapor instead of wood.

Had he whittled these the afternoon Holly told me about my family's history? He'd been felling wood.

Back then, I'd thought it was firewood—and perhaps some of it was—but then he'd told me he'd started replenishing his arsenal.

"I will carry rowan logs to your car. Burn them." The authority in his voice made me shiver. "We should call Ace."

"You said he killed Holly, yet you want to ask him for help?"

"No. We do not need his help. We need information. I want to know why Borgo has come out." Kajika released a rumbling sigh that seemed to shake the white flames dancing in the hearth. "How am I supposed to seek Gwenelda if the faerie is here?"

I pushed a strand of hair behind my ear. "I'm a big girl, Kajika, and now, thanks to you, I have weapons."

"You cannot defend yourself from a faerie."

"How weak do you think I—"

My breath whooshed out of me as Kajika cinched my throat with one rock-hard forearm. Instinctively, I elbowed him, but my elbows barely skimmed his torso.

I tried to shake him off, but his arm only tightened, pinning me in place. I swung my foot back but kicked air.

One of his hands shot to my hair. Grabbing chunks of it, he tugged hard. My neck cracked as he jerked it backward.

"Fucking let go!" I wheezed.

And he did.

I sputtered and coughed.

"You are *not* strong," Kajika said.

I raised a shaky hand to my neck and cupped the sore skin. "You —hurt—me."

"I am sorry. My intention was merely to prove that you cannot protect yourself."

"Teach me, then!" My eyes grew as soggy as my ego. "Teach me to protect myself."

"A blue moon will rise soon. Choose hunter and you will grow strong overnight."

I clenched my jaw. "I can become strong without becoming a hunter."

"You will never be strong enough if you do not pick."

"Teach me!"

He folded his arms over his bare torso that rose and fell as frantically as my own. Okay, perhaps not as frantically as mine. Not only was I out of breath, I was also incensed, and rage had the tendency to tighten my ribs.

"What if you choose them?" he asked. "Then everything I teach you, you will use against me."

I answered him with deafening silence, then turned around and stalked out to my car.

He followed me in just his stupid towel. "You told me there was doubt in your mind!"

"Doubt doesn't mean I'd turn against you! Besides, there *is* no more doubt in my mind." I raised my fist so he could read the word stamped in my skin—*human*.

My other hand still clutched the arrows. I debated tossing them into the snow, but that would be stupid. Maybe I wasn't strong like he was, but at least, I was armed.

"You retrieved your car," he said matter-of-factly.

I didn't respond. Just got inside, tossed the arrows on the passenger seat, and slammed the door shut.

One thing I was quickly learning in this new world of mine was that I had to keep myself safe. I was not a damsel in distress, nor did I want to be.

I needed to learn to throw these arrows. Since I lived in Rowan, and not in a dystopian universe, I didn't see how I could strap a bow to my back without raising eyebrows.

However, there was a dartboard in Bee's Place.

I'd start training there.

II

THE RUMOR

During the first hour, most of my darts either went wide or glanced against the wall and collapsed onto the floor like plucked feathers. Granted, I was standing as far away from the dartboard as possible.

"Are you training for some championship?" Cass asked.

"No. Just for fun." I narrowed my eyes, bent my elbow, cocked my hand back, and let my weapon fly. The steel point lodged itself on the triple ring, vibrating as it settled.

Better. Not great, but at least I'd hit the board.

"You're going to go cross-eyed if you don't take a break."

I kneaded my tired eyes, realizing only then that the room was empty. When had everyone left? "What time is it?"

"Close to midnight."

"Already?"

"You mean, 'finally?' I've been on my feet all day because the new girl who was supposed to cover lunch never showed." Cass sighed. Then she inclined her head toward one of the booths against the brick wall. "Have you had dinner yet?"

"No."

"Good. I saved you some food."

59

"Thanks, Cass." I dropped onto the bench seat opposite my friend and took a gulp of my soda before realizing it wasn't a soft drink. It tasted sweet, but also spicy, and definitely contained alcohol.

"I mixed Prosecco with ginger ale and freshly grated ginger."

I tried it again, sipping it this time. "It's really good."

"I want to be a mixologist someday."

"What's that?"

"A cocktail maker. I'd like to open my own bar."

"Here in Rowan?"

"Hell no. In Miami."

"Miami?"

"Yeah. They have such cool beaches down there, and the weather's always nice—except during hurricane season. Wouldn't you like to live on a beach?"

"There's a beach next to Astra's."

She smiled and then dug into her bowl of fragrant spaghetti. "I meant, a warm beach."

I stared at Cass for a moment and wondered how she would react if I told her she had a minuscule amount of faerie blood running through her veins. Would she be surprised, ecstatic, mind-blown? Would she want to move to Neverra? Maybe they had beaches up there . . .

I wondered if she'd ever felt different. I longed to ask, but my longing was selfish. I wanted an ally in this parallel world. Telling her would endanger her, and I didn't want to endanger anyone—especially not the sweet girl sitting across from me.

I bent my head toward my bowl and wrapped some spaghetti around the tines of my fork. Tomato sauce sloshed out and sprinkled my T-shirt. "Shoot."

"I'll get some soda water. That usually gets stains out."

I soaked my napkin in the sparkling water and rubbed the stain forcefully.

She jabbed her fork in my direction. "Who you angry at?"

"Huh?"

"You were throwing darts at that board as though it were some-one's head, and now you're rubbing a hole through your shirt."

I set my napkin down. "No one."

I ate quickly and in silence, hoping she wouldn't ask again. But it was Cass, and Cass was persistent. She reminded me of Mom in that way. Maybe that's why we got along so well.

Once I'd scraped my plate clean and done away with most of my ginger cocktail, she reiterated her question.

"I'm angry with Ace." I could've substituted his name for Kajika's.

I took a sip of my drink and swished it around my mouth, enjoying the fizzle of the bubbles against my tongue. Once they'd all popped, I let the warmed mouthful glide down my throat and settle in my bloodstream.

"Why?" she asked.

I set the glass down and twirled it between my fingers. Things were beginning to go marvelously fuzzy in my head. I felt several pounds of anger lighter and several pounds of confidence heavier.

"Because he did something. Actually, I'm not sure he did anything, but he spoke about doing it, and then it happened, so I assumed he did it, and when I told him this, he got angry with me for thinking it, but wouldn't you assume that if someone said they were going to do something, and that thing happened, then they're guilty?"

"Whoa. Slow down and rewind, because there were a lot of *its* and *somethings* in that sentence. What exactly did he do?"

I stared at the bubbles bursting on the surface. "I can't tell you," I rasped.

"Why not?"

I lifted my eyes to her bright blue ones that eternally played hide-and-seek behind her long bangs.

"Did he promise you he was single or something?"

I blinked. "What?"

61

"I don't know." She shrugged. "I know you guys have been hanging out."

Out of necessity, not out of pleasure. "How do you know that?"

"Faith said—well, she said . . . Oh, forget it." Cass leaned back in the booth. "Most things my cousin says are lies anyway."

"What did Faith say?"

Cass twisted up her lips. "She said you guys were sleeping together."

That sobered me up. "Me and Ace? No way." I shook my head. "Just"—I wrinkled my nose—"no."

I must've raised my voice because Cass shushed me. "You'll wake Bee."

I stared at the ceiling. *Bee.*

I shoved Faith's stupid gossip out of my mind. Gossip shouldn't rile me up; it shouldn't even affect me.

Gossip was nothing in the scope of things.

I nibbled on my lip, then freed it. "How is she doing?"

"I find you awfully defensive."

"Has she been coming downstairs?"

Cass leaned forward and plopped both forearms on the table. "Let's not get off topic."

"Yes, let's."

"Cat—"

"Look, if I were involved with anyone, you'd be the first to know. But right now, I really don't want a boyfriend. Relationships are too complicated."

"You've never even had one."

"I dated a guy last year," I said defensively.

"Robbie? You told me you went on two dates with him, one of which I'm still laughing about."

"Which one?"

"The movie one."

"Right. The movie one." Robbie, a BU sophomore, asked me out on a date, and then, during said date, not only had he cheapened out of buying *my* ticket, but he'd bought his own with a coupon. "Yeah. He wasn't the most romantic guy."

"We suck at picking guys." She raised her almost-empty glass and clinked it against mine. "I'm still nursing a massive crush on Ace, and he's about to be a daddy. That's plain gross. And totally evil."

"You couldn't be evil if you tried."

"I'm related to Faith. I'm sure I could be a little evil. If I tried."

I rolled my eyes. "Well then, don't try."

Cass laughed. "Do you want to go clubbing in Detroit with me on Friday night?"

I thought about it. Could I leave my father alone for the night?

Hadn't I just done exactly that?

I texted him to make sure he was all right. When he sent me a thumb's up emoji, I set my phone down and said, "I could use a carefree night."

Cass clapped excitedly. "Pick you up at ten*ish*?"

"Or I can drive? I got my car back." I didn't mention how.

"Then you're the designated driver."

"Deal."

When I left Bee's that night, I felt like I was treading air. I checked, just in case my faerie side had made me levitate. My feet were firmly planted on the ground.

Even though I probably shouldn't have been driving after my cocktail, I did. I was young and foolish, and human.

Humans did crazy things like drinking and driving. Hunters definitely didn't. At least, Kajika didn't. He was staunchly opposed to alcohol or any substance that could muddy the senses.

As I wound through the graveyard, I looked over at Ley's grave.

I shouldn't have.

My foot slammed down on the brake pedal. I rubbed my eyes and then peered at the headstone again.

How muddied were my senses?

12

THE FUNERARY VINE

Clutching the arrows inside my coat pocket, I walked on legs that felt like rubber toward Ley's grave. Bright pink roses sprouted from a thick vine wrapped around the headstone. The flowers glimmered, as though each petal were encrusted with Swarovski crystals.

I so wanted to believe that my father had planted the thing that afternoon, but there was nothing Home-Depot*ish* about these roses. I didn't even dare touch one to see if it was real. I saw through dust, so I knew they weren't an illusion, but I would bet anything they were otherworldly.

I took my cell phone out of my jeans and was about to dial Ace but stopped myself. I wasn't talking to him.

Damn.

If only I'd read Holly's book. There might have been a mention of flowers sprouting from faerie ashes.

I did the next best thing. In my browser, I typed *roses and faerie ashes*. I wasn't really expecting to find anything, but boy, was I wrong. I got a ton of hits.

As I read through them, I decided that people who'd never

actually encountered a faerie had written them. Most spoke of psalm-singing tiny folk who leapt over dead bodies as though they were rides in an amusement park. One article spoke of faerie bodies being carried on rose petals to their final resting place.

Even though I wouldn't put it past faeries to be endowed with a perverse sense of humor, it didn't explain the presence of the rose liana. And since when did roses bud from sinewy stalks? Would the flowery garland thrive? Would it take over the entire cemetery?

Even though I wouldn't mind living over a garden instead of a graveyard, these roses had thorns the size of spindle needles.

I followed the thick vine to its root in the mound that enclosed Holly's ashes. Did faeries have spirit plants like the Gottwas had spirit animals? Or was it because she was Gottwa that a rose had grown from her essence?

Had a plant risen over Ley's headstone?

Had someone uprooted it?

Should I uproot this one?

I looked upward, wishing that someone could answer just one of my questions, but the vast sky stayed empty and silent.

THAT NIGHT, I dreamed of my mother again. I dreamed she was walking me toward a mirror planted in the middle of Holly's field that didn't reflect our surroundings. The silvered glass displayed a forest full of giant trees steeped in soupy mist and garlanded by vines in full bloom.

Without words, Mom urged me to climb through the mirror, but I dug my heels into the ground. Was my mind telling me the thorns on the rose stalk were safe? Or had my cocktail and shock mingled in a perplexing dream that guest-starred Mom?

Was the rose vine even real?

Maybe I'd imagined it . . .

I stared at my dreamcatcher a solid minute before leaping out of bed and treading over to my window. After drawing the curtains open, I craned my neck in the direction of Ley's tombstone. The sight of a man with a head full of pale hair looming over the head-stone stopped my heart.

I wanted to crank the window open and yell at Dad not to touch it, but screaming would scare him, so I ran around my room, tossing off my sleep shorts and pulling on yesterday's jeans. On my way out, I stubbed my little toe on the foot of my bed.

"Son of a faerie," I muttered.

My toe ached as I pounded down the stairs and kept aching as I shoved my feet into my shearling boots and ran-limped toward Dad.

The crunch of snow made him glance over his shoulder at me. "Did you plant this?"

Breathless, I looked from his puckered forehead to the liana. "Yes."

"What sort of flower is it?"

"A rose-wisteria hybrid. I got it from Holly's greenhouse. I thought it would be a nice gesture."

"To put one of her flowers atop Ley's grave?"

Right, he didn't know I'd buried Holly on top of her mother. "Kajika put Holly's ashes here."

"When?"

My saliva sat thickly on my tongue, tasting like Cass's spicy ginger drink and bitter lies. "Last night."

Dad folded his arms. "I would've liked to have been there. I'm sure many others would have, too. It wasn't very kind of him not to take her friends into consideration."

Now Dad would think Kajika selfish, on top of dangerous and a bad influence. Ever since I'd mentioned the hunter had wrestled in a fighting ring, Dad hadn't held him in the highest esteem.

"Why didn't you stop him, Cat?" His disappointment hurt so much worse than my throbbing pinky toe.

"I'm sorry." I lowered my gaze to three rebellious tufts of ochre grass that poked through the snow. "I didn't think."

Dad sighed. "You seem to be doing a lot of that lately."

Ouch.

"I know this period of readjustment—not having a mother, moving back to Rowan, living at home—has been tasking on you, but you need to start thinking before you act."

If only he knew what else I'd needed to adjust to . . .

An idea drove my gaze back to his. "We could still organize a ceremony. I'll take care of everything. I've watched you organize so many that I know the drill."

Dad cocked an eyebrow. "I didn't mean to make you feel guilty—"

"But you're right. I've been so focused on myself that I'm forgetting about everyone else."

Dad looked at me some more and then reeled me into him. I was well aware that it was just a chest and arms, but being locked against him felt like wearing full body armor; a shield from everything that could harm me.

Too soon, the hug was over, and he took my hands, flipping them palm-side up. "Those thorns are massive. You didn't hurt yourself planting the liana, did you?"

"I wore Mom's gardening gloves."

He smiled. It was such a sad smile. "I hope Nova was watching."

I hoped not.

"She would've been so proud to see her daughter garden."

I couldn't look at Dad then, too embarrassed by my raging deceit.

Before I could add another lie to the lofty pile, Matt's postman truck careened into the graveyard. Dad waved him over.

Last time Matt had stopped by, he'd brought me the mysterious package containing *The Wytchen Tree*. It was the same day I'd ripped the iron wind chime off the porch ceiling and painted the basement door white instead of yellow. I'd tried to erase Mom that day.

I'd thought—without really thinking—that if I destroyed the visible reminders of her, her absence would hurt less. It hadn't.

Or maybe it had been one of the stages of grief. What was anger? The first? The second one? *No.* Denial was the first. Anger probably came in second.

"I got a delivery for you, Cat." Matt presented me with a box the same way a waiter in a fancy restaurant flourished a fancy dish—balancing it on one gloved palm.

I froze. Those had been Matt's exact words when he'd given me Holly's package.

He nodded to the box. Mechanically, I closed my fingers around the cardboard. And then I snapped out of my trance and checked for a return address. When I saw the name of the online store I'd ordered the replacement wind chime from, I relaxed.

Dad told Matt I hadn't been getting much sleep. That none of us had. That it had been a difficult month. Their conversation faded into the background, sounding more like white noise than dialogue.

That is, until Matt exclaimed, "Holly passed?" The postman's round face lost its rosiness.

"You hadn't heard?" Dad asked.

"No. She was such a kind lady. She always gave me a couple dollars when I dropped off her packages."

"She was a very generous person," Dad agreed. "By the way, Cat's organizing a memorial for her this weekend. We hope you'll be able to make it."

After he left, promising to come, Dad went into town to visit Bee, and I returned to the house, weighed down by my package and by the promise to celebrate the woman who'd killed my mother.

It was an accident, I reminded myself.

Holly hadn't meant to kill Mom . . . *right*?

It struck me that she hadn't apologized the day I'd gone to visit her. Had she felt no remorse or was she too guilt-ridden to confess her wrong?

I knelt by the coffee table and unpacked the box. The thoughts inside my head were so loud that I turned the TV on. When, after a half hour, I was still evaluating Holly's soul, I growled and tossed a small screw against the wall. Its dull plink was entirely unsatisfying.

I went to retrieve it, then fit it through the iron tubing and added a nut on the screw shank to hold everything in place. The screw fell out.

Was I using the right one? Or was this screw for the top of the wind chime?

Ugh! I grabbed the slats of wood that held the tubing and inserted suspension lines to secure them to the large hook. Like the hapless screw, they kept slipping out. How had Mom done this?

The metal pieces and nylon coils wobbled and blurred. I swiped my hands against my damp eyes, remembering another time I'd cried while attempting to build something.

For my sixth birthday, my grandparents had bought me a dollhouse as big as a dog kennel. It came in a kit that had to be painted and assembled. My grandfather would've made it from scratch had his arthritis not been so bad.

His fingers were perpetually bent by then. Although Mom tried to cure him with medicinal plants, his fingers never straightened.

So he'd bought a kit, and then he'd overseen its construction. I wanted to do it myself, and I didn't want any help. Not only had I attached the wrong pieces together, but when I tried undoing my errors, it splintered the wood. I'd wept tears of anger and frustration and buried myself in my bed to avoid reproof.

I was never scolded.

The next morning, Mom had fixed everything.

She always fixed everything.

I stared at all the pieces scattered on the wooden table and then stared at the manual, wiping my wet cheeks.

I can't do this without you, Mom.

A hand rested on my shoulder.

I shot up to my feet so quickly that I knocked my knee against the table. As I locked eyes on my unexpected visitor, the pain radiating from my kneecap vanished.

13
THE WIND CHIME

Kajika stood in front of me in a thick navy Henley and a pair of jeans that rested low on his waist. It wasn't a style he was giving himself, merely the unfortunate side effect of wearing my father's gifted jeans.

"I didn't hear you come in," I said, trying to recoup my wits, which had scattered like the iron cylinders on the table.

"I knocked."

"You didn't ring the doorbell."

"I forget there are bells nowadays." He gestured toward the low table. "Are you building a weapon?"

I was about to say no, but an iron wind chime *was* a sort of weapon. "It's a wind chime. To hang over my door."

"It's in iron."

It wasn't a question, but still I answered, "Yes."

The awkwardness in the room was tangible. It exuded from Kajika's every pore. It felt almost like the afternoon we'd spent in the tree house sharing precious memories about our mothers had never happened; like last night's spat had propelled us back to square one.

"Would you like help assembling it?"

I didn't want to nod, because nodding meant admitting defeat, and I had my pride. But then I thought about Mom and put her first. "I'd appreciate some help. If you have time."

"That is all I have these days." His glum tone sponged away the rest of my resentment.

Kajika was a broken man, and I didn't know how to fix broken people. My mother had been the one with that superpower.

While he set to work, I warmed two plates of roast chicken, potatoes, and green beans. When I set the steaming food on the coffee table, he hooked his plate and shoveled down every last morsel. Sensing he was far from sated, I feigned a lack of appetite and offered him my ration. He resisted for all of two seconds before wolfing down my offering.

As he got back to work on the wind chime, I returned to the kitchen and whipped up a batch of cookies, then phoned Cass to ask if the new cook could whip up mini sandwiches and quiches for Holly's memorial.

After slipping the first tray into the oven, I went to check on Kajika. I found him putting the finishing touches on the wind chime, fastening tiny bells to the nylon cords speared through the clapper.

I sidled against the wall and watched him. His features had lost some of their sharpness, and although his brow was furrowed in concentration, he appeared at peace.

"My sister loved music." He tightened a bolt on the iron instrument, before dangling it from one long finger.

The articulated instrument quivered and tinkled, and its tinny song prickled my spine and raised goosebumps over my skin.

"One day, when we penetrated the neighboring French settlement to trade our pelts for dry goods, she fell in awe in front of a wind chime. Even though our tribe needed sustenance, I traded a hide for it." His gaze tracked the contraption's slow dance. "Her smile was a thing of such beauty." A faraway gleam sparked in Kajika's amber eyes. "I studied how it was made and created others

72

using shells, driftwood, and strands of leather. Every time we would make camp somewhere, she would choose a tree and tie her collection to its branches, and then she would lie beneath it and close her eyes. She said the wind carried stories and played them for her in the form of melodies. My sister's mind was a magical place. I miss hearing her recount them."

All of Kajika's sisters had been murdered by faeries. The only surviving member had been his brother. I tended to forget this when I judged Kajika. If faeries slayed my father and aunt, I would detest them, too.

The bells and iron tubes shimmied, sparkling in the pale afternoon light.

Slowly, I pushed off the wall and took it from him. "Thank you. For helping me."

He dipped his chin against his chest. "I would help you more if you let me."

"Train me, then. Teach me."

He squeezed his eyes shut. I thought he was going to turn me down, but instead, he said, "After I find Gwen, I will teach you."

I walked to the front door and opened it. The metal loop Mom had fastened to the porch rafters shone in the afternoon sun. I dragged a wicker chair underneath and climbed up to spear the hook through the loop.

"Come with me," Kajika said.

I stared at the headstones of the sleeping hunters, at the two long empty rectangles of earth in which had rested Gwenelda and Kajika's coffins. "I have to guard the graveyard."

"Faeries cannot penetrate the rowan circle, and humans cannot dig the ground. Only a hunter can unearth a grave, and Aylen has been influenced to never set foot in it. Besides, she is no longer in Rowan."

I looked down at Kajika. "I can't leave my father unguarded. He needs me."

Disappointment strained his jaw.

I climbed down from the chair and pushed it back against the wall. The tiny bells frolicked in the gentle wind. It wouldn't really keep the faeries out—after all they could fly in through a window —but at least, they would no longer be able to walk into my house. That brought me a modicum of satisfaction, not because I was out to embarrass them, but because I wanted to make it harder for them to reach my father.

"She has a strange sense of humor, our Great Spirit," Kajika said.

I frowned.

"Ishtu also loved her father above all other men. Even above me, I believe."

The comparison to his deceased mate irked me as it always did. "Would you like me to dye my hair blonde? So that I don't resemble her so much?"

He smiled, but his smile was fringed in sadness. "I do not think blonde would suit you."

"Yeah. Probably not."

As we stood there, beneath the wind chime, with the wind playing in his silken hair and batting his scent toward me, I folded my arms in front of my chest.

"I brought you some rowan wood. Please burn it. And call me if Borgo returns." He pointed to the cell phone tucked inside his jean pocket. "I can return quickly."

I nodded.

"Do you trust me, Catori?"

The word *yes* prickled my lips. I wanted to utter it, but held back.

"It feels so strange that I must win your trust. That I do not simply possess it." A jagged swallow jostled the apple in his throat. "You trusted Blake. You trusted him with your life. Like I trusted Ishtu. With everything in me, I trusted her. It is hard to have to prove my worth when I feel like I am entitled to your respect."

"I *do* respect you, Kajika, but respect and trust are not the same thing."

His scent—wet earth mixed with blades of grass—swirled around me, blending with the music from the clinking iron. "But you do not trust me? You are unsure about me?"

"I'm unsure about everything and everyone right now. In one month, my life's been blown to pieces."

He lifted his hand to my face and stroked my cheek. "Mine too."

Could I build a friendship with Kajika, or was it as futile as erecting a house over quicksand?

"Burn the wood. And keep the arrows on you at all times." His cold fingers traveled down my neck, my arm, my knuckles. "And if *anything* frightens you, call me."

I had no doubt that *anything* meant faeries. I doubted he wanted me to bother him with my fear of furry spiders.

When he dipped his face closer to mine, I sucked in a breath and blurted out, "A rose liana sprouted from Holly's ashes."

14

THE PETALS

His eyes lingered on my parted lips, before darting over my shoulder, toward the headstone. His jaw snapped shut around a shallow growl as he set sail toward the vine. I whirled around and trailed him. He crouched and yanked on a flower head. The petals came loose.

His eyes became incandescent. "The rose petals in our graves. They came from a vine like this."

I gawked at the plant. The bud from which he'd yanked the petals was already growing new ones. In seconds, they were lush and glittery like the others.

Kajika hurled the petals over the grave and sprang back to his feet. "We were buried in fucking faerie ashes."

The curse word startled me. It didn't sound right coming from the two-hundred-year-old hunter. "That's not really accurate. You were buried in—"

"It is the same thing to me! What if faerie essence seeped into us while we slept? What if it weakened us?"

"Do you feel weak?"

"What if it was a ruse to turn us into faeries?"

"You were in rowan wood caskets, Kajika. Faeries can't touch rowan wood, so that wouldn't make sense. Besides, apparently you smell like a hunter. I'm pretty sure there's nothing fae about you." He stared fixedly at the discarded petals, which lay pristine and unbruised.

"How could Negongwa have accepted this?" he growled.

I tried to touch his arm, but he whipped it away from me.

I slanted my eyes. "It saved your life."

"I would rather have died, Catori." Disgust warped his face. "Maybe I should unbury the others right now to spare them this world."

"It's not such a bad world."

"For you. *For you* . . ." He backed away. Fast. As though sucked by a vortex.

It was still strange to see hunters move, just as it was strange to see faeries fly, but somehow I'd come to accept both.

"Kajika, don't," I said firmly.

He stood by one of the rowan tree trunks. "Do not what? Unbury the others?"

Don't do something rash.

Don't do something you'd regret.

Kajika stopped backing away. "Maybe this world is just hard for me because my mate is not in it."

I bit down on my lip, remorseful that my angular face, my obsidian eyes, my raven-black hair, my laughter resembled Ishtu's. I wished I looked different, sounded different, but I had no control over how I'd been made. The only control I possessed was over what I did.

"Find Gwenelda and bring her home. And then help me recover my book." I gave him purpose. Purpose kept people alive. "Please."

The sun was dying on the horizon, casting embers across the magenta sky, across the dark hunter. His form blurred and then reappeared right in front of me.

There was a new spark in his eyes, a new camber to his mouth. "I will find Gwenelda. And then I will return to you."

My face grew hot from the desire imprinted on his features. He was misinterpreting what I was asking, but instead of setting him straight, I allowed him to dream, because dreaming would keep his melancholy at bay.

I cleared my throat. "You wanted me to burn rowan wood."

He nodded.

I tucked a lock of hair behind my ear, gaze dropping to the ground between our feet. "Did you bring—Oh crap, the cookies!" I lurched back into the house, careened into the kitchen, and tossed on kitchen gloves, grousing when I removed the tray and found the dough crisp and blackened. *Damn it.*

As I dumped them into the trash, a new aroma layered itself over the charred scent of my baking. Kajika was kneeling before my hearth, spinning the tip of an arrow into a white log. In seconds, smoke curled off the dried bark and wrapped around his hunched form.

"You found Nova's wind chime?"

I startled at the sound of my father's croak and whirled to face him. "Dad, you're home!" Why did I sound like a kid caught with her hand in the cookie jar?

"Oh. You have company." Dad's voice was tight. "Hello, Kajika."

The hunter unfurled from his crouch like a stalk of pondweed dragged by a slow current. "Mr. Price."

"I'm sorry about your loss," Dad added, as he hung up his coat. "Did Cat tell you we're organizing a memorial service for Holly this weekend?"

"I didn't have time." I slid the oven glove off my hand.

Dad sniffed the air. "Is something burning?"

"I forgot a tray of cookies in the oven."

His blue gaze met mine, and I could tell he was wondering what had made me forget. I could also tell, from the press of his lips, that he believed the hunter at fault.

"We hope you'll be able to attend," he finally said.

"I will try, but I must—"

"—return to Boston," I supplied, before he could tell my father he was setting out on an expedition to find Gwenelda.

My father was not a fan of the woman who'd posed as my 'Canadian cousin,' because he still believed she'd murdered her medical examiner husband.

"We'll hold you in our thoughts."

Kajika nodded. "I should be on my way. I will see you soon, Catori."

"Safe travels Kaji!" I was acting extra-spastic.

Once the pick-up turned out of the graveyard, Dad said, "He's related to you."

"God, Dad, not this discussion again. There's nothing going on between Kajika and me. I promise."

Even though Kajika clearly had wanted something to happen. As I returned to the kitchen to slide in the next tray of cookies, I wondered why I'd pulled away. The hunter was kind, undeniably handsome, strong, and tremendously protective.

He considers you a spare, my conscience pitched in. *A replacement for his dead mate.*

I didn't have *that* many requirements when it came to relationships, but I did want someone to want me for *me*, not because I was their beloved's doppelganger.

Until I was certain that Kajika wasn't seeing Ishtu every time he laid eyes on me, I'd keep my distance.

Kᴀᴊɪᴋᴀ ᴄᴀʟʟᴇᴅ me four times the first day.

He didn't say much, merely seemed to want company, so I provided chatter.

I talked about Rowan, and Cass, and the incredible movie I'd watched with my dad the night before.

I told him about the new playlist I'd created on Spotify, and explained how to download the music app.

I reassured him that no faeries had paid me a visit.

I asked him how he was going about looking for Gwenelda. It wasn't as though he could drop by a police precinct and file a missing person's report.

He said he'd caught the hum of her opal necklace. Opal apparently purred to hunters. Pretty neat tracking device.

Faeries had blazing brands; hunters had semi-precious stones.

I studied the opal necklace Gwen had given me the night of my mother's wake. Illuminated by the lamp on my nightstand, the neon-veined milky stone gleamed like a fireball. I slipped it on and then clicked my light off.

I wondered if Kajika could feel the hum of my pendant. Would it scramble the signal he was getting off Gwen?

I asked him before hanging up, and he said he couldn't feel mine. He was too far away.

The following day, he called me twice. The second time, he'd sounded excited, breathless. Someone had seen a woman fitting Gwenelda's description in a Burger King off the freeway in Kansas. Plus, the vibrations rolling off her necklace were becoming clearer.

Kansas? What the heck was she doing in Kansas? Sightseeing to forget her pain?

The next day, he didn't call.

At nightfall, I called him.

There was no answer.

I5

THE CLUB

That night, I dreamt I was trying to fit a key in a lock, but the key was twice as big as the lock. It had been incredibly frustrating. I thought about looking up the meaning in Mom's beloved dream dictionary when my phone buzzed.

I snapped it from its charger and all but punched the screen.

CASS: Food will be ready around 10:30.

The disappointment that it wasn't news from the hunter made my heart feel like a dumbbell.

I tried his cell, but like yesterday, he didn't answer. I tried again before Holly's memorial service but was met with more empty ringtones.

Maybe he'd lost his phone. Or maybe he'd found Gwenelda and hadn't had time to call. After all, they had a lot to catch up on, right?

Still, I couldn't shake the dread creeping through me as the hours passed. What if faeries had gotten to them?

Even though I didn't feel much like partying that night, I'd promised Cass to go clubbing, so I slipped on my favorite black leather leggings and a black tank top. After I made up my eyes with mascara and eyeliner, I sent Kajika a text to call me back.

He didn't.

He'd definitely lost his phone. Who went from calling someone four times a day to nothing?

Worrying about him was pointless, yet I couldn't help it.

After two of Dad's friends arrived at the house for the poker and pizza night I'd suggested he host, I left to pick up Cass. I connected my music to the car's stereo and was about to hit play when I noticed a new playlist had been added to my library.

It hadn't been there that morning when I drove over to Bee's to grab the food. The only person who had my login information was Kajika. He'd had enough time to listen to music, to create a playlist, but not to·call me?

Irritation squashed my concern and made me drive too fast. I was still fuming when Cass trundled out of her one-story clapboard house wearing a pink tutu, a white graphic tee, and Stan Smiths.

As she settled in beside me, I side-eyed her choice of skirt. "You look like a piece of bubble gum."

"Why, thank you. And you look like the Grim Reaper."

I smiled, and it struck me that it was the first time I'd smiled in days. "Appropriate for a girl living over a graveyard, no?"

She laughed. "I can't believe we're making jokes about death."

"May as well. So, where to?"

She typed the address into my GPS. As I drove away from Rowan, she said, "I want a pair of pants like that, but in Ferrari-red."

I bet. Where I favored understated, Cass loved loud colors. My mother had loved color as well. Especially red and yellow. The memory put a damper on my mood, but Cass's constant flow of chatter and bubbling excitement didn't let me wallow. Soon, I was almost as pumped as she was for the carefree evening ahead.

Where Rowan went dark after 10 P.M., Traverse City came alive. There were people everywhere. It didn't hurt that the night was surprisingly mild for February.

We parked a block away from the club and left our jackets in the car so we didn't have to lug them around. I was heading to the back of the line when Cass hooked her arm through mine and yanked me toward the fridge-sized bouncer beside the door.

The man took one look at us and unclipped the velvet rope, ushering us through.

"You come here often?" I whispered as we entered the loud, dark club.

"Nope."

"Then why did he let us through?"

Cass rolled her eyes. "Because we're hot."

The club was housed in an old library. Two-story high bookcases wrapped around a dance floor as big as our school gym. There were no books on these shelves, though, only objects of curio—skulls, beakers, dried flowers, and birdcages.

There was even a cauldron, which made me think of faeries, which made me look around. Ridiculous, I know, yet I couldn't help but peek behind the bar to see if anyone was crawling out of a hidden portal.

"Okay, so I had Cutie make us two Tonguebreakers." Cass shoved a drink into my hand.

It was neon-green, like the opal pendant nestled between my breasts. "Doesn't sound very enticing."

"They're just super sour Manzanas." She took a sip from hers. "You're going to L-O-V-E it."

So I tried it. It was awful. Acrid. I coughed and asked for water to rinse my mouth.

"Can I get a beer?" I asked the bartender.

Cass pursed her lips. "How can you not like this?"

"I've never been a fan of sour things."

After I'd gotten my cold beer, Cass grabbed my hand and dragged me through the writhing crush of bodies. As I swayed to the music, my stress and anger fizzled like the bubbles inside my beer.

"We should go out more!" I shouted over the deafening music.

"Yes! Absolutely yes! Now that you're back for a few months, we can go out all the time. We could even go see another ultimate fighting match. That was fun, wasn't it?"

Even though her mouth kept moving, her voice stopped penetrating my ears. And not because she'd just brought Kajika front and center, but because, sitting at the bar, one dainty leg folded over the other, a faerie was watching us.

Lily's long blonde hair glimmered in the revolving strobe lights, and her doll-like gray eyes blazed like pyrite. I expected her brother or Cruz to be with her, but neither kept her company.

Which didn't mean they weren't there.

I told Cass I was going to get a fresh beer and beelined toward the faerie.

"Is this a coincidence?" I asked Lily loudly.

Her eyes zeroed in on the iron chain around my neck. If I touched her, I'd singe off a layer of skin. I thought of the wind chime then. Did it really affect faeries if they didn't touch it? Had Cruz lied to me when he'd asked me to get rid of it?

She propped her phone in front of my face. **Don't come any closer or I leave.**

I folded my arms across my chest. "Because you think I want you to stay?"

Would you rather be alone with Borgo Lief and Ace?

84

16

THE KILLING

I whipped my gaze from side to side, scanning the club for the silver-haired faerie and the blond one. "I don't see them."

Lily typed for a while and then propped her phone in front of my face. **Why do you think we're here? Borgo followed you from Rowan, and Ace followed Borgo. My brother's been monitoring the old man to make sure he doesn't misbehave. Has the faerie made contact with you?**

"No. I mean, I saw him once, but we didn't talk."

Lily's fingers danced over her phone. Her message hiked up my eyebrows. **Ace is worried he wants to take you to Neverra.**

Ace had worried about me? Guilt twanged against my ribs.

Nobody wants a hunter up there.

My remorse evaporated. *Of course . . .*

Silly me.

Why I'd imagined Ace worrying about my safety was ludicrous. "Hunters can't enter Neverra, so his concern is misplaced."

Apparently, you're also a faerie. So maybe you could go through a portal.

I blinked. "You know?"

It's all anyone can speak about on Neverra.

85

I was the talk of the faerie world? Well, shoot.

Stella's been blabbing about it nonstop, Lily wrote on her phone. **Now that she's become a** *caligosupra.*

"A what?"

A mist-dweller. It's just a fancy title that allows her to build an abode over the mist.

"What mist?"

You really know nothing about Neverra, do you?

I shook my head. However curious I was about this mist, I asked a more pressing question, "Does Borgo know Kajika is back?"

Yes.

"Lily!" Cass's gleeful timbre clapped my eardrums. "Fancy seeing you here!" Cass pressed her clumpy bangs from her sweat-slicked forehead and hugged the faerie.

Lily froze, clearly not expecting to be embraced by my effusive friend. I mouthed, *Don't hurt her.*

The faerie's dark eyebrows slanted in annoyance. What? Did she expect me to trust her?

As she pulled away, Cass slurped up the Wood heiress's attire with her twinkling eyes. "That top! Where did you get it? I want it. It's *gorge.*"

Lily gave Cass a tight-lipped smile and a rigid shrug.

I had to admit Lily's silky red halter-top was nice—an outlandish consideration when a dangerous old faerie lurked nearby. Surely this was my psyche's defense mechanism: *think of inane things to avoid worrying about critical ones.*

"Want something to drink?" the bartender asked Lily, whom he was eating up with his eyes, and clearly not because he admired her taste in fashion.

"Another beer," I said, since Lily was otherwise preoccupied, typing out a message to Cass.

"That'll be eight dollars," he told me distractedly.

I peeled a ten from my purse and laid it on the sticky bar.

"Is Ace here?" Cass asked, way too eagerly.

Lily nodded. She dipped her chin toward a corner of the room. I turned at the same time as Cass. This time, I saw both faeries.

As though they could feel us staring, they interrupted their conversation and stared back. Eyes couldn't burn, yet theirs felt like laser beams. Especially Ace's.

It could've been a trick of the strobe lighting or a trick of his faerie fire, but it nonetheless made me clutch my beer bottle nearer to my pounding chest. Its coolness did little to slow my quickening pulse, but it did chill my flushed skin.

Ace turned back toward Borgo and jerked his head toward the door. The old faerie pressed his lips together, but then he tucked his chin into his neck like a cowed dog and walked away.

I tracked his retreat with my gaze, half-expecting him to duck inside a coat closet, but he left through the front door. I supposed faeries didn't build portals everywhere.

When I turned back toward Lily, my nose almost brushed up against Ace, who'd reclined against the bar as though he'd been standing there, watching the room for hours instead of a smattering of seconds.

I jolted away, my heart bumping against the walls of my chest, igniting the brand on my hand. Ace's gaze dipped to it, before skating over my collarbone and the chain wrapped around my neck.

I dragged my glowing hand down to my side, balancing the beer bottle between my index and middle fingers. "Why was Borgo here?"

He trailed the chain right into my tank top, his attention lingering there.

If he'd been any other guy, I would've assumed he was checking me out, but he was a faerie, and I was wearing the equivalent of rat poison around my neck.

"He thought you were Ishtu." His tone was perfectly flat. "Back from the dead." His eyes finally made their way back to my face, and although I tried to read the emotion they contained, they were too guarded.

"Who's Ishtu?" Cass asked, sucking a pink cocktail through a straw.

"Kajika's ex . . . *girlfriend*," I said.

She grimaced. "And you look like her? How weird is that?"

It was most definitely weird.

Then again, my whole life was weird.

"You guys want something to drink? The bartender is awesome-sauce," Cass said.

"We're good, Cassidy." Ace hooked one ankle over the other, getting comfortable, as though he was planning on staying.

"Where's the third stooge?" my friend asked.

Sister and brother both frowned.

"Cruz. Where is he?" she asked.

"He had some urgent business to attend to," Ace said, eyeing me.

"What sort of business?" I wrapped my mouth around my bottle's neck and took a long pull to quiet my ticking nerves.

Ace tilted his head to the side. "Why don't you tell me?"

"Why should I know Cruz's business?"

"*Why* . . . because of your *closeness* to the hunter." Could Ace sound any more sickened?

Cass's gaze ping-ponged between the faerie prince and me. "Hold on a sec. You hooked up with Adonis Ali, Cat?"

"Adonis Ali?" Ace arched an eyebrow at me, even though I hadn't been the one to come up with the moniker for Kajika.

Lily's eyes didn't waver off my face.

"No." My lips barely parted around the word. "As for Cruz, I have zero fucking idea where he is or what he's doing, because unlike you, Mr. Wood, I don't go around snooping on people."

A spasm hijacked Ace's falsely calm exterior, making his left eye twitch almost maniacally. "If I didn't *snoop around*, you'd be hanging with Borgo right now."

"Maybe I would've preferred that."

Ace straightened his head with an audible pop, then proceeded to stretch it from side-to-side, all the while spearing me with a barbed stare. He could stare all he wanted, I wouldn't be intimidated.

A lit phone snipped the tension stretching between me and the prince of Lalaland. *Where did Kajika go, Catori?*

Hoping an answer would make the siblings leave, I said, "He went to find Gwenelda."

"*The* Gwenelda who killed her medical examiner husband?" Of course, Cass would know this since her brother Jimmy had been the investigating officer.

"She didn't kill him," I said. "It's complicated."

Cass's eyebrows curled high.

"Lily loves to dance, Cassidy." Ace's gaze was so hot on my cheek that I rubbed the skin. "Why don't you get her off her stool and show her how girls in Rowan shake it?"

Although faeries didn't have influence, Cass grinned, only too happy to get away from our tense conversation. "It'd be my pleasure."

She seized Lily's hand and tugged. The faerie stumbled from the sudden jolt and almost collided into me, but I stepped aside before my skin could fry hers. When she regained her balance, her face teemed with relief.

"Like to *shake it*?" I asked as they faded into the thick crowd.

"Where's Kajika, Catori?"

"Something wrong with your hearing, Your Highness?"

Another satisfying twitch took hold of Ace's eye. "I meant geographically."

"And why, do tell, should I share anything I know with you?"

"Because a faerie died yesterday. I didn't love the guy, but did he deserve a bloody arrow through the heart? Surely not."

17

THE ANGER

The intensity of Ace's scrutiny rivaled the chilling force of his news.

I sucked in a breath. "In Rowan?"

"No. In Kansas."

My blood ran cold because that was Kajika's last known location. "You—you think Kajika killed him?"

"Only hunters can kill faeries, and since there are only two, that places him pretty high up on my list of suspects."

"But he's looking for Gwenelda. He's not hunting down—" A thought hurtled through my mind. "Maybe the faerie attacked him, and he had to defend himself."

"So he *is* in Kansas." It wasn't a question.

"I didn't say that."

"I leave for a week, and suddenly, you're a hunter-hugger?"

I squeezed the bottle's neck hard between my fingers. "I'm not a hunter-*hugger*."

"Yet, you refuse to impart sensitive information. Information that could potentially help me stop a bloody war before it begins. *And* you're wearing their necklace."

90

"Because Borgo's in town. I'm not strong like Kajika or endowed with magical dust like you, Ace. I'm just trying to protect myself."

"You're marked. The only faerie that can kill you is Cruz. Don't you get how our system works?"

"I could still be hurt."

The apple in his throat rolled. "How do you know it isn't the people who gave you the necklace who'll hurt you?"

"Don't, Ace."

"I bet you still think I killed Holly."

"She had a rash all over her body. Which means she was *gassed*."

His gaze turned icy. "That's a convenient conclusion."

"Can you prove you didn't asphyxiate her?"

He folded his arms over his white dress shirt and glowered. I childishly glowered right back.

Two songs played before I said, "Her ashes turned liquid and produced a rose liana."

His pupils seemed to shrink, giving way to more brilliant blue.

"Does that happen to all faeries?"

He slid his lips against one another as though evaluating how much of an answer to give me. Perhaps, he wouldn't give me one at all.

Lo and behold, he said, "Yes. We all turn into flora when we die. The first exotic species on this Earth came from a deceased fae."

I thought of all the flowers Grandma Woni had turned into jam; pictured the petals as bits of faerie flesh and gagged.

"Beats becoming worm food," he pitched in.

I shook both images from my head and refocused on the liana. "Apparently those are the same roses the hunters were buried in. Did you know that?"

"I assumed. Hunters aren't endowed with that sort of magic."

"And you didn't tell me?"

"First off, why should I share anything about my world with

91

you?" His tone was clipped. "And secondly, would you even have believed me?"

I discarded that first part because I felt the same, but I did give that second part actual thought. *Would* I have believed him?

"Did you ever wonder how your mother got the coffin out of the ground all by herself?"

I stopped raising my beer bottle to my lips, shocked by his enquiry, because no, I hadn't wondered, but I really should have. "Let me guess"—I took a sip, but the beer tasted warm and flat now, like ash and tears—"you know?"

"Actually, I don't. No faerie could've assisted her, and Gwenelda was still in there. She couldn't have helped, either. So no, I don't know, but you should wonder about these things instead of wondering if I killed a decrepit *calidum*."

"Don't call her decrepit."

"Fine. A *timeworn calidum* who, by the way, got your mother killed."

I gritted my teeth at his reminder but chose not to engage on the subject. Holly's death hadn't brought Mom back, so it didn't please me that she was gone.

"She chose *your* species." I jabbed my pointer finger toward him.

"Species?"

"You should show her some respect."

"She wrote a potentially harmful book about us, so no, I don't think I owe her anything."

"There's nothing harmful in there, Ace!" I tossed both hands in the air out of frustration, sending what little beer remained in my bottle sloshing onto some guy's boots. "If you give me the book, I'll prove it to you by reading it out loud."

No way in hell would I divulge her secrets to the people she'd hidden them from. If I got the book back, I'd make sure to sit under the wind chime, wearing pounds of iron jewelry, and read it cover to cover until I'd committed every last word to memory.

Someone bumped into my back so hard it sent me flying toward Ace. He whipped one arm out in front of him, effectively breaking my fall. Flames engulfed his fingers and wrist.

I gasped.

He yanked his hand back, grabbed a random glass from the bar, and dumped it on his crackling flesh. It hissed as the fire extinguished.

I sort of felt bad. "That's pretty much how my hand feels every time the brand lights up."

Ace's blue eyes were as neon as the drink Cass had ordered me when we'd walked in. "I highly doubt the pain of a faerie brand is anything like that of iron."

"Do I owe you something?"

"For saving you from getting a faceful of beer-basted wood?"

"No, for bringing my car back."

"I don't need your money. Got plenty of my own."

Guilt that I hadn't even offered to pay him layered itself over the vast range of other emotions the faerie seemed to always bring out in me. "I meant a *gajoï*, Ace."

"No."

"Why'd you do it, then?"

"Because I knew where it was, and I assumed you'd be needing it."

He wasn't a total jerk, but that was a very selfless thing to do. *Too* selfless. "How about the real reason?"

When his gaze dropped to my mouth, I freed the lip I was biting.

"Why do you assume I have some ulterior motive?"

"Because I highly doubt you had nothing better to do with your time. The same way I highly doubt you're looking to—how did you say it again? Oh, yeah. *Seduce* me into being your friend."

His lips quirked but the smirk held all of three seconds. "Fine. I did it because I felt bad about the book."

I tilted my head, and my long hair slipped over my shoulder. "Not because you want me to tell you what's inside?"

"No. But if you feel like telling me, I'm all ears."

"Find a way to get rid of this"—I lifted my branded hand—"and I'll tell you everything I saw."

His eyes traced the faint white V, and I swear there was something feral in his slow study of my brand.

"*Without* killing me," I added, assuming that was where his mind had gone.

"You and your silly requirements."

"Yes, staying alive is so silly." I attempted to tamp down my growing smile. "So, do we have a deal?"

"We do."

"Shall we shake on it?" I asked sweetly.

He raised a smile to match my own. "Wait until I tell Borgo you're actually Ishtu."

My glee vanished. "You wouldn't."

"Apparently I kill dying *bazash*, so why wouldn't I?"

"He'll kill me."

"He can't."

"He'll torture me."

"Maybe I'll watch."

"I hate you."

"Hate you too, Kitty Cat. So very much."

The nickname made me forget my comeback.

"What? No *don't call me that*?" he said in a high-pitched, nasally voice.

"I don't sound like that."

"That's the way all women sound to me."

"You're such a pig."

"You mean faerie prince."

"More like woodland swine."

He chuckled. "It's so easy to rile you up. So easy."

94

I glared at him, and then I moved toward the bar. He shifted away, no longer smiling.

He probably thought I was about to sauté some other body part of his. It wasn't my intention, but if by chance my arm were to brush his and set fire to his crisp little shirt, I'd feel minute remorse. He healed quickly.

"Can I get another beer, please?" I asked the bartender.

"Coming right up."

"Want a drink, Ace? My treat. Perhaps something with cyanide?"

He peeled three hundred-dollar bills from a wad of cash in the back pocket of his skinny jeans and slapped them on the bar top. "Cyanide doesn't kill us."

"What a shame."

"Still dead set on offing me, huh?"

Yes, we'd just bantered like old buddies, but I still didn't know for sure if he'd had a hand in Holly's death.

"I might trust easily, Ace, but I don't forgive easily. You helped steal from me. And then Kajika sees you at Holly's right after she dies." My anger was jumbled with disappointment, and that was the worst sort of anger. "Please, take your little sister and leave me the hell alone."

His features hardened into a steel mask. "Very well." He signed something, I imagined to Lily, who returned to his side, obedient little sister that she was.

I nodded to the three green bills on the bar. "Don't forget your cash."

His nostrils flared, once, twice. Then he flicked his gaze toward the bartender, who was ogling Lily—*again*. "Keep the change, but no more drinks for these two. And stop eye-fucking my sister. She's a minor."

The harsh words popped Cass's eyes wide and sent a blush careening over Lily's cheeks, a shade of red that rivaled her top.

95

Cass's shock and Lily's mortification had nothing on my anger, though.

I balled my fists. "Where do you get off thinking you can boss Cass and I around?"

Ace took a step toward me, getting so close that the fire beneath his skin licked a path down the front of my body, and his scent— clean, expensive, male—punched up my nose. "If you want to get shitfaced, by all means do, but then my sister and I fly you home. You want us gone, you stick to water. What'll it be?"

The opal pendant vibrated with my raging heartbeats. "Water."

Oh, how I wanted to punch something—preferably something Ace-shaped. This need grew as the hours ticked by and didn't abate when the sun cracked over the horizon.

I was so consumed by my wrath that, come dawn, I drove over to Blake's old house, let myself in with the spare key he'd given me, unearthed his punching bag, and pummeled the stiff leather until my knuckles bruised and sweat basted my spine.

And still I kept punching.

I probably would've kept up my assault if a scarred faerie hadn't had the balls to show up in Blake's garage.

18

THE LOVERS

"Stay back!" I yelled at Borgo.

He was standing close enough that I could see the white, caterpillar-like scar straining over his collarbone.

I flicked my gaze to the hood of the old Buick on which lay my windbreaker. Inside the zippered pocket were the little white arrows Kajika had fashioned for me. Slowly, so as not to alert the faerie, I backed up toward the car.

"Don't come any closer." If only my voice sounded authoritative instead of tremulous.

Borgo took a step toward me. I bolted backward. When the base of my spine met the cool body of the car, I whipped out my arms and scrabbled for my jacket. Instead, my hand met glass.

Excruciating pain shot through my palm and up my wrist. It traveled like an electrical current up my forearm, icing the blood in my veins.

I tore my fingers away from the car window, and almost fainted at the sight of the gash leaking blood. Even though common sense urged me to keep my attention on the faerie, I twisted my neck to see what I'd cut myself on—the serrated edge of a shattered window glowed red.

97

It took me a millisecond to link the smashed glass to Blake's suicide attempt. When Cass had found him, she'd bashed the window in with a bat. I could really have used that bat right about now. Although I wasn't sure I could actually swing it.

Unfortunately, my wound didn't miraculously heal like it had the time I ran into the faeries in Ruddington and one of them charred my fingers. The deep cut gushed blood that dribbled in rivulets down my forearm.

I snapped my attention back on Borgo. Black and white dots sprinkled my eyesight, and cold sweat trickled down my neck from the loss of blood.

It's just a flesh wound, I reminded my woozy self. *You didn't nick an artery.*

My stomach heaved nonetheless. I gritted my teeth. Now was so not the time to hurl or swoon.

Borgo zipped closer to me, appearing between me and my windbreaker—between salvation and certain death.

I whipped my hand out and held it in front of his face. "Get back! I have hunter blood on my hands."

He smiled. I had to blink several times to make sure I wasn't imagining it.

"I'm dead serious, Borgo Lief!"

The brand on the top of my hand started to burn, but the pain was nothing compared to the one blistering my palm.

Shallow blue flames enveloped Borgo's hand. Reflexively, I shut my eyes and mouth and tried not to breathe through my nose. I even raised my arms to shield my face, which was utterly useless. He was about to set fire to me, not *gas* me.

When I'd pictured my life ending, it had never been in a dusty garage after a boxing workout, incinerated by faerie fire. Then again, who *would* imagine such a death?

I waited for the kaleidoscope of memories to click through my mind; for the white light to blind me and Mom to collect me; for the fear to subside and turn into numbness.

I waited and waited, but all I saw were the burgundy insides of my lids, and all I felt was my furious heart rate. I tasted metal at the same time as the pain in my hand receded. If I wasn't hurting any longer, the end was near.

When I'd left the house that morning, my father had been asleep. I would've given anything to go back in time, to climb over him and hug him like I used to when I was a child. I would've given anything for a few more minutes with him.

My eyes became wet and hot. My cheeks, too. Senses darting out of me like octopi tentacles, I listened.

Someone exhaled. "You're okay." The man's voice sounded like a crackling gramophone.

Was it the Great Spirit? Wasn't the Great Spirit female? Maybe She had a gravelly voice. Tentatively, I lifted my lids up.

I was still in Blake's garage.

And Borgo was still in front of me.

I checked my palm quickly. It was clean of blood and devoid of the slenderest blemish.

"You didn't kill me," I whispered.

"Kill you?" He sounded borderline pained that I'd jump to that conclusion. "I'm not sure what you were told about me, but I'd like to introduce myself to you, Catori. I'm Borgo, former head of the Lief family, one of the noble families on Neverra."

"I know who you are," I croaked.

"If you think I wanted to end your life, then no, you do not know who I am, because I'm no murderer."

"You killed Ishtu."

The lines around his eyes and the grooves in his forehead became as pronounced as claw marks. "I did not"—his throat bobbed with a thick swallow—"kill her."

"Kajika told me everything." I creeped sideways until I was an arm's length away from him. "He saw you. You and Lyoh. He was *there*."

The blue in Borgo's eyes seemed to whirl. "He arrived too late to see anything."

"Right. You'd already killed her."

"No." He delivered the word like a punch. Mouth tight, he shifted his gaze to the Buick and studied the hood's curves. "I left Neverra because I was told Ishtu . . . I thought—"

"You thought you'd botched the job and returned to see it through?" My voice was so strident I prayed a neighbor would hear me.

I searched the dawn-lit road for incoming cars or a sprinting savior. I'd even take a flying rescuer for once.

"I didn't kill—" His voice caught on a . . . *whimper*? "Ishtu."

My gaze snapped back to his like a rubber band.

His face had grown several shades darker, and his feet had lifted off the cement floor. "I didn't."

Slowly, the ruddiness drained from his face, but the spark in his eyes didn't abate. Emotion rolled off him.

It slowed the pounding of my heart, made it thump deeper, longer, more intensely. It was as though Borgo had hijacked that organ and was molding its beats.

The gentlest caress brushed my cheek, pressed my face sideways. No hand stroked my skin, though I felt one, and then that same hand stroked my veins.

My blood bloated and floated sluggishly through my body.

Although I'd never been interested in older men, Borgo's charming smile, his brilliant eyes, and his steadfast confidence attracted me.

He'd healed my hand. He'd helped me. Saved me from bleeding out.

I felt indebted in a way I hadn't felt since Cruz had saved Gwenelda.

The absolute tenderness of his deed hit me with a force that made me step toward him and kiss his cheek. His skin was soft, hot, and smelled of sand and sunshine and fire.

He gasped, leaped back.

Smoke curled off his flesh.

Why was there smoke? *My necklace!* I reached my hand out to nurse his ashen cheek, but he zipped farther away from me, hissing.

"I'm so sorry. Oh, Borgo, I'm so sorry."

"It's okay," he said, his voice hoarse. "I've felt worse pain."

"What have I done?" I moaned. "Oh. What have I done? You don't even have dust to heal yourself."

"It's okay. It'll heal."

"Can you use fire?"

"Fire doesn't heal faerie wounds." He was still breathing hard, but his voice had grown steadier. "It would be like healing human wounds with blood."

As he spoke, I looked at the ragged scar on his neck and hated the person who'd given it to him. I hated Kajika. He'd bragged about hurting Borgo, about usurping the faerie's dust. *Bastard!*

"I'll get your dust back," I said. "I know who has it. I'll go—"

"I'm going to switch it off now, Catori."

"Switch what off?"

"When I turn it off, promise you'll still hear me out."

"Anything for you, Borgo."

His nostrils flared slowly. "Say the words."

I frowned but spoke them. "I promise you."

He held my gaze the same way a man holds his lover's hips— possessively, preciously, passionately. It reminded me of the way Cruz had embraced me the day he'd brought Gwenelda back to life. How could I have loved a boy when a real man was standing before me, though?

"You make me feel like"—I studied the magnificent blue depths of his irises—"like I'm the most extraordinary woman on this planet. Like ..."

The end of my sentence withered in my throat. Somehow, though, my mind remembered it.

Repugnance flooded me.

Had I just professed my love to this . . . this executioner?

"What did you do to me?" I growled.

The man's face was so lined. More lined than my father's, and yet, somehow, I'd looked upon it with enchantment and tenderness.

I rubbed my mouth, my cheek, feeling utterly filthy. "What the hell did you just do to me?"

"I used *captis* on you."

Even though the faerie was still close and emitting heat like an inferno, the air lost several degrees.

I shivered, and then my teeth chattered, and I wrapped my arms around myself. "You what?"

"I made you desire me, Catori."

The words reverberated through my skull like a dull headache.

"I'm sorry. I didn't want to use *captis* on you, but there was so much hate in your eyes. I couldn't stand it." He sighed deeply. "I need you to listen to me. You promised. Please keep your promise."

"Do I have a choice, or will it tear me to shreds if I tell you to get the hell away from me?"

"You have a choice but—"

"Did you come here to kill me?"

"No."

"Did you kill Ishtu?"

"No."

There was no reason for me to trust his answers. "If I hear you out, do you promise to leave me alone after that?"

He nodded.

"And do you promise *never* to use *captis* on me again?"

"I promise."

I watched him warily, detecting pain and sadness in the droop of his mouth and eyes. The sorrow surprised me so much that it stopped the gush of adrenaline and steadied my heart.

Was he doing that? Making me feel something again?

I tried to pick apart my feelings, but it was as futile as monitoring the evolution of a single cell without a microscope.

"I loved Ishtu," he said quietly.

Had he just said . . .? *No.* I must've misheard.

"I loved her."

This time, there was no mistaking his declaration.

"And she loved me."

19

THE PUNISHMENT

Borgo stared around Blake's garage, gaze lingering on the Buick's shattered window. "Did you break the window?"

Was he really discussing the state of Blake's car after he'd just bowled me over with his declaration? "Ishtu loved you?"

He looked around at the shelves that still held Blake's toolboxes, at the work bench topped with curled wood shavings, at the row of school trophies my friend had won for swimming. "Who does this house belong to?"

"My friend." My body felt like a room in which the power had gone out. Darkness swamped my insides, smothering any lingering light.

I didn't want to discuss Blake, not with this stranger and not when my heart was still tripping over that stranger's revelation.

Borgo must've sensed my disquiet because he didn't ask any further questions. "Could we take a walk, Catori?" He slid his gnarled fingers through the wave of silver hair that crested over his tired forehead. "I will not hurt you, I promise."

I bit my lip. I supposed that if he'd wanted to hurt me, he would've done so already. Besides, being out in the open with this man was preferable to being locked in a garage with him.

"I was on my way to breakfast." I hadn't been, but Bee's was a few blocks away. It felt smart to head to a populated area. "We can talk on the way there."

I grabbed my windbreaker and stabbed my arms through, then zipped it up over my bright-pink workout bra and sheer-black tank top. Curling my fingers around an arrow, I led the way to Bee's, maintaining a wide distance between us.

Although he glanced at me several times, he didn't speak. Not even when I told him that the stage was his.

As we neared Morgan Street, he said, "I'm still trying to get over the fact that you aren't her."

Where he watched me with curiosity, I regarded him with suspicion.

Since he still had said nothing by the time we reached the restaurant's threshold, I sighed and gestured for him to follow me inside.

Cass, who'd dropped the little pitcher of milk she'd been frothing when I'd walked in with Borgo, trotted over to our booth, gaze pinballing between the old fae and me.

Although clearly desperate to know who he was and why I was sitting with him, she thankfully didn't ask. His eyes lingered on my friend, as though he recognized her. Maybe he recognized what she was—fae, like him.

Well, sort of like him, since she was mixed.

As she retreated toward the coffee machine with our order, she drew her cell phone out of her apron pocket. A second later, my phone vibrated with a message from Cass—a bunch of question marks. I sent her a quick thumbs up emoji so she wouldn't worry, then I slid the phone back into my windbreaker's pocket.

Since Borgo still hadn't volunteered any information, I asked, "Can all—can all of you use *captis*?"

What I'd felt for Borgo reminded me acutely of what I'd felt for Cruz. Had the black-haired faerie coerced me? Would it lessen my guilt if he *had* used magic?

Borgo nodded. "But the older we become, the more we can control it. The younger generation just puts it out there whenever they're attracted to someone to guarantee the attraction becomes mutual. Men—especially fae—do not fare well with rejection."

So the fae really could manipulate hearts...

"Why do you ask?"

I didn't want to admit what I feared. Plus it was none of his business. "Did you use *captis* on Ishtu?"

"We can't use it on hunters, just like they can't use their influence on us."

"I have hunter blood."

"But it's not pure." His eyes glided over my nose, lips, chin, but there was nothing lustful about his scrutiny. If anything, his expression seemed to waver between awe and sorrow.

"If you didn't kill Ishtu, then who did?"

"Lyoh Vega."

My lungs loosed a breath that he hadn't spoken Kajika's name. Yes, my mind had gone there. How could it not after Borgo confessed the hunter's mate had loved a faerie? Spurned spouses often committed crimes of passion.

Cass returned with two mugs of chamomile tea and mouthed something that sounded like, *What's that smell?* but I guessed it was, *What the hell?*

Later, I mouthed back.

She glanced over her shoulder at me so many times on her way back to the bar that I thought she'd trip on a chair leg, but Cass had worked here long enough to have the layout memorized.

"Why did Lyoh kill Ishtu?" I asked.

"Because she found us together one day. In the woods. There was a small cave where Ishtu and I would meet. When Lyoh discovered our relationship, she did what I might have done before Jacobiah introduced me to hunters. Before he showed me they weren't evil-incarnate." He lowered his gaze to the steam curling off his tea. "She reported me to Maximus Wood."

A single tear trickled out of his right eye and dripped down his ashen cheek. The skin had smoothed out over the burn my iron-laden kiss had inflicted, but it was still the slightest bit leaden.

"She killed Ishtu, and then she reported me," he repeated in a thick whisper.

I didn't think Borgo had much to gain from fabricating a false love story, and yet . . . "Kajika never mentioned that his"—I'd been about to use the word *mate* but switched it for the more acceptable —"wife was having an affair."

"Because he wasn't aware of our tryst. Kajika was so busy chasing faeries he often forgot he had a young, beautiful wife at home. A wife who wanted peace, like her uncle Negongwa." Borgo knotted his fingers together on the table, pain or shame—perhaps both—rippling across his brow. "She and Kajika fought about Negongwa's desire for an armistice often. When she'd accompany her uncle to his meetings with Jacobiah, she'd tell me about how deaf he was to her pleas."

"And you were at those meetings because . . .?"

A deep swallow jostled the time-loosened skin of his throat. "Because I was Jacobiah's first guard—his *draca*—and a *draca's* duty is to protect the *wariff*."

"*Draca*? Is that a type of *lucionaga*?"

"Something like that." Borgo's lips quirked at my use of a Faeli word. "I transformed into another winged creature."

"Which one?"

"One you'd rather never encounter."

My heart sped up the slightest bit; not quite fast enough to ignite my brand. Speaking of brand, I clearly remembered it lighting up in the garage, yet neither Ace nor Cruz had shown up.

I drummed my fingers, watching the tattoo roll over my metacarpal bones. "Which bird?"

"It's not really a bird."

"Then what is it?"

"I believe you Earth-dwellers call them dragons."

107

Even though I was no cartoon character, my jaw slackened, drawing my lips wide. First faeries, then fireflies, now dragons?

A normal girl might've challenged the existence of a mystical beast, might've told the faerie in front of her that he was clearly off his rocker, but I was no longer a normal girl. I shifted in my seat, my Lycra leggings sliding over the blood-red leather like silk over skin.

"Are you still—" I cleared my throat to untangle my voice from the sticky threads of my disbelief. "Can you still *transform*?"

"No. Once you're stripped of the title, you're stripped of the power to transform."

"Who's the current *draca*?"

"Lyoh Vega."

I shivered at the name. I already didn't want to encounter her in human form, but even less in *mythical-fire-breathing-creature* form. "Is there more than one?"

"Many are trained at birth for the station—they earn the title of *lucionaga* and serve to protect the royal family—but until chosen as *draca,* none are given the power to shift into more than a fire-wielding fly."

I smiled at the description, but then I stopped because this wasn't a convivial tea party; it was a very serious hearing.

There were few patrons at Bee's, but the few sitting there—especially old Mr. Hamilton—kept darting curious glances our way. Hopefully, no one had caught a word of our conversation.

Still, I decided to rein in my curiosity about the faerie world and focus on the reason I was sitting across from Borgo. "How do I know you're not lying to me about your relationship with Ishtu?"

He looked up from his mug, eyes stained red. "Do you know what the punishment was for faeries who took hunters as their lover?"

"They imprisoned them, right?"

"Under Linus, yes. Under Maximus, punishment was castration."

The blood drained from my face. "They—you were—"

A red slash brightened his sallow cheeks. "I would rather have been killed, Catori."

I was too horrified to say anything.

"Even though, in a way, I already was. The day Ishtu died, so did I. So did I . . ."

The air in the room grew suffocating and loud as though thousands of *lucionaga* were beating their tiny, scorching wings against my eardrums.

"Death is all I've yearned for these past two centuries, but I stayed alive because Lyoh and Jacobiah had a child, and Jacobiah wasn't there to take care of him. I stayed to remind Cruz what an extraordinary man his father was. I stayed so that he could have someone in his life to run to since he could not run to his hateful mother.

"But Lyoh, being the manipulative witch that she is, took him away from me as soon as she could secure a good marriage for him. We still met, but Cruz became busy with court life; he made friends. In the past few decades, our friendship became a hindrance to him. *Caligosupra* do not like *caligosubi*, and that's what I'd become after my castration." My raised eyebrow incited him to add, "*Caligosupra* are mist-dwellers, and *caligosubi*, marsh-dwellers. *Caligosupra* employ us, remunerating us with sunshine and mallow, but that's the extent of our contact."

I rolled the paper napkin between my fingers. "Why are they called 'mist-dwellers?' And how does one pay in sunshine?"

"A silver ribbon of fog drapes over Neverra. It serves as a border between the castes and blocks the sun from reaching the land."

It seemed strange to have created a border from a fluid cloud. In my mind, borders were solid, tangible, like walls.

"You still have fire, so why don't you just fly over the mist?"

"And rub shoulders with *caligosupra*? I would rather die for good, Catori. The only reason I stayed on Neverra instead of leaving was for Cruz, but now—" He took a sip of his tea, lids slipping shut.

"Now, I've no plan to return. Especially since your tribe is back. I want to help."

I didn't doubt that he did, but I doubted the hunter would let him.

"I will start by apologizing to Kajika."

My heart stumbled as I imagined Borgo walking up to Kajika. The hunter would stab him in the heart before Borgo could utter a single word. "I don't think he'll listen to an apology. He really despises you."

"But I did not kill Ishtu."

"But you loved her, Borgo. Not only is the hunter proud, but he's still obsessed with Ishtu. With her memory. So confessing your love would be worse."

"Have you ever loved anyone, Catori?"

I nodded.

"Well, if someone who loved them too thought you'd killed them, could you live with yourself?"

"I completely understand your reasons, but I've come to know Kajika, and he's—well, he's hotheaded and not easy to talk to."

"I appreciate your concern. Truly I do."

The door to Bee's Place jingled.

"Does your concern mean you believe me?" Emotion lanced in his jaw.

I was about to say *yes*, that I did believe him, but was interrupted by the two newcomers that strolled up to our booth and plopped their unwelcomed asses down.

20

THE CONTAMINATION

Ace leaned back in the booth, making himself right at home. The nerve of this faerie. "Sorry to crash your little rendezvous, Borgo, but we have a few questions for your lovely companion."

Even though I still wore my iron necklace, I scooted as far away as possible from the blond male, all but gluing my back to the brick wall.

"What? Not happy to see us, Kitty Cat?"

"When am I ever happy to see you?" I muttered.

"I can think of a few instances. Like the time your aunt and father—"

"What do you want?"

Murmurs spread like bushfire around the restaurant. Everyone —which was thankfully only Mr. Hamilton, Cass, and a handful of regulars—had pivoted to look. I felt myself blush, so I inched the zipper of my windbreaker down to cool off, which had the added benefit of exposing my iron necklace.

Ace didn't inch back even though I willed him to. His complacency both annoyed me, because it meant he wasn't threatened, and satisfied me, because he clearly underestimated me.

"You should really scootch back," I suggested sweetly.

"I would, but then I'd have to speak really loudly, and I doubt you want everyone listening in on the conversation we're about to have about your boyfriend."

My stomach hardened into a fist. "I don't have a boyfriend."

The green depths of Cruz's eyes called out to my own. "Don't you?"

The room and everyone inside started disappearing, as though individual spotlights were being switched off.

I could almost hear the circuit breakers tripping.

Click.

Click.

Click.

Only Cruz remained incandescent, wreathed in some sort of unearthly glow.

"Catori?" The disembodied voice felt as though it were calling me from the bottom of a cave.

There was a loud clapping sound. Two hands colliding dangerously close to my nose.

I blinked. Like a spider whose silken web was abruptly torn, I plummeted out of my daze.

What the— I stared around the booth, my gaze stopping on Cruz. "Did you just use *captis* on me?"

"Yes." Cruz laced his fingers together on the table and studied his nails as though they were some newly-sprouted body part.

"Have you used it before?"

Slowly, he lifted his gaze to mine and nodded. "I have."

"When?" I demanded, even though I was almost certain I could pinpoint the exact instances he'd performed his little magic trick.

"In my car and after I brought back Gwenelda."

I knew it! I knew the pull I'd felt to him was unnatural!

"*Captis* calms people down," he said slowly.

"Do I fucking seem calm to you?"

Cruz didn't even flinch at my hiss. As for Ace, he just smirked.

Bastard.

I turned the full force of my glare on the prince of Neverra. "Have *you* ever used it on me?"

"The fact that you have to ask makes me wonder *when* you felt like tearing your panties off in my presence."

My cheeks flamed. "Never."

"Relax, Cat, I'd rather flagellate myself with that necklace of yours than get you hot and bothered. Even for fun." He picked lint off the lapel of his sports jacket and flicked it off. "Now that we've cleared that up, Cruz, can you please fix Borgo's cheek, and then can we move on to the matter at hand?"

I folded my arms over my chest as Cruz inspected Borgo's ashen skin before pressing his palm to it. Sparks erupted and glittered, swirling in the restaurant's inert air.

I watched the dust carefully, afraid it might drift toward me, slide into my mouth or up my nostrils. Reflexively, I held my breath. I didn't shut my eyes, though. I didn't want to miss a single beat of what was happening.

When Cruz finally lowered his hand to the table and slotted his fingers back together, I gasped for breath. "Why can I see it but not your illusions?"

"What exactly *do* you see, Catori?" Borgo asked.

"Sparkling dust."

"*Wita*—so you stop referring to it as dust or *gassen*," Ace said, "is fluid, like a ribbon. What you see are particles." He finished his explanation just as Cass bustled over to our table.

"What can I get you all?" She flicked her pen against her notepad, beatmatching the pulse in my neck.

Ace smiled up at her, and a blush stained her cheeks. The Great Spirit help him if he was using *captis* on her.

"Why don't you whip us up a round of cocktails? Nothing too sour."

Was that for my benefit? I supposed it was for his since he didn't

113

know the first thing about my likes and dislikes. "I don't want a cocktail."

Cass's eyes darted to me. "I can make a virgin one for you."

One corner of Ace's mouth tugged up. "Had too much to drink last night?"

"Screw you," I muttered under my breath.

"Can I get another tea, Cass?" I grumbled, because mine had gone cold, and there was little else I disliked more than tepid beverages—although admittedly, my list of aversions was growing exponentially fast these days. "I've interacted with toddlers more mature than you, Ace."

"What did I say this time?"

Borgo and Cruz glanced at him.

"Just show her the picture." Cruz was staring at his clenched hands again. Did he not trust himself to look at me without using magic?

"So? Have you ever seen her?" Ace jabbed his cell phone screen that was lit up with the picture of a twenty-something blonde with a razor-sharp bob and thin brown eyes.

The woman was staring straight into the camera, one palm held aloft as though she were shielding herself.

"No. Who is she?" I asked.

Ace's lips curled in disgust. "*She* is a new one."

I frowned, until I computed that *new one* probably meant *new huntress*. And then my frown metamorphosed into surprise, which was closely followed by dread. I unknotted my arms and leaned forward to further inspect the picture.

"Another one was awakened?" I asked, even though none of the twelve had blonde hair. At least, not in the hand-drawn portraits in Holly's book. Perhaps the woman had dyed her hair?

"No."

"Then how? Is she family?"

Ace's phone turned dark. He lifted it and returned it to his pocket. "Did Kajika ever tell you how he became a hunter?"

"He did." My lids drew up and up. "*Oh.*" Even though the air was stiflingly hot, a chill raced down my spine.

I remembered the hunter's story as though he'd recounted it yesterday. Negongwa had pressed a bloodied hand against one of Kajika's open wounds so that their bloods mixed.

"He *made* her?" I whispered.

"Either he or Gwenelda did," Cruz said. "And then they abandoned her, because she clearly didn't understand what she was, even though she managed to kill one of ours."

"Who did she kill?" Was Borgo hoping Cruz would speak Lyoh's name?

Cruz stretched his neck which cracked more than once. "Simoni."

"Oh," Borgo said flatly. "Your mother must be upset. Wasn't he her latest plaything?"

Cruz's head straightened and his jaw flexed.

For a long while, neither spoke, merely stared at each other in charged silence until Cass bustled over with the cocktails and two bowls of salted corn nuts.

I shifted in my seat, catching Ace's full attention. His gaze darted to my necklace and then to the limb nearest him.

I relished the security iron gave me. I'd never felt more invincible. If only it worked on everyone and not just on faeries.

Once Cass was gone, I asked, "Did you apprehend her?"

"She unfortunately got away," Cruz said.

"Really? You had time to snap a picture of her, but not to catch her?"

"She wore iron," he answered, as though that explained why they hadn't been able to capture her.

Our gazes intersected, but nothing happened this time. No out-of-nowhere desire, no heightened pulse, no hatred, no love, nothing.

"Her reflexes were unnaturally developed." He dropped his

attention to the thin stream of bubbles rushing around the large ice cubes in his clear cocktail.

I frowned. "Meaning?"

"She was fast."

"I thought it took time for their powers to develop." When Kajika recounted the story of how he'd become a hunter, he'd mentioned it had taken days before his supernatural skills kicked in.

"Perhaps it's an effect of their lengthy slumber," Borgo suggested.

It made sense. "Did you have time to ask her about Gwen and Kajika?"

"Yes. She didn't know who they were."

"So they made her and left her? How did she know to wear iron? How did she know how to"—I leaned forward and whispered —"kill your kind?"

Ace drummed his fingers against the table. "All great questions we'd love for you to ask your little boyfriend."

"Stop calling him my boyfriend."

"I'll stop once you stop acting like he's the Great Spirit's gift to womankind."

"How am I giving off that impression?" My voice was strident. *Too* strident.

Cass, along with the new cook, glanced in our direction.

"You're wearing *his* necklace." Ace's clipped tone could shear metal.

"It's not *his*; it's Gwenelda's."

"And the little arrows in your pocket? Are those Gwenelda's, too?"

I looked down at the sticks that were jutting out of my pocket.

"We were hoping you could call him, Catori." Cruz rubbed his thumb against the condensation hazing his glass, making the ice cubes shrink. "And tell him that if he creates any more hunters, we'll have to take action."

"How do you know he has not created more?" Borgo lifted his tea and took a sip.

Steam curled off Cruz's thumb as his fire dried the dampness. "We haven't sensed more."

"What sort of action?" I crossed my legs, and the burgundy leather squeaked beneath me.

"We'll annul our peaceful accord, and then I'll gas him." Ace said this so matter-of-factly that I froze.

"And you don't understand why I think you killed Holly?" My voice was low and full of disgust.

His eyes became shards of aquamarine, sharp and cold. He could glare all he wanted. I wasn't intimidated.

"Move. I'm all *faeried* out." I started sliding to get out of the booth, but he didn't budge. I stopped before our bodies touched, not wanting to create more of a show than we were already giving Bee's customers.

He stayed put.

"Move out of my way, Ace," I gritted out.

Still, he didn't.

"Fine. You asked for it." I scooted closer, until my wrist connected with his thigh.

He lurched off the banquette and hissed as tendrils of smoke wafted off his stonewashed gray jeans, from a hole no larger than a cigarette burn. He slapped his palm against his pant leg.

Wita pulsed from his hand like face powder. It stopped the burn but did nothing to mend the hole in his jeans.

Good.

A nerve ticked in his jaw. He was angry with me. Well, I was angry with him.

"If Kajika calls," Cruz said calmly, "please tell him what we spoke about."

Since it was in everyone's best interest, I nodded.

"Thank you for listening to me, Catori." Borgo's lips bent into a soft smile.

I nodded again and then I streaked out of Bee's.

Cass trotted out after me. "Are you all right? Who was that old guy? And what the hell happened back there?"

"Nothing. Nothing happened."

"Then why are you leaving in such a rush?"

"Because I'm late for lunch with Dad." I jogged off before she could pursue her line of questioning. There were only so many lies you could feed a friend who knew you inside out.

After picking my car up from Blake's, I tried phoning Kajika. When my call clicked to voicemail, I tossed my phone on the passenger seat with a growl.

I had half a mind to drive to Kansas, but who was to say they were even there?

"Damn it, Kajika!" I slapped my steering wheel. "What the hell are you and Gwen doing?"

Here I thought they'd wanted peace, but instead they were growing an army, and an army meant war, and war meant dying.

Even though I usually disliked any and all comparisons to Ishtu, I realized we were alike in more ways than our looks.

If only she lay in the graveyard . . . I may just have awakened her so I wasn't so alone in the battle between hunters and faeries.

What was I thinking? Waking her would cost me my life, and I wasn't ready to give it up. The same way I wasn't ready to snuff out anyone else's life.

Well, maybe Ace's. He was insufferable.

In my rearview mirror, I caught sight of someone standing on Blake's roof. Someone with golden hair kissed by the sun and tousled by the wind.

Think of the devil, and the devil appears.

I powered down my window and stuck my hand out, making sure the faerie prince didn't miss my raised middle finger.

Why couldn't he stay the hell away?

21

THE IMPRINT

I spent the next few days holed up inside my house, doing laundry, rearranging my closet, ironing Dad's shirts, realigning shoes, cooking, vacuuming, scrubbing, dusting, and catching glimpses of fireflies.

No blond princeling, though. Either Ace had finally gotten my message through his thick skull, or he was off preparing his people for war.

I hoped it was the former.

Four times a day, I'd try Kajika's phone, but the hunter seemed to have dropped off the face of the planet. Which should've unsettled me but I was growing too frustrated with everyone and everything to be flustered by his silence. He was probably declining my calls because he knew I'd disapprove of what he and Gwen were doing.

Dad crouched down next to me in the hallway that separated our bedrooms. "Cat, honey, if you keep scrubbing that spot, I'll have to put in new floorboards."

I'd been trying to get a grease spot out of the wood for the last hour, but no amount of scrubbing worked. I sat back on my heels and stared daggers at the stubborn stain.

"What's going on with you?" he asked.

War is brewing, Dad. Since I refused to alarm him, I said, "I'm working through some anxiety."

"Well, if you're done for the night, can I take you out to dinner? Even though I love your cooking, there's this new Japanese restaurant that opened in Ruddington."

Ruddington reminded me of Kajika.

Why did everything have to remind me of hunters and faeries?

Tonight, I would make new memories and new associations. "I'd love that."

Dad rose and then offered me his hand. I took it and let him pull me up.

"We need to start having some fun again. I feel like someone pressed pause on our lives when Nova left us, and I still haven't found the remote to set it back in motion." Although dark circles still marred the skin around my father's pale-blue eyes, they'd stopped being perpetually pinkened by tears.

I changed into my leather leggings and a red shirt that was so bright it was almost blinding. Aylen had given it to me when I was accepted into BU two years back. It was soft and draped across my chest, giving the impression I had more cleavage than my modest B-cup.

I blow-dried my hair stick straight. The ends almost grazed my tailbone. I'd been growing it out since the summer I turned sixteen and thought it would be neat to chop it into a pixie-cut.

After darkening my eyes with kohl and mascara, I grabbed my only small bag—a black clutch with lots of decorative golden zippers—and stuck my phone, keys, wallet, and rowan wood arrows inside.

How I hated the fact that my new normal was lugging around magical wooden sticks.

"I'm ready, Dad," I called out as I descended the stairs.

He clicked off the TV and walked over to the front door, sliding his arms through the sleeves of his coat. "Look at you." His gaze took on a hazy sparkle.

I prayed he wouldn't cry.

"When did you grow up?" There was a definitive hitch in his voice. "Nova would've—"

"No crying, Dad. Not tonight." I squeezed a smile onto my face. "*And* we're taking my car. Rolling around in a hearse greatly diminishes my street cred." I added a wink that lifted both corners of my father's drooping mouth.

As we settled inside my little SUV, he added, "That makes you the designated driver this evening."

"Damn. Here I was planning on getting plastered with sake."

Dad snorted and shook his head, good mood firming up. He toyed with the radio dial, tuning in to the Elvis satellite channel, and we—yes, *we*—sang along to the music all the way to Ruddington.

I wanted to bottle this moment up because I sensed it wouldn't last.

WE WERE SEATED at a small table by a window that overlooked Lake Michigan. The water shone like dark ink in the light of the rotund moon. Even though I'd always wanted to move away, we did live in a beautiful place.

"That lake," Dad said.

"Yeah."

"I wanted to buy a houseboat when we were newlyweds, but your mom"—a forlorn smile bent his lips—"she did *not* want to live on a boat."

"You think it was because of the way Chatwa died?" My great-great grandmother had drowned a few years before the Second World War. She'd been only fifty-five.

121

Even though my mother hadn't known her, brutal deaths left scars.

Dad tore his gaze off the lake. "Possibly. After all, before you were even crawling, she'd signed you up for swimming lessons."

A woman dressed in a yellow kimono sashayed over to us and extended leather-bound menus. I was so ravenous I wanted to order everything. Except for the blowfish. I would never willingly try something that could kill me. Then again, I'd kissed a faerie and taken a ride with a mysterious hunter. How much more dangerous was blowfish?

As I closed my menu, having selected what I wanted to eat, I traced the symbol stamped into the soft leather cover with my finger—a whimsical rendering of a tree. I frowned at it, inspected it closer. Where had I seen it before?

A chill slinked up my spine as I remembered.

On the front page of Holly's book.

I was so stunned that the menu slid out of my hands and landed on my chopsticks, catapulting one to the floor. The waitress bent down to collect it and then returned a moment later with a fresh pair.

"Excuse me, but can you tell me what this symbol means?" I asked, pointing to the menu.

"It's printer who made menu," she said.

"Which printer is that?"

Dad arched a brow. "Why such interest in a printer?"

"For a writer friend." I tapped the tree and refocused on the waitress. "Do you know the name of the printer by any chance?"

"It's small press in Detroit. Forest Print. Ready to order?"

We ordered, and then Dad grilled me about my writer friend. I tossed my former roommate's boyfriend under the bus. Dad was impressed I had such industrious acquaintances.

Our boatload of sushi and sashimi was quick to arrive, and we were quick to devour it. For dessert, we had green tea ice cream and a teeny glass of sparkling sake. While Dad paid, I excused myself to go to the bathroom.

I looked up Forest Print and discovered it was located by the Detroit River, across from Belle Isle. I took a screenshot of their main page, then emailed them, asking if they had a record of a book called *The Wytchen Tree*, which they'd printed in 1938.

1938. A year before World War II.

My stomach churned. Chatwa had died around that time. Had her niece's book gotten her killed? Had the faeries tried to make *her* read the book, and she'd refused?

Chilled by my theory, I walked out of the bathroom brushing the goosebumps off my arm.

Dad was waiting for me in front of the door with my coat. "I was beginning to worry."

"What year did Chatwa die, Dad?" I asked, hoping he'd say 1936 or 37.

He draped his hand over my shoulder. "Chatwa?" He scrunched up his forehead. "Hmm. I think it was 1938."

"Are you sure?"

"Pretty sure. It should say on her gravestone."

A fresh wave of goosebumps coalesced with the last one. "Thank you for dinner, Daddy. I hope you know you're my favorite date."

He kissed the top of my head. "I don't think I'll ever tire of hearing you say that."

I settled in front of the wheel and was about to pull out when a text message appeared on my phone.

KAJIKA: We are coming home.

22

THE NOTE

Although I'd had no plans to go out, the message I'd received from Kajika made me race over to Holly's after dropping off my father.

The house was dark, quiet, and cold—creepier than most of the houses in Rowan on Halloween. I attempted to stifle my overactive imagination as I pressed the front door open and its hinges creaked.

"Hello? It's me, Catori!"

I tried the light switch, but no bulbs flickered to life. The power company must've cut the electricity again.

I turned on my phone's flashlight app and directed the beam around me. It looked exactly the same as it had the night I'd last seen Kajika, except that tonight no fire burned in the chimney.

Clutching my phone in one hand and an arrow in the other, I walked slowly through the kitchen. A rank smell flooded the space around the closed refrigerator. I imagined food rotting inside.

Although I was tempted to toss the moldy contents, I didn't touch the fridge door, afraid of how much worse the stench would become if I gave it an exit route.

I shone my light over the kitchen counters. Stacks of yellow post-its were neatly piled next to a ceramic pot filled with pens and a beige rotary-dial phone. That phone inundated me with memories.

Each time Grandma Woni and I had visited Holly, I'd ask to use the phone to call home—which was the only number I knew by heart. No one else in Rowan owned a *spinning phone*. Soon, someone would throw it away.

I hesitated to take it, but did I really want a reminder of the woman who'd tucked my mother into her deathbed?

I turned away from the phone and strode toward her bedroom, my gaze lingering on the bare mattress and the discarded yellow bathrobe that was draped over the flowery chair I'd sat on the day she'd told me our story.

Beyond her mattress was her dresser. The first drawer had been pulled out.

Since the rest of the apartment didn't look tossed, I imagined Kajika or Gwen had riffled through it. I crossed the room to close it but stopped when my phone's torch made something shine within. I slid my arrow into the back of my jeans and reached inside the drawer. My fingers met cool, smooth glass.

Delicately, I extracted my plunder—a framed picture of two young women who looked to be about my age.

One blonde; one dark-haired.

I recognized Chatwa right away. We had many pictures of her in our family albums. However, I didn't recognize the girl she was with. It struck me that it had to be her twin, Ley. I'd never seen a picture of her. After their fight, Chatwa had removed her sister from her life. In the picture, both girls smiled and had their arms slung around the other's shoulder.

Mom resembled Chatwa with her square jaw, full lips, and dark eyes that slanted upward. The resemblance made my heart ache, so I tore my eyes off her face and focused on Ley's.

She had the same light eyes as Holly, the same small nose. She even had the same scar on her hand. I brought the flashlight closer to the image thinking it was a crease in the glossy paper, but it wasn't. There really was a scar. Had she gotten it from gardening like Holly? Had she loved flowers and plants as much as her daughter?

I decided I would ask my father. He might know. Although, we hadn't even known Holly was related to us until a few days before she'd died, so maybe he wouldn't be any wiser than I was.

Clutching the frame, I walked back toward the door but stopped when something fluttered in the cold hearth. I approached slowly in case it was an animal. When I was close enough, I realized it was just a piece of paper.

With my index finger and thumb, I plucked it from the dusty, white mound of ashes. I brushed the powdery residue off the singed vellum, then tried to make out words, but they weren't in English. I shone my phone's light onto it. A large char mark obliterated the top left corner of the letter, but three letters remained: *ika*.

Had Holly written Kajika a letter?

Unfortunately, the bottom half of the letter had crumbled, so there was no signature. I recognized two words, though: *manazi* and *pahan*. If I wasn't mistaken, they meant *book* and *faerie*.

The front door's hinges creaked. I jumped, but then I took a deep, calming breath and walked back out to the living room, assuming it was Kajika.

I froze when I caught sight of my visitor. Moonlight lacquered his silver hair and made his exposed skin glow. I clutched my arrow tighter. "What are you doing here, Borgo?"

"My apologies, Catori. I saw a car and thought Kajika had returned."

His face was so crumpled with disappointment that I relaxed my grip on the arrow.

"You really have a death wish, don't you?"

"I'm hoping the hunter will hear me out *before* he kills me."

I doubted Kajika would listen to the faerie's apology. Especially considering his apology was almost worse than his presumed act.

"He is not here, is he?" Borgo asked.

"He sent me a message that he was on his way back."

I was almost going to invite the faerie to come inside and wait with me but thought better of it. If Kajika saw me with Borgo, he would flip, and I wouldn't blame him.

"How about I speak to him before you do, Borgo? So I can prepare him."

"I've been waiting two centuries to speak with him."

"I understand, but he might not give you all of two seconds to explain anything, and then those two centuries would be wasted. Let me prepare him. It's not going to be pleasant news for him."

What was I getting myself into? Was I really volunteering to tell Kajika that the love of his life had cheated on him?

Borgo's throat bobbed with a swallow as he relented.

I shot him a relieved, albeit tight smile.

"You know, I was practicing my apology in Gottwa."

"You speak Gottwa?"

"That's how it began with Ishtu. She taught Jacobiah and me Gottwa. Learning the hunter tongue was a way to show our respect for the tribe." His eyes glazed over. "After some months, I began to teach her Faeli."

I stared down at the piece of paper squashed against my still-blazing cell phone. I debated all of ten seconds before asking, "Could you translate it for me?"

I had a Gottwa dictionary in my sock drawer, but I didn't want to leave Holly's until Kajika arrived, and I wanted to know what the letter said before facing him.

"I will try my best."

Hesitantly, I stepped closer to Borgo.

"Catori, I will not hurt you. Besides, rowan wood was burned here so I cannot enter."

The air smelled of organic decay, not of a cold fire. "You can smell it?"

"No."

"Then how do you know?"

"I tried to enter, but my arm began to itch. My kind is allergic to rowan. But you know this already, don't you?"

"I do." I was starting to know a lot of things. "I heard hunters smell strong to faeries. Did it never bother you with Ishtu?"

"I cannot smell anything. Since birth, I've been immune to scents."

My eyes widened. "Oh. You have congenital anosmia? That's really rare."

"Congenital anosmia?" He smiled. "Three hundred and forty years and I never knew the name of what ailed me. Thank you for teaching it to me."

"You're welcome, I guess."

"You are a smart girl. Ishtu was very bright as well."

I knew it was a compliment, but gosh did it feel weird to have yet another point in common with the dead huntress.

"So, do you want me to decipher your paper?"

"I'd appreciate it." I tendered the charred letter.

When his fingers came in contact with it, he hissed. The paper fluttered to the floor. The pads of his fingertips swelled and bubbled, and violent red blisters erupted over his skin. "Rowan wood ash," he said, his breathing labored. He squeezed his eyes shut, gritted his teeth. "Give me a second."

"I'm so sorry, Borgo. I didn't realize they were rowan wood ashes."

Beads of sweat coated his forehead and upper lip. "It's all right," he finally said, opening his eyes. "The rash will go away."

"I really didn't mean to hurt you."

"Thank you."

"What are you thanking me for?"

"For not wanting to hurt me." He managed a smile.

His gratitude stunned me . . . touched me.

"Can you hold the paper up?" he asked.

The paper. *Right.*

I crouched and grabbed it. And then I held it in front of his face. I followed the movement of his eyes as they hopped over the words and loped over the lines. When he raised them back to me, they'd dimmed considerably.

"What? What does it say?"

"A lot of words are missing, so maybe my interpretation will be wrong."

"What does it say?"

"Holly worries faeries"—he paused—"demand read book"—another pause—"kill her with smoke."

Goosebumps annexed each one of my limbs. If it weren't scientifically impossible, I'd have said they coated my organs too.

"Does this make sense to you?"

"It does." Holly had been killed with rowan wood smoke, which meant I was right to believe she'd been murdered, but wrong about the culprit.

"Who is Holly?"

"The faerie who lived here."

"I did not know her; then again, I do not mingle on Neverra. And I have not come back to Earth for two centuries." Since I'd become very quiet, he added, "Someone killed her?"

"Apparently."

"Death by *alinum* is horribly painful. Like death by *wita*."

"*Alinum*?"

He raised a forlorn smile. "I forget you don't speak Faeli. *Alinum* is rowan wood."

It explained the welts on her face and arms. Tears coursed down my cheeks. Borgo raised a hand, but retracted it when he saw my swinging iron chain. It felt as though it were choking me, the same way the smoke had choked Holly.

I grabbed it and yanked it off, and then threw it so hard against the sooty Spanish tiles I expected both to shatter, but the opal simply skidded until it met the wall.

I wiped my tears away.

"She meant something to you, didn't she?"

"She was"—I gulped, seeking out oxygen in this stifling house—"she was family."

Considering the circumstances of her death, it felt slanderous to bring up her involvement in my mother's demise, so I shoved that aside.

His eyes widened. "*Alinum* doesn't affect hunters."

"Holly wasn't a hunter."

"It doesn't affect humans either."

"She wasn't human."

"Your kin was—was fae?"

I was breathing too hard to answer, too incensed by what I'd just uncovered.

He stared at me as though my face had peeled off and revealed another. "What are you?"

"Both."

"Both? You mean a faerie had a child with a hunter?" he asked.

"Taeewa"—I shut my stinging eyes—"wed a *bazash* named Adette."

"I remember Taeewa. He was one of the kind ones. One of the curious ones. We spent a lot of time together."

Not only did I open my eyes, but I opened them wide.

"You descend from him?" There was wonder in his tone.

"I—" My phone pinged so loudly it made my train of thought scatter in time with my pulse, and my brand light up.

KAJIKA: I will not be back tonight. I am sorry. I will explain.

I squeezed my phone between my fingers and then slapped the note on the couch in plain sight, so that when he *did* get back, it would be the first thing he'd see.

"He's been delayed," I muttered, clutching the framed picture of my ancestor.

I walked past Borgo, no longer scared of him even though I'd forsaken my necklace.

When I returned home, I debated whether or not to phone Ace

to apologize. I felt horrible for having accused him. He might've been guilty of colluding with Gregor, but Ace hadn't asphyxiated Holly.

The hunters had.

I opened a text message and typed, **I'm sorry for having accused you of Holly's death.** I almost sent it, but in the end, I decided to call him in the morning, once I'd calmed down and sorted through my thoughts and feelings.

I didn't want to risk telling Ace I was choosing my faerie side or something ridiculous along those lines.

In the faint glow of my bathroom light, I fell asleep looking at the rescued picture of Ley and Chatwa on my nightstand, and wondered how two people who loved each other so much could've picked opposing sides.

What had happened to them?

Had some man come between them?

23

THE CAVE

When I awoke, it was midday. My hair was matted to my forehead, and my T-shirt was damp with sweat. I slid my window open and welcomed the cool breeze. With my hands sprawled on the ledge, I gazed down at the rose-covered headstone.

"I'm sorry for what they did to you, Holly. I'm sorry I wasn't there to stop them."

Had they planned it?

Had Gwen told Kajika to keep me away?

Is that why he'd sat with me, congenially discussing our mothers?

Was it all just a ruse?

I felt dirty and used, the same way I'd felt when Cruz reclaimed his bargain. When would I grow strong enough to prevent people from using me?

After splashing water over my face and tying my hair up in a high ponytail, I dressed in sports clothes, secured an armband around my bare bicep, stuffed my phone inside, and grabbed my headphones. I was about to forgo the rowan wood arrows, but given

132

I no longer had my iron necklace, I slid one between the armband's Velcro.

Darts were more convenient than running with a wind chime hooked to my purple and lime tie-dyed leggings. I cringed at having to wear them outside the house, but my good—i.e. black—leggings were in the wash.

Whatever. They'd serve their purpose.

"Dad!" I called out, skipping down the stairs. Overnight, my pent-up rage and guilt had converted into energy.

"In here."

He was watching a basketball game on TV.

"I'm going out for a run."

"Go, you. Want to have lunch at Bee's after?"

"I'll meet you there." I plugged my headphones into my ears and clicked on a workout playlist.

I hadn't run in a long time—for exercise, I mean.

My feet dragged as though I'd strapped on ankle weights, and my lungs burned as though they were being shredded against a cheese grater. By the time I reached the small cabin in which Gwenelda had held Jimmy hostage, my limbs screeched.

The loathsome memory made me run faster. It also made my V-shaped brand spark—or perhaps that was my escalated heart rate.

The forest glistened with sunshine. The snow had completely melted, leaving the ground softer, spongier. It sucked at my sneakers, but I kept running. I headed down the familiar path that led to the cauliflower-shaped lake I skated on in the dead of winter.

Mom and I had gone there last winter. On Christmas Eve. We'd packed a thermos of hot chocolate and hiked to the lake. We'd discussed many things that day. Most of them trivial, like my social life.

Mom had been concerned I was burying myself under home-work and not meeting people. *We're proud of you, honey, but don't forget to have fun. To meet people.*

I am having fun, and I am meeting people.

133

Then why don't you bring any here to visit? Your friends are always welcome.

Because we live over a cemetery, Mom. No one wants to spend their vacation in a graveyard. Which wasn't even true. A lot of people were fascinated with death.

No friends visited because *I* didn't want them to see where I lived. I was embarrassed by it. Embarrassed by my parents' line of work. Even though Mom hadn't said anything, her forehead had been all rumpled.

I'd made her feel guilty.

I was a horrible daughter.

Sweat trickled down my neck and collarbone, dripped between my breasts. My hand was on fire. I expected to smell burning flesh soon, but thankfully, the fire was contained in the brand. I ran faster, harder, as though there was still a way to catch up with that day months before. To beg my mother for forgiveness, or simply tell her how much I loved her.

Faeries, hunters, and magic inhabited this world, so why couldn't there be ghosts?

I veered right, ducking to pass under the thick branch of a crooked juniper tree, my knees pumping to a new Shakira song, lengthening my strides, invigorating my calves.

I felt strong. I probably wasn't.

I carved a path down the lakeshore. Yellow reeds bent and swayed as I passed them, as though stretching after the bitter winter that had entombed Rowan.

I loped around the glimmering water, through clouds of nascent midges, and circled around the one-story, teal clapboard house with its large windows and slate-shingles, the only property in the area with a private pontoon.

I'd dreamt of living in that house when I was younger. I would tell my parents each time we hiked by it, hoping they'd trade the graveyard for the lakefront gem. Now, the house seemed small and desolate. Not that I loved my graveyard house, but it *was* home. The only home my mother had known.

Perhaps I'd have another home someday. Once I no longer needed to babysit the slumbering hunters.

I gave the house one last look before sprinting in the opposite direction, back toward the town, down the swirling, sandy trail that led to the boathouse. I came to an abrupt halt when something moved to my right.

I popped out my earphones and scanned the woods. Only tawny bark and silence surrounded me. I strained to hear crackling or buzzing, but there was no sound.

Not even birds chirping.

My pulse rattled.

When a forest hushes, danger rushes. It was a saying Mom had told me so many times it had become anchored deep within me. She'd repeated it to make me aware, not to frighten me.

Frankly, it did both.

I imagined a bear observing me from behind a trunk, readying to charge me. I was being ridiculous.

Another movement caught my eye. I squinted to make it out, but it was half a mile away, by the rocky gorge I used to scale with Blake during family picnics. Water from the lake streamed through the rocks and created a small wading pool. We'd play for hours in that pool.

This time, when the form moved, I established it was human. Another hiker?

But if it was human, then why didn't its feet touch the ground? Why was it hovering over the rocks?

I should probably have continued down the trail, left it alone, but it waved to me. I shaded my eyes and made out pale hair.

I approached cautiously. "Borgo?" I asked when I was close enough to spot the faerie's brown cowboy boots.

"Morning. Or rather"—he looked upward, at the sun streaming over our heads—"good afternoon."

"What are you doing here?"

"This is where I sleep."

"Here?"

He tipped his head toward a crawlspace in which I'd played many games of hide-and-seek. "The cave I spoke to you about."

I blinked back at him. "This is where you met Ishtu?"

"Yes." He gestured around him, to the wooden picnic benches and tables and stone barbecues. "It's no longer much of a hidden place, is it?"

"No. It's one of the most popular places for a picnic."

"Did you come to picnic?"

"No." I found myself smiling. "I was running."

His relaxed expression stiffened. "From what?"

"Huh?"

"What were you running from?"

"Nothing. I was just running."

"Why?"

"Because it helps me think."

"You humans are a bit odd."

"Don't people ever exercise on Neverra?"

"Not for pleasure. Unless you consider dancing an exercise. *Caligosupra*—mist-dwellers," he added, even though I remembered, "they dance a lot, but not the others. The others—humans, *calidum*, the ones who live below the mist—they work too hard to dance."

"What do they work on?"

"Cultivating crops to feed the nobles; herding animals; manufacturing the spirals; carving abodes into the *calimbors*."

"*Calimbors*?"

"Did Ace and Cruz not tell you about Neverra?"

"We haven't had much time to speak about your . . . world."

"Would you like me to tell you about it?"

"Are you allowed to?"

"I can do whatever I please."

"Won't you be punished for telling a potential hunter about the faerie world?"

"Catori, there is no punishment left in your world or in mine that scares me."

I supposed that pulling out his teeth or filling his airway with dust couldn't be worse than castration.

"So, would you like to hear about Neverra?"

"Actually, I would. Just a minute, though." I pulled my phone out of my armband and called Dad to tell him I'd be late. "Love you, too," I whispered before hanging up.

Borgo had lowered his gaze to the narrow cave again, except he wasn't actually looking at it. His eyes were closed. "The last time I heard those words, I was here." Slowly, he raised both his lids and face.

It chipped a piece off my heart that no one had spoken those words to him in two centuries. "Cruz loves you." I was guessing this; I'd never discussed Borgo with Cruz.

"I'm sure he does." Borgo exhaled slowly, heavily. "Shall we sit?"

I walked toward the nearest picnic table, straddled the bench, and slid my armband off. As he took a seat across from me, Borgo eyed the little white arrow lodged between the Velcro.

"So what are *calimbors*?" I asked.

"Sky-trees. We have three different types of trees on Neverra —*mallow*, *calimbors*, and *volitors*. *Mallow* grow on the marshland."

"They're the ones with the hallucinogenic leaves?"

"Yes. You've heard of them?"

"I have." I didn't tell him that Stella Sakar had tried to make me ingest one of her mallow-spiked cupcakes to prove I wasn't just human.

"*Calimbors* are hollow trees that rise two to three thousand feet and in which we build our homes."

"You live inside trees?" I exclaimed.

"Yes."

"Wow."

"It's not that impressive, Catori. We do not build houses like yours. I've seen abodes made of glass and metal that are a thousand times more impressive than our homes."

I supposed people were always more impressed with what was uncommon to them. "You have a king. Does that mean you have a palace?"

"Yes. It is the only dwelling not built in the sky-trees."

"Is it built on the ground?"

Borgo smirked. "Royals descending below the mist? That will be the day."

I wondered if his dislike of the royal family stemmed from the atrocity they'd inflicted on him or if it was more ancient than that.

"The palace is built on the mist. It rises and falls along with it. Every hundred or so days, when the mist descends and drapes over the land, the palace almost touches the ground."

"You mean the palace moves?"

He nodded.

"Is it made of *wita*?"

Borgo smiled. "Few can concretize *wita*. As for the few who have that ability, their creations fade when they die. If the Woods had built their floating palace out of dust, it would've vanished eons ago."

"What is it made of then?" I asked, but Borgo didn't answer.

He shot to his feet and gaped wide-eyed at something behind me. I prayed it wasn't a bear.

When I whirled around and found what he'd spotted, or rather, *whom* he'd spotted, I wished it had been a bear.

24

FIRST FLIGHT

Kajika stared at Borgo, amber eyes pulsing with alarm. "Catori, get away from him!"

I stood up, but it wasn't to walk away. It was to protect the faerie behind me from the hunter's wrath.

"Catori, that's Borgo Lief. The faerie who murdered Ishtu. Get away from him!"

"I know who he is."

"Then what are you doing standing next to him?"

"I'd rather stand next to him than next to you right now." My voice wavered. I wished it hadn't. I wished it could have matched my solid stance.

The line of Kajika's shoulders stiffened.

"I guess you didn't stop by Holly's house yet," I said.

He didn't move.

Didn't speak.

Didn't breathe.

"I found the note you tried to burn in Holly's fireplace." I folded my arms in front of me. "You know, the one about filling her with rowan wood smoke."

Silence stretched between us as wide and treacherous as a ravine.

"You lied to me." *Thump, thump, thump* went my exploited heart. "You told me Ace gassed her."

A nerve ticked in the hunter's angular jaw. "Holly asked Gwen to help her pass to wherever faeries go to die. Holly feared *pahans* would force her to tell them what she had written inside the book."

"You pretended not to know about the book!" Pain rumpled my voice.

"I am sorry I lied, but I thought the truth would hurt more."

I pulled my arms tighter against me as the air iced my sweat. "It never does."

Kajika closed his eyes a millisecond. When he opened them, they seemed dimmer, bleaker. "What are you doing with *him*?" He spoke the word as though he were referring to trash.

"I'm not done asking questions. Were you really looking for Gwenelda, or did you know where to find her?"

"I did not lie about not knowing where she had gone."

"Did you know what she was doing? Or was turning humans into hunters your idea?"

"Catori, I will explain everything to you after you get away from the vicious faerie."

"Vicious?"

"Murderous."

"I understand what vicious means. What I don't understand is what you're even doing here?"

"This is where she was killed. Where I buried her."

Borgo took a tentative step forward. "Kajika, I—"

The hunter whizzed over to me at super speed and knocked me behind his back. I lost my balance and latched on to the bench, but then the bench was torn from my fingers and the ground vanished from underneath my feet.

My stomach dropped as grass and rock became smears of green and gray, and the tepid wind turned brisker and whipped my ponytail into a frenzy. In front of me, loomed the crown of a red pine.

I reached out toward the uppermost cluster of needles, thinking I could grab ahold of it to get away from the faerie who'd scooped me up, but I was yanked back and then twirled around. I shrieked as the hands that held me left my body.

For a terrible moment, I was freefalling, surrounded only by air. Then hands and arms slammed back around me, and I gasped.

This time, I didn't try to rip the scalding arms from my waist. I was too high up to survive the fall.

"You can thank me in kind later," Ace said.

Should've known it was him. "What the hell? Put me down!"

"Good thing you weren't wearing your hunter collar today."

"Are you not hearing me? Put me down," I shrieked.

"Sound doesn't carry up here. Especially high-pitched notes."

"I know you can hear me. PUT. ME. DOWN!"

He swooped toward the right, jerking me along with him.

My stomach heaved along with my body. I thought I was going to be sick. I closed my eyes and breathed through my nose.

"You don't have a fear of heights do you?"

"No, but I do have motion sickness."

"Are you insulting my flying skills?"

I flung my lids up. "What the hell are we even doing up here? Why did you snatch me? I should be down there. Kajika is going to kill Borgo."

"Why do you think we're up here? So I could compliment you in private on your leggings? I'm holding you hostage."

For the space of a heartbeat, our eyes held, and I stopped trying to break free. But then I remembered Kajika and Borgo were facing off below, and I clawed at Ace's shirtsleeves to unshackle myself from his unyielding grip.

"Careful, Kitty Cat. Last I checked, you didn't know how to fly." His eyes churned like the surface of the shallow stream pooled at the bottom of the rock formation, violet and gold flecks throbbing against the blue backdrop. "You're safer up here with me than down there with them."

"Are you keeping me safe, or are you keeping me hostage?"

His eyes burned into mine. "Why would I keep a budding huntress safe?" He flicked his gaze to my right, onto a circling red-tailed hawk. After watching it a moment, he hissed, and the bird of prey swooped upward and away. "We have too many new ones running amok as it is."

"How many?" I asked, watching another bird swoop past us.

"Last I counted, there were seven new ones. Gwen and Kajika have been busy swapping blood with strangers. The good news is, they're explaining things to them this time. The bad news is, they're explaining things to them. One tried to slice my head off with an iron cord."

My gaze snapped to his neck. Sure enough, there was a faint white line.

"I'm not a liar, but you know that now, don't you?"

"I do," I admitted, before raising my gaze back to his. "How do *you* know *I* know?"

"I heard you telling Kajika. Just like I heard you asking your new faerie buddy questions about Neverra. Are you thinking of making a trip to our isle?"

"Why would I willingly visit a place infested with creatures that want to kill me?"

"They don't *all* want to kill you. If Borgo could still get it up, I'm pretty sure he'd—"

"He's kind, Ace. Don't speak of him like"—my voice juddered—"like he's some animal. If anyone is an animal, it's your family. It's Gregor. They maimed him. All Borgo did was love! Since when is that a crime?"

"He loved a huntress," Ace replied coldly.

I turned my face away because I couldn't stand to look at him.

Something pumped hard in his chest. I guessed it was a heart, but I must've imagined it because he clearly didn't have one.

"Before being a huntress, she was a woman," I murmured. "Now fly me down. And don't you dare consider it a bargain."

He didn't move for so long that I thought I would have to gnaw off his arm, but then we fluttered down like leaden feathers.

He stayed by my side after he released me.

I wished he'd just left.

25

THE WAVE

Even though I was angry with Kajika for lying to me, the look on his face when our gazes collided, the redness dyeing the whites of his eyes and blotching his brown cheeks made all that anger recede. Borgo must've told him about Ishtu.

The hunter clutched an arrow, but it wasn't raised. He stared at me, but I didn't think he was seeing me. It was as though he were looking straight through me.

What did one say in a moment like this one? What did one tell a man who'd gotten both his heart and ego crushed? That you were sorry for him?

Kajika wouldn't want my pity. He'd detest it.

Since I couldn't come up with any suitable words, I walked over to him and touched his arm to tell him I was there. Yes, he'd lied about Holly, but in that instant, it didn't matter. What mattered was coaxing the arrow out of his hand before he launched it at one of the faeries.

He looked down at my hand, then at my arm, and then at my face. When his eyes met mine, he ripped his arm away. "You are just like her," he said in the lowest, harshest voice.

My lips parted with a gasp. "That's not fair."

"She slept with a faerie." His gaze slid over my shoulder to Borgo. "And so did you."

I balked. Did he think I'd slept with Borgo?

I glanced over my shoulder to find that Borgo wasn't alone. Standing next to him was Cruz.

My molars clenched as I returned my attention to the hunter, too taken aback by the childishness of his attack to refute his accusation.

"I came back for you, but I should not have bothered." A strand of silky black hair fell into his reddened eyes, and he raked it back. "You cannot be trusted." He spit on the ground between us.

He was hurt, but he had no right to throw that hurt in my face.

"Don't confuse me with Ishtu," I said in a placid voice.

"Oh, I am not confused. Ishtu loved me. You do not even care about me. Just like you never cared about Blake."

"Don't you dare speak of Blake!"

"You made him kill himself."

Something swelled inside me, like a ball of ice. It expanded with such fierceness I thought it would crack my veins and tear off my flesh.

It tasted bitter and sweet, cold and scorching.

Like a snowball acquiring speed, it rolled through me, swelling, and then it exploded from my body.

Kajika's eyes shot to a spot above my head.

He backed up, but not before a wave slammed into him.

His lips parted, his hair dripped, and his olive-green T-shirt clung wetly to his thudding chest.

I was wet, too. More like drenched.

Moisture was evaporating off the three faeries, whose eyes were riveted to me.

"I thought she didn't have any hunter powers," Ace told Cruz.

Hunter powers? Had I . . . had *I* just moved water with my mind? I checked my hands. I wasn't sure why I was looking at them. To check if they'd turned into hoses?

Thankfully, they were still just fingers.

"You did it, Catori," I heard Cruz say. He stood next to me, amazement stamped in his blazing green eyes. "This time, you really did it."

This time. When was the last time? When the memory of the dusky parking lot behind the sheriff station slotted back into my mind, I pressed my lips together. Cruz had convinced me I'd unlocked his car with my mind, and then he'd laughed.

At me.

He'd laughed *at* me.

Like that night, Cruz smiled. Why was he smiling?

"Are you screwing with me?" I asked.

His delight faltered. "No."

"Then why are you grinning?"

"Because you moved water with your mind, Catori. You should be thrilled."

Thrilled? This was awful.

Awful, and a little bit amazing, but mostly awful.

Had there been a blue moon, or was I so genetically odd that my body had decided to become a hunter without my mind's consent?

I looked back toward Kajika, who still hadn't moved. "Tell me *you* did this."

I willed him to nod. Willed him with all my might to take the blame. I just wanted the wave to have originated from him. Not from me.

"It was not me." Many emotions saturated his voice—wonder, but also apprehension.

I shut my eyes, squeezed my fingers into fists, and attempted to quiet my seething mind before it uprooted a tree. "Well, shit," I whispered.

There probably were a million words better suited to describe the present situation, but my mind—which had been able to lift water from a rock bed—couldn't seem to come up with a single better one.

I cradled my face with my palms, wishing the five-letter word I'd tattooed into my skin could stop the progression happening within me. "I don't want this."

"You should be thankful for such a gift," Kajika said. "You have not even pledged yourself to Her, and She bestows upon you humongous power."

I lowered my hands. "With humongous power comes humongous responsibility."

Kajika shook his head, spraying the grass with drops of water. Unlike the faeries, he hadn't dried. "I can teach you to control it."

"You mean, you can teach her how to use it to kill more of us?" Ace said.

Kajika glowered at him. "I spared Borgo."

"You knew Cruz or I would fill your lungs with *wita* if you tried to kill him." Ace was hovering next to me.

"I did not spare him out of fear." Kajika bared his teeth like a cornered fox. "I spared him out of pity for having believed a huntress could have loved him. She was exploiting you, Borgo. Just using you for information on Neverra. You think I would not have known if she had loved another? She told me about your incredible coupling. It always lasted all of a minute. And before you assume she enjoyed it, know that she suffered many days after she met with you in your little cave, so charred was she from within."

I spun toward Borgo, whose face had crumpled like a squashed soda can.

"Kajika, stop it!" I yelled. Even if the love affair had been in his mind, Borgo had pined for Ishtu his entire life; he'd lost his manhood because of her.

"Huntresses are master manipulators. Perhaps that is why the Great Spirit bestowed power upon you, Catori."

I kept my gaze fixed on Borgo, refusing to lower myself to the depths of Kajika's pettiness.

The old faerie raised his eyes to mine. And then, quicker than a lizard snatching a fruit fly, he filched my running armband from the picnic table.

"I am sorry," he croaked into my ear right as he punched my arm.

Or at least, I assumed he'd punched me. When I looked down, I found blood spurting from a tiny wound.

Borgo hadn't punched me; he'd stabbed me.

26

THE BLACK OUT

Cruz and Ace jumped on Borgo. I thought it was to neutralize him, but I was wrong. It was to stop him from using the arrow dipped in my blood to pierce his own heart.

As though looking through a fisheye lens, I watched them struggle. Somewhere in the back of my mind, I heard them shout.

I saw dust sparkle, flames sizzle.

The faeries tore open his shirt and yanked on the Velcro armband that was still attached to the arrow, ripping it from Borgo's chest. The small, bloodied spear and synthetic holder flapped through the air and landed soundlessly onto a patch of sand.

I was going to be sick.

The world sparked and faded around me, then sparked and faded again.

The noise, too, came and went.

There was wind and screams, and then there was silence. Complete, horrible silence.

Bile surged in the back of my throat when my gaze locked on Borgo's skin. Like Holly, his flesh had turned elephant-gray.

I dropped to my knees.

"Her blood is poisoning him!" someone shouted. I wasn't sure if it was Ace or Cruz.

I touched Borgo's face. It was cold and chalky. I willed him to open his eyes. I willed it as fiercely as I'd willed the water to rise, even though I hadn't known what I was doing then.

Slowly, they opened.

Fresh hope coursed inside of me. "Borgo?"

Cruz and Ace were taking turns trying to mend the tear in his flesh with their dust while coaxing the poison out of him with their fire.

"Ishtu." His white lips barely moved over the name of his beloved.

I wasn't sure what got into me, but instead of correcting him, I said, "Yes?" and brushed strands of silver hair off his forehead.

"Were we . . ." His voice was so quiet I had to lower my ear to his mouth. ". . . a lie?"

I bit down hard on my lower lip that had started to tremble. Although I lifted my head, I didn't break eye contact. Tears dripped off my chin and plopped onto his sallow cheeks.

"No," I rasped. "It was real. We were real." How I got my voice to work was beyond me. My throat kept clenching in time with my heart.

I brushed Borgo's hair back but stopped when I realized I was smearing blood onto his forehead. I snatched my hand back, staring wildly around me.

Cruz's forehead rested on Borgo's chest, but Ace was looking at me.

"My blood. It's everywhere. Am I . . . am I making it worse?"

"You're making it better," he said.

Was Borgo healing? Just as I gazed back at the ancient faerie, he exploded into ashes.

I yelped, which made me inhale a mouthful of him. I gagged, shot up to my feet, and vomited at the foot of the picnic bench. When the sourness stopped spilling out, when the world stopped spinning, I straightened and rubbed my mouth. Gray dust clung to my hands, coated my clothes. My wet leggings were no longer lime and purple. They were gray. My shoes were gray. My tank top was gray. My arms were gray.

Cruz's forehead was also covered in soot. Even Ace hadn't been spared, but at least his face was clean. I instinctively looked at where Borgo's body should've been, but instead found a patch of wet earth. A flower would grow . . . a strange and beautiful bloom.

I focused on the soil, wishing it would sprout out at that very moment so I could forget about the decomposing body and the ashes that had painted my body with death.

Cruz was still kneeling with his eyes closed. If his lips had moved, I would've said he was praying, but his mouth was as motionless as the rest of him.

As though my body was finally remembering what had led to Borgo's suicide, my arm began to throb violently. The skin around the torn flesh pulsated, and my muscles seized.

To calm the fierce pulse pounding in the wound and ease the blood flow, I elevated my arm, but it came crashing back alongside my body in no time, angering the agonizing injury.

I must've yelped because the next thing I knew, Ace was inspecting my arm. When he made to clutch it, I jolted back. The sudden movement sent a shockwave all the way into my shoulder blade.

"My blood, Ace. My blood just killed a faerie."

"Just give me your arm already."

"It could kill you."

"It would have to come in contact with my heart, and since I don't have one, I'm safe."

I blinked, not understanding if he was joking or serious. And then I didn't care if he was or not as teeth-grinding pain surged down to my elbow and up into my shoulder socket.

My body stiffened, and my lids squeezed. I collapsed backward.

I prepared to hit the ground but instead felt myself being

airlifted and laid out. I opened my eyes, and the world swam into focus.

Something gold and blue shimmered over me, and then it faded.

Everything faded to black.

I CAME to like a child being ripped from her mother's womb —shrieking.

When I tore my lids open, the sun flared white against my pupils, and two familiar faces hovered over me.

"We can't heal the wound, Catori." Ace's voice sounded as though it were coming all the way from the graveyard. "We tried, but our magic doesn't work on rowan wood."

I swallowed and wet my parched lips with the tip of my tongue. When I tasted ash, bile simmered at the base of my throat. I clamped my teeth shut and swallowed down the vile sourness.

I wasn't sure how deep Borgo had stabbed me, but the wound made my entire bicep throb. I inhaled slowly, held my breath.

The pounding abated when I kept perfectly still, but when I gasped for air, fresh pain raged fiercer in my veins. I nonetheless concentrated on my breathing, attempting to ease the pressure crimping my lungs and throttling my heart.

I wiggled my fingers, making sure there was no nerve damage, and felt something rough and splintery beneath them. I turned my face and realized I was lying on the picnic table.

Slowly, I jimmied my body into a sitting position, putting all my weight on my good arm, then delicately collected the wrist of my injured arm and nestled it against my chest.

"I need to get home. Disinfect the wound." I sounded like a robot. "I'll probably need a few stitches."

"Shouldn't we get you to a doctor?" Cruz asked.

"I can do it myself." My grandfather had been the one to teach me, dexterous as he was at all manual tasks.

Ace and Cruz exchanged a look.

"Can you even walk, Catori?" Cruz asked.

I lowered myself off the table. "He stabbed my arm, not my leg."

Ace snorted.

When my feet touched the ground, the world spun, and I wobbled. I released my wounded arm to catch hold of the table until the sky, the ground, the trees and rocks settled back in their rightful places.

"Would you like me to fly you home?" Cruz asked.

Pride urged me to refuse but walking home would take me hours in my woozy state. "Yes," I conceded.

"I'll do it." Ace leaped over the table toward me. "You head back to Neverra and report what's happened."

A nerve pinched in Cruz's jaw. "Very well." He hopped into the air. "Just so you're aware, Ace, I'll ask for permission to avenge Borgo's death."

Even in my loopy state, the word made me tick. "Avenge? Kajika didn't kill him, Cruz."

"He killed him with his words."

I spun to face him, my ponytail whipping across my cheek. "Put yourself in his shoes, Cruz. If you learned that Lily was in love with another man, how do you think you'd react?"

The faerie's green gaze was affixed to the horizon peeking through the red pines. "Lily's free to love whomever she wants."

That won him a hard stare from Ace.

Although a frown tipped my eyebrows, I decided not to poke at their relationship any more than I already had. "Kajika still didn't drive that arrow through Borgo's heart. If anyone should be punished, it's me. After all, it's *my* blood that killed him."

Had I seriously just invited the faeries to chastise me? Blood loss and coherent thinking clearly didn't mesh.

Ace folded his arms in front of him. "Kajika was despicable to

153

you, left you bleeding out in the middle of the forest, yet you protect him?"

The wind snatched my ponytail and tossed it at my mouth. I pressed it away. "He wasn't himself." I averted my eyes so he wouldn't see the threads of resentment weaving themselves around my disenchantment.

My gaze ended up skimming the ground upon which Borgo had lain mere minutes before. Only my armband remained. I took a few steps that felt like lunges and bent to pick it up. I snapped the Velcro open, plucked the bloody arrow out, and with my good arm, hurled it as far as I could. It was not a very impressive throw.

"We are fools to believe that peace is possible." The wind carried Ace's embittered murmur to my ears, amplifying it.

"Don't say that. Borgo and Kajika's quarrel was personal. They fought over a woman; not over regulations and land."

Cruz rose higher. "Perhaps you can forgive Kajika, Catori, but I can't. Borgo was like a father to me. Besides, I'm not asking for your permission to end the hunter's life. I am telling you that if Linus sanctions his death—"

"This is why it never stops! Because of revenge. Gwenelda killed my mother, but you don't see me proclaiming I will murder her. Please, Cruz, please don't spill more blood."

I willed him to nod, but all he did was stare at me through those neon-green eyes of his that had once fooled me into believing him more friend than foe.

"Oh, and, Cruz, what Catori did stays between us, capeesh?"

"What I did? What did I do?"

Ace cocked a single eyebrow. "Your little water show."

Oh.

That.

Cruz nodded before rocketing skyward and whizzing like an arrow over the tree line. I watched him for a long minute, and then I looked at the water I'd stirred with my mind.

Was I a huntress now? But if I was a huntress, then why wasn't my wound sealing?

I turned to ask the remaining fae but lost my train of thought when my nose bumped against his stubbled jaw. Had I gotten closer to him? Had he?

I took a step back, tripping over my own two feet. He snapped an arm out and snagged my waist, holding me upright and far too close.

Close enough that I could count every one of his eyelashes.

His warmth sizzled over my skin, wicking moisture out of my tank top and eliciting shivers from my limbs. "Cold?" Was it me or had his timbre dropped?

I swallowed. He had to know I wasn't since I was pressed up against his fireball of a body. "No."

"Then why did you shiver?"

"Because all the dying is getting to me." It wasn't a complete lie, albeit it wasn't why my skin was coated in goosebumps and my nipples hard as beads.

He's engaged and he's having a kid, I reminded myself. I was done coming in between couples.

Not that I was interested in Ace romantically.

Nope.

He was just an above average-looking male who happened to be in possession of a crown and nifty magic.

Nothing more.

Nothing less.

I cinched his wrist with my good hand and attempted to tug his arm down, but there was no give to the limb keeping our fronts flush. This was the attic all over again.

"I really doubt your fiancée would approve of you holding a woman so close."

His mouth slimmed.

When his hold still didn't slacken, I added, "Especially a despicable huntress. Think of the stain on your reputation."

155

The hollows beneath his cheekbones seemed to deepen as his jaw flexed. "Have you never heard the old adage: *keep your friends close and your enemies closer*? Proximity facilitates the snapping of necks."

Cool sweat beaded between my shoulder blades and trickled down my spine, icing my feverishly warm skin. "Is that your plan? To snap my neck?"

A ray of sun draped across Ace's face, chasing away the shadows roughening his features. "Like a green bean, Kitty Cat."

My pulse quieted because any murderer who took themselves seriously didn't use vegetables as metaphors. "Green beans don't have necks. I take it you don't do your own cooking?"

The corners of his mouth twitched. "Why lift a finger when hundreds of people live to serve me?"

"Has anyone ever told you that your personality gives whiplash?"

The twitching turned into an incandescent smile. "Few people are familiar with my *sprightlier* side. You should feel honored."

"What I feel, is too hot, so let go?"

He indulged me with one more sly tic of lip.

Was it my imagination or did his fingertips brush across my backside and thigh on their way down?

27

THE STITCHES

After he released me, Ace said something but my blood beat too harshly against my eardrums to make out what. I could still feel the path his blunt fingernails had taken, as though he'd raked them across my skin instead of stroked leisurely down my lurid lycra leggings.

He tilted his head to the side. "You look a little flushed."

I choked on a swallow and proceeded to pound my fist against my solar plexus. "You'd be flushed, too, if you'd been squashed up against a human-shaped radiator."

His grin was so casual and smug that I sobered up real fast. "I don't know what game you're playing, Ace, but I'm not interested in participating."

"Game?" His smugness faded, leaching out of him like—*hope-fully*—the blood in my cheeks. "I'm not playing any games, Cat. You lost your footing; I broke your fall. That's called chivalry. Last I heard it was a pleasant trait in a man."

What about holding me close? What about touching my ass? I wanted to scream both at him, but I was still unsure if the second one actually happened.

"You want peace," he muttered, "yet you treat me like the enemy."

I blinked in surprise at the hurt and anger blistering his tone. "You're the one who thinks hunters are hateful."

"Are you a huntress?"

"I don't know, Ace. Am I?"

He eyed my wound, nostrils flaring as though my blood was tainting the air. "Your wound would've closed had you been one."

My pulse quieted at his answer. I'd assumed as much but it was nice to hear it said out loud. "Can we please stop fighting? It's exhausting."

His gaze lifted off the oozing puncture wound in my bicep. "Hunters have killed two of our own. The fighting is just beginning."

Okay then. "I was talking about you and me, Ace, but since you bring up the bigger picture, you have Neverra. Why come here, to Earth, and stir trouble?"

"What are you suggesting? A travel ban?"

"Your world sounds beautiful."

"Why did you go to Boston to study? Why did you travel to Mexico with your parents last summer, or to Europe the summer before that?"

"How do you know where I traveled?"

"You don't think fae have been keeping track of your graveyard? Of you? But that's beside the point, Catori. Why do *you* travel?"

"To get away from Rowan; to see more of the world."

"That is why we, fae, come here. Our goal isn't war. Our goal is knowledge—meeting new people and discovering new cultures. Because of what we've gathered and watched, we are building the first ever elevator on Neverra which will allow the marsh-dwellers to rise over the mist whenever they please. They won't have to spend hours, days walking up the spirals. They won't have to bargain with faeries for a lift." His tongue swiped almost angrily over his upper lip. "Hunters believe we're ill-intentioned . . . that we wish Armageddon on this planet so that we can take it over. We have no such ambition."

His words fell into me one by one, like bricks in a game of Tetris.

And like in Tetris, I swept them to the side or flipped them so they could interlock neatly. "You come to Earth to sightsee and explore?"

"You just moved water with your mind, yet you find my insight shocking?"

"Well . . . yeah."

Ace's mouth canted but then its curve flattened. He was eyeing my arm again. "We should really get you patched up before you bleed out."

"Why?"

"Why what, Kitty Cat?"

"Why do you care if I bleed out? Wouldn't it be convenient?"

"I'd have no one left to pester if you expired."

I shook my head. "For the life of me, I can't figure out your end goal."

"Perhaps I don't have one." He scooped me up, one arm underneath my knees and the other beneath my shoulders.

I just had time to lock my uninjured arm in a vise around his neck before he shot upward. On instinct, my eyes shut as we ascended into the cool, crackling air. Wind brushed my cheeks and danced in my ponytail, while Ace's heat spread like ointment over my skin and loosened my taut muscles. It reminded me of lying on Blake's grandfather's fishing boat when it coursed at full throttle over Lake Michigan in the summer heat.

Too soon, we stopped moving, and Ace set me down on my front porch. The faerie's forehead scrunched up, and his eyes moved to a spot over my head.

He jolted off the porch and pressed his palms over his ears. "Why the hell does iron swing over your door?"

I looked at the wind chime, then back at Ace, and then I smiled smugly. "I was wondering how it worked."

And now, I knew—like an ultrasonic, dog collar.

I walked over to my front door and tried opening it, but Dad had locked it. And I hadn't taken my keys because I was supposed to meet him at Bee's. My phone indicated it was 1:30 PM. I texted him that I was taking a shower so he wouldn't worry, and then I checked the living room windows, but they were locked. I remembered opening the one in my bedroom that morning. I stepped off the porch and shielded my eyes. Here was to hoping that Dad hadn't closed it. I really didn't want to meet up with him looking like an injured rat that had rolled around in a dustpan.

Lo and behold, it was open.

"Can you fly me up to my bedroom?"

He glanced at the wind chime. Gritting his teeth, he grabbed me, pushed off the ground, and flew up to my window. I tried to remember if Cruz had been in that much pain the first night I'd met him. He hadn't pressed his palms to his ears. I would've remembered that.

I sashayed my legs through the opening and limboed in. Ace vaulted into my bedroom, then slammed my window shut so hard it made a loud whoosh.

"Are you going to tell me to take it down?" I asked.

"It's your house. If it makes you feel safe, keep it."

"If faeries can still get into my house, then it doesn't serve much of a purpose, does it?"

"It would keep most faeries away."

"But not you?"

"It takes a lot to keep me away."

I bit my lip. "I'm sorry I blamed you for Holly's death."

"Yeah. So am I." He rubbed the back of his neck that was still coated in ashes, like most of his body.

"You want to take a shower?"

His pupils flooded his irises, and then the corners of his lips

160

perked up. "You think a simple apology will win you a shower with a prince? Not sure what you've heard, but I'm not *that* easy."

I blushed, and then I rolled my eyes. "Oh my God, get over yourself. I don't want to shower *with* you. I'm offering you to take a shower in my house. That's all."

"I was just teasing you."

"Sure you were."

The silence thickened between us, coalescing until it filmed my skin. I toed off my sneakers, concentrating on their sooty fabric.

Ace cleared his throat. "I'll grab a shower when I get home."

"Go." Why did my voice sound so scratchy? "You can go." I peeled off my socks. "Thanks for flying me home."

"Don't you want help darning your arm?"

Borgo had stabbed my right arm. Even though my penmanship was all right with my left hand, sewing myself up would probably prove a shakier endeavor, and trembling needles were *not* pleasant.

"Steri-Strips should work." *Hopefully.*

"Rowan wood wounds don't seal by themselves. At least, not when you're a faerie. The skin has to be reattached for it to heal."

"But I'm not a faerie."

"I'm not sure what you are, Cat."

Neither was I.

"Look, if you want to risk having a hole in your arm for the rest of your life, then by all means, scotch-tape it shut. If it doesn't heal, it'll make a great conversation starter during boring dinners."

I gawked at my wound. No way was I risking keeping a tiny crater in my arm. "Fine. Yes. I'd like your help." I went inside the bathroom and closed the door.

"You want some help getting your clothes off, too?" Ace asked. "I'm good with spandex." Even though I couldn't see him, I could tell he was smirking.

In answer, I locked the door, making sure the click resonated through my bedroom.

28

THE CALM

Washing your hair with one hand was tricky, but when covered in someone's ashes, one made do with whatever limbs worked. Once my locks were clean, I scoured my skin with Aylen's lavender-scented soap, reducing the bar to the size of a credit card.

After towel-drying myself as best I could, I unlocked my bathroom door. Ace was standing by my window, inspecting the cemetery.

"You know quite a bit about this graveyard, don't you?" I asked.

He turned toward me, and his eyes caught on the hem of my towel. If he'd been any other boy, I might've been embarrassed standing before him in a towel, but considering how much he reviled huntresses, I knew that any flirtatious talk was just that . . . *talk*.

"Don't you?" I repeated.

His eyes returned unhurriedly to my face. "What is it you want to know?"

"When Ley was buried, what plant did she turn into?"

He cast his gaze on my yellow dream-catcher. "Don't know. Why?"

I wanted to know if she really had been buried in the cemetery, since no plant graced her headstone before Holly's vine. "Do you know someone who would?"

"Have you asked Astra?"

"Not yet. I heard she wasn't doing too well."

"She's not." Ace flicked the feathers, making my nightmare trap shiver. "She's been at Mercy Hospital for the last month."

"How do you know that?"

"I visit her. When I was a kid, she took care of me; only fair that I take care of her now."

Who is this man?

He stabbed his fingers through his hair, ridding the dark-gold of the streaky gray. "Do you plan on getting dressed? Or is that your outfit of the day?"

I smirked. "Right, fire-beings probably don't need towels. Are you dry the second you turn off the shower?"

"Want to find out?"

"I doubt your fiancée would appreciate that," I volleyed back.

Not the faintest hint of a smile lit up his face. "Where's your first-aid kit?"

"In the kitchen. Under the sink."

He went to collect it while I yanked on the first thing I found—a short, liberty-print dress. I'd just finished pulling up my burgundy tights when my door opened.

"Ever heard of knocking?"

"No. Is that some strange human ritual?"

I shook my head, suppressing the smile that was trying to crawl over my lips. I didn't want to encourage Ace. "Have you ever sewn anyone up?"

"No."

"So I'm your guinea pig?"

"Worried?"

"How bad can you be at it?"

Wincing from lack of anesthetic, I felt every pierce of metal, every drag of thread. Cold sweat coated the back of my neck. I willed myself not to pass out from the pain.

"What's your favorite thing to eat?" Ace asked.

Food, really? Just the thought of eating made my stomach heave. "I don't know."

"Everyone has a favorite food."

"Spaghetti." I held my breath as the needle went in. "With butter and ketchup."

"I should've known you'd have such poor taste. Muddled genes and all."

I glowered. "I'll have you know the combo's delicious." Although the rest of my family's opinion on the dish aligned with Ace's, it was my grandfather's favorite. He'd make it for the two of us when I'd had a bad day or when I was feeling under the weather.

"My favorite meal is a burger."

"Really?" Here I'd expected a faerie prince's favorite meal would be caviar peppered by some magical herb that grew only on Neverra.

He pricked my skin. "Earth-dwellers make them so well. I think it's the meat. The meat on Neverra doesn't taste the same."

I pinched my mouth shut to keep from yelping.

"What's your favorite thing to drink?"

"Water."

"Don't be boring, now."

"Anything that sparkles." I took a deep breath as he pulled the needle out and dragged the thread slowly. "You?" I managed to ask.

"Whiskey. I like the flavor of smoke." He snipped the thread. "Okay, we're all done. I'm all out of lollipops, though."

Even though my throbbing arm felt as though it was roasting over an open flame, I smiled. "I was always a sticker girl." I went to look at his handiwork in my bathroom mirror.

As he disinfected the needle with a burst of fire from his fingers, he said, "Better than the hole?"

"Better than most stitching I've seen. Are you secretly a surgeon on Neverra?"

He clicked the white plastic box closed. "Nope. Just extraordinarily skilled with my fingers."

I didn't miss the hefty innuendo. Again, I didn't encourage it. "Are there doctors in your world?"

"Are you looking for a job?"

"Why can't you ever give me a straight answer?"

My phone buzzed. I swiped it off my comforter. It was Dad asking me what I wanted to eat. I typed, **Spaghetti.** Then I shrugged on a sweater so that Dad wouldn't see my injury.

"Want lunch?" I was hoping he'd turn me down, and not because he was still covered in ashes, but because bringing Ace Wood to lunch with my father at Bee's would raise eyebrows and spark the rumor mill.

"Got to get back."

Had he sensed I didn't want him to come?

"If you need anything, get your heart rate up. Phones don't work on Neverra."

I filed the information away. "Get my heart rate up?"

"So that your brand flashes." After a beat, he added, "Lope around the cemetery or watch a scary movie. Or better yet, use a toy."

"A toy?" Wooden blocks flashed across my lids.

When he nodded to my nightstand, I understood what *toy* he was referring to and turned crimson.

The corner of his mouth lifted a fraction.

"You really enjoy making me uncomfortable," I mumbled.

He chuckled.

I spun my hair into a bun and knotted it. "Thanks, by the way."

"For the advice?"

"No. For the stitching. I owe—crap, *do* I owe you?"

He shot me a brazen smile. "Maybe."

"Give me a straight answer."

"Hand me your pillow."

"My pillow?" I asked eyes wide. "What do you want with my pillow?"

"Hand me your pillow, Catori."

My stomach began cramping, and it wasn't from hunger pangs. I really *did* owe Ace. Before the pain intensified, I lunged toward my bed, yanked up my pillow, and tossed it at him as though it were a hot potato. He squeezed it between his long fingers, and the cramping stopped immediately because I'd fulfilled my end of the bargain.

"There. Now you no longer owe me."

"Can't believe you used up a favor from your sworn enemy on a pillow."

"I'm a surprisingly stand-up guy, huh?" After frisbeeing the pillow back against the headboard, his hand rose between us and knuckled my jaw closed. "You're gawping."

Instead of removing my face from his fingers' perch, I froze. The fire beneath his skin pulsed against my chin, warming my cheeks further.

He was slow to drag his hand away. "I'll use your kitchen window to leave. It's farther from the swinging mind-shredder."

And then he was gone, and I was alone, heart playing hopscotch. Rubbing the patch of skin that still tingled from his touch, I descended the stairs, grabbed my car keys, and drove over to Bee's, replaying every minute of my morning on a loop.

Soon, my head throbbed as insistently as my arm.

After parking in front of the restaurant, I sat in my car and observed the animated dining scene through the glass.

I pictured my mother sitting next to my father, clasping his hand like she always did, laughing at one of Bee's stories.

I saw Blake slalom out of the kitchen to personally deliver our meal like he always did.

I imagined myself sitting across from my parents, long braid tucked over one shoulder, asking Blake if he wanted to go to a movie with me after his shift.

When I blinked, only Dad and Bee remained.

29

THE TREASURE HUNT

T he following day, I received an email from Forest Print. They had a basement full of archives, but not enough staff to go through them to offer me a timely response. I replied asking if *I* could go search them myself.

A day later, I received an invitation to explore. If I hadn't misread the logo, Holly's book was a mere two hundred miles away. I phoned Cass to see if she was game for a road trip and digging through stacks of files.

A half hour later, Cass jogged out to my idle car, pigtails swishing.

"Go, go, go," she said, tapping the dashboard.

"Who are we getting away from?"

"Mom. She wants me to go to Home Depot with her to pick up gardening supplies."

I pulled away from her house and drove toward US-37. "You love shopping."

"For clothes. Not for mulch and Miracle Gro. Plus, she can spend her *whole* day there. A cell phone only has so much battery."

I chuckled but then recalled fragments of my conversation with

Ace. "I heard your grandmother's in the hospital. Why didn't you tell me?"

Her delight at having escaped her mother faded. "I thought you had enough on your plate between your mom and Blake."

"But that doesn't mean I don't want to hear what's going on in your life." I reached across the car's center console to squeeze her hand. "For the next three hours, you are telling me everything that's going on in your life."

"Honestly, there isn't much."

"You never did tell me why it ended with Declan."

After I mentioned her ex, Cass had no trouble coming up with three hours' worth of conversation. I must've spoken a grand total of twenty words during the drive, and that included my lunch order at a diner in Lansing.

By the time we parked in front of Forest Print, a riverfront, square, brick building with loft-sized windows across from Belle Isle Park, I was up to date on everything in Cass's life.

"That's one heck of a piece of real estate," she said as she got out of the car.

A metal plaque above the large doors indicated the year 1906. I wondered if a century ago, the area was already affluent.

We entered the enormous, light-filled building filled with digital printers and sleek computers. The owner, a Mr. Thompson, greeted us, gave us a tour of the facilities, and finally escorted us to the basement. He was extremely chatty—he probably didn't get that many visitors.

"Fourth generation," he said proudly.

"You don't say," Cass replied politely. It was the third time he'd told us this.

I turned toward the row of shelves and forced myself to think of something not funny to hide my grin. What came to me was Holly's book. It worked wonders.

"So, where should we start looking? Are these organized by

date?" I inspected the rows of metal shelving crammed with cardboard boxes.

"Used to be, but the basement flooded a decade back, and then boxes were rearranged helter-skelter."

Cass cracked her knuckles. "I guess we're sleeping here tonight."

"Oh, you can't sleep down here." The man rubbed the bald spot on top of his head.

"Um, it was a joke," she said.

"Bathrooms are down the corridor to the right. There's also a water fountain." He started walking back toward the elevator. "We close at six, girls. Hopefully you'll have found your metal plates by then."

"Hopefully." As the elevator door closed, I laid my bag on the floor and pulled out a random box. Inside were rows of thin, etched metal sheets and a folder with a yellowed printout that read: *Acts of Grace*. I pushed the box back. "So we're looking for a book called *The Wytchen Tree*."

"Tell me why, again?"

"Family history," I said cryptically.

"That *isn't* on Wikipedia?"

I shook my head.

"You owe me a really nice meal after this," she said, disappearing down the first row.

"CAT, I'm going to go get us some lattes, okay?" Cass yelled from behind one of the metal racks.

A moment later, the elevator dinged and *whooshed* shut. How lucky was I to have such an amazing friend? I remembered yelling at Kajika and Gwenelda the night he awakened that by taking Blake away from me, they'd left me with *one* person—my father—but I had Cass.

170

And Aylen.

And Bee.

Rowan truly was a good town.

I had presented today as a road trip/treasure hunt. The road trip bit had been accurate, but the treasure hunt part was way less thrilling than I'd made it sound.

We'd been down there for three luckless hours. My arms ached from shifting boxes around. The wound was nowhere near healed. Thankfully, it wasn't infected either. I'd been popping Tylenols as though they were M&M's to counter the dull throbbing.

I strained to read the words on yet another metal plate that wasn't accompanied by a printout. A mirror would've come in handy considering the letters were back to front. After ascertaining it wasn't the one I was looking for, I shoved the box back in place, massaged my temples, and then reached for the next box.

Most of the archives had been repacked after the flood in blank boxes. How was I supposed to find one box in this sea of unmarked cartons?

I peeked before pushing it back in its place. *Nope.* I rubbed my palms together to get rid of the fine layer of dust—the basement most probably had not been cleaned since the flood. The dust reminded me of Borgo, which made me think of Kajika and Cruz.

Hurt by the hunter's unfair criticism, I hadn't called him. What exactly would I say? You owe me an apology? Would an apology suffice to erase his cruel words? Even if they were spoken in anger, they were voiced. Which meant they were thought.

Flinging Kajika far from my mind, I reached toward the highest shelf for a box. Even though I was tall, I had to press up onto my toes to grab ahold of it. Just as I managed to latch on, the lights went out.

I jerked, dragging the box off the shelf. I sprang backward, and swung my arms out of the way, which angered the stitches and reawakened the tender wound. Like a ton of bricks, the box toppled down and hit the floor with a loud clang. I groaned and squinted to make something out, but it was pitch-black. The only source of light was the faint glow of my brand, but it was nowhere near bright enough to guide me.

So as not to walk into a wall, I extended my good arm in front of me. My fingers met cool metal. Slowly, I dragged them along the shelves, following their path. When cardboard and metal turned to air, I established I was back in the aisle.

Hand still extended, I edged toward the elevator. My heart pumped in my chest frantically. It reminded me of the fair that came to Rowan in August, or more precisely, of the house of horror where mannequins with glowing green eyes leapt out as you meandered through the dark labyrinth.

I used to seek thrills, but that was before they sought me. These days, I could do with less excitement.

A door clicked, and I jumped.

"Cass?" I called.

No one answered.

Had my mind made the sound up, so desperate was it for companionship in the dark? I kept walking, but so slowly a snail might've beaten me to the elevator. My palm hit something hard. If it hadn't been warm, I would've assumed it was a wall.

30

THE LIAR

A heartbeat fluttered beneath my fingertips. I pulled my fingers off the chest.

"Cass?" I asked softly, praying I hadn't just groped Mr. Thompson.

No answer. I backed away, heart pounding.

"Who's there?" My voice cracked.

There was a low chuckle. And then a candle flickered. No, not a candle. A palm. And the palm rose to light up a face.

I huffed when I saw whose body that palm was attached to. "For God's sake, Ace, you couldn't have said something? Did you have to creep up on me?"

"I don't creep; I fly."

I rolled my eyes.

"Plus, I assumed you would guess it wasn't Cass. She's about a head shorter and has boobs. Not that I ever looked."

"Right . . ." Like I'd ever believe Ace hadn't checked out Cass.

She was part-faerie like him, *and* she was a woman. I was pretty sure it was a winning combination for the prince of Neverra. Although, maybe being a woman was enough. As long as that woman wasn't a huntress.

"Who did you think it was?" he asked.

"Someone who worked here."

"Where exactly *is* here, Catori?"

"A basement."

He circled his flaming hand around. "I can see that. I mean, why are you in this basement?"

"I'm searching for something."

He eyed me.

"With which I don't need your help," I added.

"But I'm here. Might as well put me to use."

"I have Cass."

"I don't see her."

"Because she went to get us coffee."

"And why are you in the dark? Does that thing you're looking for glow?"

"No." It would make the search a hell of a lot easier if it did. "Don't you have stuff to do?" I asked, trying to get rid of him. "Maybe a pregnant wife to tend to?"

"She's not my wife, and she has a court full of servants to do her bidding. She doesn't need me."

"Maybe she wants you there."

"She doesn't."

Okay. So the needy fiancée line wasn't working. "No new hunters to check up on?"

"*Lucionaga* are presently in charge of them; I've been relieved of my duty."

The faerie guards were vicious pests. They sliced through flesh and filled the wounds with dust. They were the ones who'd attacked and poisoned Gwenelda.

I must've turned pallid because Ace added, "They're not allowed to kill."

"Do they abide by orders?"

"Better than Cruz and I do, apparently."

"What about Kajika?"

"What about him?"

"Why isn't Cruz here?"

"Would you rather have Cruz here?"

"I would rather have no one here."

"Father didn't sanction the kill. Borgo committed suicide after all."

Relief filled me just as the rows of fluorescent bulbs buzzed back to life, swamping the room in brightness. I blinked.

"I thought you'd lef—" Cass stopped talking at the sight of Ace. "Oh, hey." She frowned at me. "Um. You didn't tell me he was coming."

She tugged on her pigtails, then combed out her bangs like a preening bird. I wondered if Ace was interested. If he was, would he tell her what *she* was? And if she found out what she was, would Cass hate me for what *I* was?

"I didn't know he was coming," I said.

"Then how did he find us?"

"I was getting my sister's wedding invitations printed. Small world."

Cass didn't balk at his convenient explanation. "I heard you're doing the wedding on Beaver Island. Any chance we can score invites?"

I gaped at Cass and then at Ace. "You're doing the wedding in Michigan?"

"Beaver Island is our home."

Right. This was where they said they lived. Linus Wood had bought the island and built houses for his family and friends on it. I'd assumed no one actually used those houses, but maybe I was wrong.

Ace's eyes moved from my face to the arm I was nursing against my chest. Before I could react, he hiked my blouse sleeve up. "Has it been bleeding a lot?"

"Something's bleeding?" Cass hated the sight of blood. She'd

175

fainted during biology in junior high when we had to prick our finger and smother a drop on a glass slide.

"It's nothing," I told Cass. "Don't look."

She took a step toward me. I yanked my arm loose and tugged my sleeve down over the bloody bandage, but the fabric was soiled too. Her eyes started to roll to the back of her head.

"Grab her," I told Ace.

He leaped forward and caught her right before she fell, then sat her down with her back against a wall. Unfortunately, he didn't have time to catch the two paper cups of coffee she was carrying. They collided onto the floor, caps flying and coffee sloshing out. Ace's jeans took the brunt of it.

"You okay?" I asked Ace.

A long strand of dark blond hair had fallen into his eyes. He shoved it off his forehead. "Me?"

I pointed to his jeans.

"Oh. Can't feel heat."

"Right."

After darting a glance at Cass, whose head had lolled onto her shoulder, his palms ignited. He ran them over his pants. The flames ate the stain without singeing the cotton. He made a fist and squelched the fire just as Cass came to.

"Wh-what happened?"

I crouched down next to my friend and held her hand. "Blood."

"Ugh." She rubbed the back of her neck. And then she yelped, "Our coffees!"

"We can get more."

"But the mess," she said.

"I'll get some paper towels," I said, standing up.

"I'll take care of it, but first, let's take care of your arm," Ace said.

Cass glanced at my arm, then squeezed her eyes shut. "What happened to your arm?"

"Bumped it into one of the shelves."

"Seriously?" Cass groaned.

176

"Don't try to stand up until I come back," I said.

She nodded, eyes sealed tight.

I went to collect my bag, then walked over to the restroom. Ace followed me inside.

"I'm fine, Ace."

"Hunters usually heal fast."

I tipped my head to the side. "You already have me labeled, don't you? Sorry to disappoint you, but I don't seem to fit in a neat little box." I gripped the cool edge of the sink. "I want the truth. Have you been ordered to babysit me to insure I don't *join* the other side?"

He jerked at my tone. "I'm here because your brand lit up, and Cruz couldn't come."

"But why are you *still* here? I'm not in any danger."

His nostrils flared.

"Did *you* turn off the light so I would freak and my mark lit up? So you'd have an excuse to swoop in and spy on me with me being none the wiser?"

"You got me."

I stared at him, shocked he'd just admitted to a conspiracy theory I'd made up on the spot. After the shock came disappointment, and then anger.

"Can you please leave?" I hated how my voice cracked.

He released a deep sigh. "Cat . . ."

I stopped him with a raised palm and a stern, "No." I was tired of the emotional seesaw he and I were sitting on.

Besides I was hunting down the book he'd helped steal. If he stayed and I found the plaques, the Great Spirit only knew what he'd do with them. Bring them up to Neverra? Melt them with his fire?

I couldn't risk it.

"How do you say *leave*?"

"*Vade.*"

I startled. "I thought that meant 'fuck off.'"

"I lied. Shoot me." His gaze dropped to my pockets, seeking out rowan wood arrows. "Actually, I'd prefer you don't."

I gripped my hip. "Why is it that everything that comes out of your mouth is a lie?"

His razor-sharp cheekbones darkened in infuriation. "Forgive me for not wanting to soil your pretty mouth with curse words, Cat." With that, he spun on his black boots and pounded out of the diminutive bathroom.

Hopefully I'd wounded his pride deeply enough that he'd keep away this time.

FIVE UNSUCCESSFUL HOURS LATER, we dragged our carcasses back to the car. Instead of driving home, we booked a hotel to stay the night in Detroit.

Mr. Thompson had invited us to return in the morning since we'd only gone through a third of the archives. Although Cass would take the first bus back to Rowan, because she needed to be at work, I was determined not to leave empty-handed.

"This is heaven." Cass lay starfish-like on the bed.

"Hopefully, we'll get lucky tomorrow," I said.

"Hopefully, we'll get lucky tonight," she said, squeezing her pillow.

"We can't break in."

She waggled her eyebrows. "I'm not talking about your book."

I grimaced.

"I booked us a table at Nona Gina's, which turns into a club at midnight. It's gonna be awesome." She rolled up into a sitting position, then tossed her legs to the side and all but bounced onto her feet. Where did she find all this energy? "First things first, we need clothes. You obviously can't wear that."

She scrunched up her nose at the brownish stain I'd tried to clean when I was re-dressing my wound. So we went shopping.

After purchasing dresses at a little nearby boutique, we stopped by CVS for stockings and toiletries.

Cass, who'd brought a pencil case stuffed with makeup, dolled me up like she'd done for prom—for every school dance, for that matter. "That color. You should get all your clothes in that color from now on."

"I look naked."

Cass had convinced me to buy a nude dress with spaghetti straps. I was the first to admit it was pretty, but I looked uncharacteristically girly. Then again, with my sheer black stockings, combat boots, and leather jacket, it was subdued girly.

"I'm so excited for tonight," she said.

Even though I tried to muster up excitement of my own, between our fruitless archive-spelunking and infuriating Ace, my mood was, if not in the dumps, suspended right over them.

As we walked toward the restaurant, I looked for stars, but the streetlights overpowered the sky. I lowered my gaze, aware that if the moon shone, I could spot faeries. If any were even in town. Maybe they were hiding in their magical bunker. Still, I kept my hand in my bag, wrapped around one of the arrows I'd brought from Rowan.

When we arrived at the restaurant, the maître d' didn't seat us straight away. He had us wait at the bar. Since Cass was the smiley one, I let her charm the bartender into one, not carding us, and two, concocting two colorful drinks.

"Kir royal," she proclaimed, sticking a champagne flute in my hand. "Not sour. I promise."

I took a cautious sip of the bubbly red drink, which turned out to be so deliciously fruity, I drank it way too fast. So did Cass. We ordered two more just before we were shown to our table.

I froze halfway there. "What are *they* doing here?"

31

THE BOND

Ace and Lily sat at a round table set for four. I assumed the vacant seats were for Cass and me.

My friend blew her bangs out of her eyes. "I thought it'd be nice to all hang out."

I breathed in slowly, then breathed out slower.

"What? You didn't want me to invite them?"

"It's fine." I started walking again.

As we approached, the two faeries looked up.

I slid into the seat beside Lily and pasted on a super fake smile. "How *fun* to meet up."

Her expressive dark eyebrows tipped toward her nose. She looked at her brother, who signed something, no doubt an explanation for my substantial lack of enthusiasm.

"How are your wedding preparations going? Did you find your dress?" Cass asked.

Lily shook her head, and her stick-straight blonde hair brushed past the sparkling choker encrusted with a mix of pearls and diamonds and her strapless white dress that made my nude number look like a nun's habit.

I shrugged my jacket off, warmed by the alcohol and the annoyance of having to spend the night making small talk with two faeries—or just one, since Cass roped Ace into a conversation.

Lily glanced at my arm. When she didn't ask any questions, I deduced she either didn't care or Cruz had relayed the events that led to my stab wound.

"Are you going to do a joint wedding?" Cass asked when the appetizers were set in front of us.

Ace raked back his hair, even though it was stiff with gel and needed no readjusting. "Haven't found my dream tux yet. Can't get married until I do."

"I didn't realize grooms were so concerned about looking pretty," I quipped.

Lily smiled, while Cass looked at me wide-eyed, shocked I dared tease Ace Wood.

"Can't you get a tailor to custom-make one for you?" Cass asked.

"Our tailor's busy making Lily's dress," Ace responded.

Lily pressed her lips together and glanced at her brother, and that single glance was heavy with meaning.

Did he *not* want to get married? He had a baby on the way. Weren't children way more binding than an ordained union?

"Do you have pictures of your dress, Lily?" Cass asked.

Lily shook her head but smiled at my friend.

"I bet it's going to be gorgeous," Cass said.

"Excuse me. I have to get this." Ace stood, slid his ringing phone out of his dinner jacket's pocket, and walked out of the restaurant.

"I'm going to go freshen up." Cass patted her mouth on her napkin. "Be right back."

As I watched her wind her way toward the bathroom, I asked Lily, "Why are you really here?"

She typed on her phone: **I'm here because I needed to speak to you. Ace accompanied me because I begged him.**

I sat up straighter. Well, that was unexpected. "What do you need to speak to me about?"

The bond, she wrote.

I frowned.

I found a way to break it without death.

I sucked in a breath. "You did?"

She nodded.

"That's . . . that's the best news I've gotten in forever." I could've hugged Lily, but Lily did not strike me as the hugging type. "How?"

We'll transfer your bond.

"Transfer it?"

To another fae.

"What? No!" I said too loudly. "I mean—I thought you found a way to break it, not pass it along to someone else. How is *that* a better solution?"

She lowered her eyes to her phone and typed. Her frosty pink nails glittered underneath the wide conical bulb hanging over our table.

It's better for me. When she lifted her gray eyes back to mine, they shimmered just as brightly as her nails.

I realized she saw the magical bond that linked me to Cruz as a threat to their relationship.

This might not be your ideal solution, but you don't understand what it's like. Every time the bond glows, someone makes a lewd innuendo. And if no one is around to make one, he becomes distant. He worries. It hurts, Catori. It really hurts. Even though Ace goes to see you instead, I don't want Cruz to even think about you. You can understand that, can't you?

I nodded. Of course I understood.

Ace was striding back to our table, slipping his phone back into his navy jacket's breast pocket, forehead ridged in concern. I felt it had to do with the hunters but bit the question off my tongue. I didn't want to talk to Ace if I could avoid it.

"Does Ace know about your solution?" I asked Lily quietly.

Apparently, not quietly enough. "I *am* the solution," he announced, dropping back into his chair.

182

I stared between brother and sister, horrified Lily had elected her brother as my new keeper. "Absolutely not."

"Because you have someone else in mind, Kitty Cat?"

I glared at him.

He folded his arms. "Come up with another candidate, and I'll gladly recant my proposal."

"Astra."

"It only works with unadulterated fae blood. *If* it even works," he added, glancing at his sister. "The . . . *person* who gave us this solution is a little"—he flexed his jaw—"well, she's a little unreliable."

"Who's a little unreliable?" Cass asked, popping back into her seat. She'd fluffed up her bangs and reapplied a hefty coat of red lipstick.

"A friend of the family's," Ace muttered.

I stared across the table at him, wondering if this *friend of the family's* was a friend at all.

Cass got sidetracked by the sight of our main courses and proceeded to discuss food and drinks with Ace, while I seethed in silence, mechanically dumping bites of steak and vegetables into my churning stomach and tossing back the wine Ace had ordered.

By the end of the meal, my head felt as light as a helium balloon, and my heart, surprisingly, too. The music grew louder; it pounded inside of me. I splayed my fingers on the tabletop and rose. The room spun a little, but in a lovely way. It was like looking through the kaleidoscope I'd built with Mom.

Lots of people had gotten up to dance in the narrow space between the tables. I swayed right along with them, and so did Cass a minute later.

"Well, someone's in a better mood."

Courtesy of alcohol and good music.

She leaned close. "I met a guy on my way to the bathroom."

I gave her a thumbs-up. "Go, you! Point him out."

She nodded toward a guy in a gray suit. "Isn't he a bit old for you?" His face wasn't wrinkled or anything, but he had gray in his hair.

"I like mature men. I'm going to go dance with him."

"Okay, but . . ." I didn't get to voice my caution because she'd already stepped out of hearing range.

Lily pushed her chair back and stood. Although she wore sky-high glittery heels, her head hovered in the vicinity of my chin.

She popped her phone in front of my face. **Why aren't you wearing your necklace?**

"Because it gave me the illusion I was safe."

Her delicate chin bobbed with a nod. After flicking her attention toward her brother, who watched us like a grumpy hawk, she replaced her last question with a new one. **Why are you angry at Ace?**

Because he's keeping tabs on me, I thought but didn't say.

He didn't kill Holly.

I frowned, until I realized she thought I was mad about that. "I know," I said. Then louder, for Ace's benefit, I added, "I just don't like to be spied on."

Tendons pinched in his neck as he reclined in his chair.

"Can you really think of no one else for the transfer, Lily?" I pleaded with her.

I can, but they might actually want to be bound to you so that they can kill you. Would you like me to ask around? Her question dripped with sarcasm.

"When are we doing it?"

As soon as Cruz gets here, she typed. **He's on his way.**

Ace's blue eyes snapped to the restaurant entrance.

Cruz wasn't on his way. He was here.

32

THE CHANGELINGS

Dark circles marred the skin beneath Cruz's eyes, deepening the hue of his irises. Borgo's death had clearly taken its toll on the guy.

"You okay?" I couldn't stop myself from asking.

He nodded, the same way I'd nodded when people had asked me if I was all right after Mom's passing. A nod made people leave you alone. Everyone dealt with grief differently, but apparently, Cruz and I dealt it with it the same.

"Are we doing this here?" I asked over the loud music.

Lily shook her head, then gestured for us to follow her. Cruz walked next to her. She slid her hand into his and turned her pretty face up to look at him. He shot her a weary smile. How could he believe she loved him like a brother? How?!

When I turned back toward the dance floor in search of Cass, I found myself face-to-face with Ace. Even in the dim lighting, his eyes blazed blue. Color didn't make eyes beautiful, didn't make them sparkle more, Mom would say. I could still hear her tell me, *What makes eyes beautiful are the souls looking out through them.*

Ace's soul wasn't all that great, yet his eyes were mesmerizing.

He has magical fire, Catori. Fire makes things glow. Like eyes.

"Having second thoughts?" he asked.

I whisked my lashes down, forcing myself to stop admiring any part of my future keeper. "Aren't you?"

"It makes my sister happy, so no."

I sighed. "I'll just go tell Cass we'll be back in a few minutes. That's all it'll take, right?"

"Hopefully."

I went to speak to Cass, but she was so busy flirting with the older guy, she barely listened to me. "Don't leave with him while I'm gone, okay?" I murmured in her ear.

"Geez." She blew air out the side of her mouth, which tossed up the pieces of her bangs that sweat hadn't stuck to her forehead. "Okay, Mom."

"Cass, I'm serious. Swear it."

"I swear."

Before he whisked Cassidy deeper into the crowd, I gave the guy the evil-eye, hoping he got the memo of what would happen to him if he didn't treat Cass with the utmost respect.

"Is it me, or does he look sleazy?" I asked Ace, who was still standing next to me. Probably to make sure I wouldn't bail. "Your kindred spirit."

Ace didn't smile at my joke—which wasn't much of a joke. Instead, his Adam's apple jostled. "If he's anything like me, we should hurry, or you won't see Cass until tomorrow evening, and she won't be in any shape to help you."

Conceited much?

As we walked out of Nona Gina, I asked, "Does your fiancée know you're taking on a bond?"

"My fiancée doesn't give a shit who I bond with as long as it isn't her."

I was taken aback by the harshness of his comment. "Perhaps you should've reevaluated your relationship before deciding to bring a kid into this world."

"Yeah," was all Ace said.

We met Lily and Cruz on the sidewalk. They glowed as brightly as the seashell-shaped nightlight my parents would plug in the hallway outlet at night to guide my tiny footsteps after a bad dream.

The faeries interrupted their silent conversation when they saw us approach. Then they began leading the way down the street.

"Is your sign language the same as ours?" I asked Lily, before I remembered she'd communicated with Dad.

I was about to add, *Never mind*, when Ace said, "We adopted the one they use here. No one else is mute on Neverra. We were lucky Father spared Lily." A chilling darkness coiled off each of his words.

I frowned. "What do you mean *spared*?"

"Ever heard of changelings?" The apple in Ace's throat clenched. "Disabled faeries are abandoned here."

"You mean . . . you mean . . ." I stopped walking, whatever buzz I'd felt back at the restaurant fading like ink under sunlight. "You exchange babies with disabilities for healthy human ones?"

"Yes. That was the olden way. They also disposed of faeries they deemed unpalatable look-wise," Ace explained. "Perfection and strength are two of the most important traits in faeries. Makes for a healthy society, doesn't it?"

I must've looked horrified, because Cruz turned slightly to look my way. "Thankfully, Linus passed a law after Lily's birth stating that changelings were prohibited."

"*Our father, our hero*, right, Lil?" Ace's tone was pitch-black this time.

Lily pursed her lips and swallowed. Then she gave him a half smile that was no smile at all.

I caught Cruz watching me watch them and raised an eyebrow. I didn't expect him to explain the Woods' dysfunctional relationships to me—I had no right to even ask—but that didn't stopper my curiosity.

I pressed my mind off matters that didn't concern me. "What happened to the abandoned faerie babies? They had fire in their veins, didn't they? Didn't they fly out of their cribs?"

"Flying is like walking; you don't master it at birth," Cruz explained. "By the time they could learn to fly, they'd often passed on."

"Faeries can't survive more than a few months on Earth without visiting Neverra." Ace's gaze scrolled over the lit establishments lining the darkened street, lingering on the giddy crowd beyond the glass façades. "Our bodies aren't made to live here."

"But *bazash* live here," I countered.

He flicked his gaze toward me. "*Bazash* aren't made purely of fire."

Lily gestured toward a quiet alley that smelled of piss and beer. A cat jumped out of a black trash bin, arched its bony back, and hissed at the faeries.

"Animals can see through our dust," Cruz said. "They don't quite know what to make of us."

When the feline didn't quit hissing, I worried it would attack.

Lily tipped her face upward, toward the flat roof of the brick building before us, and then she levitated and shot upward. Cruz glided after her.

When I looked back at Ace, he was hovering off the ground. "Need a lift or do you want to try that fire escape ramp? Looks pretty sturdy."

Not only was it rusted, but some of the steps were also missing.

I sighed. "I'm more worried about the cat guarding it."

A corner of his mouth ticked up. "Looks mutual. Didn't think cats could be so wary of each other."

"Funny," I mumbled and raised my gaze to the rooftop. "Does this have to be performed on top of a building?"

"Fewer human eyes up there." He bobbed like a lantern caught in a summer breeze. "And fewer cats."

I nibbled on my lip, anxiety churning in the pit of my stomach. "After this, will you leave me alone, Ace? Even if my brand lights up?"

The cat paced, eyes gleaming like the safety reflectors on my bicycle. The one that had been stolen from me the night I got my 'human' tattoo; the night I ran into two faeries who charred my fingers with their fire.

"If I don't come, some other faerie will. You're a liability for our race."

My lids reeled high. "I'm not a huntress."

"But you have hunter abilities."

"Doesn't mean I'll use them."

"Doesn't mean you won't, either. Now come on. Let's get this over with before the sleazy dude abducts Cass."

I stiffened.

"I'm kidding. I promised the maître d' a thousand bucks if he kept an eye on her. Now turn around. I'll carry you up."

A thousand? The Woods were evidently not only made of fire.

Exhaling slowly, I turned so my back was to Ace.

He landed so softly that his boots barely registered against the pavement and then he wrapped both his arms around my waist. Although this wasn't the first time he was carrying me, there was something cautious about his grip, as though it repulsed him to touch me.

"Ready?" His murmur brushed the shell of my ear, eliciting goosebumps.

"No."

His heart beat fiercely against my shoulder blades. "Think of how happy this will make my little sister."

I could reproach Ace many things, but not the lengths he went to for the people he loved. "Fine."

His arms tightened around my abdomen just before he soared up to the rooftop to seal my fate with his.

33

DARK MAGIC

A sea of glittery buildings sprawled around the rooftop atop which Ace and I landed. Fixing my gaze on gently-lit Belle Isle, I stepped out of his arms.

The wind whisked Cruz's black curls, sending them toppling into his eyes. "Your branded hand, Catori."

I extended it. "Will it hurt?"

"Did it hurt the first time?" he asked.

"It felt like an electrical jolt."

"It shouldn't be more painful than that, right, Lily?"

She nodded.

"Ace, put your hand on top of Catori's."

The faerie prince hovered his palm over my knuckles, features tight, almost as tight as the navy blazer stretched over the rigid line of his shoulders.

Cruz wrangled back his wild hair. "Your hands will need to touch for this to work."

Before my next breath, Ace's hand collided with mine, revving up my tottering nerves. Now that the alcohol had completely deserted my system, my edginess had no buffer. My brand flared, but Ace smothered its light.

Under Lily's watchful gaze, Cruz placed his glowing palm atop Ace's hand and began chanting something in Faeli. For a moment, nothing happened, but then a slow crackling sound burbled from our piled hands and sparks sprang off like embers.

I watched—one part mesmerized, two parts freaked out. My hand dropped, and cool air buffeted my skin.

"Hold her hand, Ace," Cruz commanded between gritted teeth, before resuming his foreign incantation.

Ace closed his fingers around mine to keep them in place. The heat became almost unbearable. It was as though his veins were leaking fire into mine.

I closed my lids and focused on my breathing, inhaling deep lungfuls of the musty air that was thick with the promise of spring. Between the soothing coolness and the musicality of Cruz's voice, the pain began to ebb. And then the prickling stopped. Just stopped.

I cracked my eyes open and looked around me. "Is it—" I was going to say, "done," when a sensation, akin to a warmed blade, sliced into my skin.

I tried ripping my hand out of Ace's, but he held on tight. I grit my teeth to bite back a scream. The direction of the blade turned sharply then plowed through my tender flesh. I watched our hands, expecting blood to drip, but only magic dripped. Glittery flecks swirled and spun around our stacked hands.

It became pure agony.

Tears bloomed in the corners of my eyes, trickled down my cheeks. I whimpered.

I didn't think I could feel anything other than pain, but suddenly something soft caressed my palm. I looked over at Ace. His eyes, like his face, were incandescent, his pupils reflecting the sparkling dust.

I felt the gentle stroking again. It momentarily tore my mind off the pain.

Was he twitching, or was he trying to lend me comfort?

Scents erupted around us—rain, sunshine, and musk. They rushed across the rooftop like a storm, lifting my hair and lashing my cheeks. Whatever words Cruz had spoken seemed to have awakened more than his magic . . . it seemed to have awakened the elements. The eddying wind was rich and warm, ribboned by threads of coolness that offered a welcome respite to the churning inferno.

As suddenly as it hit, the storm rolled away. Our three hands glowed as one, and then only mine and Ace's blazed, and then the fire was snuffed from both.

"Shall we see if it worked?" Cruz lifted his hand off first.

Even though my throat felt raw, I croaked, "Because it could have *not* worked?" Shakily I pulled my hand back toward me and inspected it.

"I've never used Unseelie magic before," Cruz said.

My stomach fluttered. "Unseelie?"

"Did Ace not tell you about Neverra during his many visits?" An undercurrent of prickliness ebbed in Cruz's timbre.

Ace glared at the boy he considered to be a brother. "Most times I've *visited*"—he said the word as though it tasted foul—"Catori was accompanied by her little hunter. And I didn't care to explain to Kajika how our world worked."

That wasn't true. The part about me being in Kajika's company. Most of the times Ace had visited, I'd been alone. I folded my arms in front of me. My newly marked flesh no longer hurt.

"Would you mind explaining it to me?" It was definitely not a question.

"*Wita* is light magic—Seelie magic," Cruz said. "Unseelie magic is dark and performed by the *forma*."

"*Forma*?" I asked.

"They're a malevolent caste of faeries who live in the *hareni*—grottos beneath the ground," Ace explained. "Picture an ant hill."

Although the wind wasn't whipping my skin, every inch of me felt iced. "You have people living underground on Neverra?"

Lily cleared her throat and shot her brother a warning look that said, *Don't give away information about our world to the maybe-huntress.* At least that's what I imagined it said.

"And how did you get this spell from these evil Unseelie?" The word wasn't totally unfamiliar to me, but I doubted I'd read it in Holly's book. Maybe I'd heard it in a movie?

"Lily met with one." The shadows, which hadn't dissipated from Cruz's features, turned almost opaque.

"Which was incredibly stupid and dangerous." Ace's razor-sharp tone made his sister flinch. "Never again, Lily! You hear me? Never."

The gray in her eyes trembled until a single tear slipped out, silvering her cheek.

Cruz sighed, tucking Lily's hand in his. "What's done is done. Your hand, Ca—"

"What did they ask for in exchange?" I asked, even though perhaps I should've been more concerned with whether it had worked.

"Nothing," Ace muttered.

"You mean to tell me the *good faeries*"—I added air-quotes—"don't do anything for free but the *evil ones* do?"

"Don't concern yourself with what we traded to relieve Cruz of the mark."

"I will concern myself with what concerns me, Ace. And *this* concerns me. What did you trade?"

Silence stretched between us as wide and dark as the Detroit River.

"The book," Cruz admitted.

"Holly's book? *My* book?" My gaze vaulted onto Lily. "You gave them *my* book?"

"They won't be able to read it," Cruz said. "In case Ace hasn't shared this with you, the ink disappeared when Stella brought it to Neverra."

I blinked. Not only had Ace told me, but he was well aware the ink was still visible to me. The fact that he hadn't looped in Cruz made me wonder if a rift was forming between the two friends.

Was that rift me?

34

THE THEFT

I looked at Ace, and he looked at me. I tried to read his thoughts, but he'd built a wall around himself. "Why would they accept a blank book?"

"The *forma* asked for it because they heard talk about it during the Night of Mist," Cruz explained.

What the hell was the Night of Mist? I didn't even bother asking, as I was way more concerned by the fact that my book was now in the hands of evil faeries. What if *they* could see the ink?

"I'm working on getting it back before Gregor notices it's gone," Ace grumbled.

Lily was biting her pink nails. If I'd double-crossed this Gregor guy, I'd probably be chomping on my nails, too.

Cruz rubbed the hand not clutching Lily's down his tired face. "Catori, could you please show us if it worked?"

"How exactly would you like me to do that?" I stretched out the fingers of my right hand and peered at my skin, but the air was too black to make out my faerie-inflicted scar.

"You could throw yourself off this building," Ace suggested, "and wait for one of us to catch you."

My mouth went bone-dry. "You probably wouldn't try all that hard."

A dark smile crackled the wall guarding his expression.

"You don't have to do something that extreme, Catori." Cruz's gaze bore into the side of Ace's face, as sharp as the rowan wood arrows I was not, at present, carrying. "Just hop in place to get your heart rate up."

"Seriously? You want me to hop?" The idea was ludicrous.

"Fine." Ace lunged toward me and grabbed the back of my head.

I gasped as his lips crashed into mine, hot as a branding iron. My thoughts scattered from my brain, my breaths from my lungs, my pulse from my heart. My entire body felt as though it were short-circuiting.

I inhaled sharply, and his scent sank into me, jolting me out of my daze. I ripped my lips off his and smacked my palms into his chest, shoving him hard. Since his body was stone, I ended up being the one to totter back.

Ace rubbed at his chest as though I'd hurt him. I hoped I had.

His hand glowed. Just like mine. But instead of there being a single 'V' for Vega, there were two interlocked ones—'W' for Wood.

The rooftop faded as my mind whisked me back to that strange dream I'd had. The one in which I'd stood in the middle of a snowstorm clothed in a red gown, conversing with my mother about the brand on my skin that had transformed from a 'V' to a 'W' right before I'd awakened.

Goosebumps puckered along my spine as I landed firmly back in the here and now, on this darkened rooftop surrounded by three glowing faeries.

Impossible.

My rational mind—yes, I astoundingly still had one—refused to accept that I'd somehow foreseen wearing Ace's brand instead of Cruz's.

The irrationality of it sparked a hard shudder.

And then the taste of Ace's mouth on mine shook me anew. How dare he kiss me!

"I'm glad Lily's trade wasn't for nothing," Cruz said, his pitch toneless. "I need to get back to Neverra. Lily?"

She signed something to her brother. He didn't sign anything back.

Tears spilled down her cheeks as she took off.

The 'W' hadn't vanished. Then again, neither had my anger. I was still seething, flushed with indignation and—

No. Just indignation. "I would rather have jumped off the building."

Ace's eyes gleamed like cut sapphires. "Well, I didn't feel like diving after you."

"Well, I didn't feel like kissing you." I made a fist, trying to calm the chaos raging inside me.

I searched the night for the top rung of the fire escape. Once I spotted it, I marched toward it, the need to get away from Ace overpowering my sound judgment. I reasoned, as I notched my boot onto the first rung, that rusted didn't mean broken.

I held on to the ramp and moved carefully down the zigzagging stairs. The metal jangled underneath my weight. I looked down. There was still a long way to go.

"What the hell are you doing?" Ace hovered on the other side of the balustrade.

"Climbing down."

"I can see that. You do realize how fucking unsafe this staircase is, right?"

I gritted my teeth. *Like he cares . . .*

I kept descending. Ace kept hovering.

"I'll fly you down."

"No thanks."

"Catori Price," he growled, ramming his hand through his gelled locks, mussing them up. He added nothing more after my name, yet the air smacked with lots and lots of words.

I quickened my stride to escape Ace Wood. As if that was an actual possibility. Only way to escape him was throwing myself off the railing and I didn't feel like killing myself over a stolen kiss.

Since I was stuck with him, I decided to make the most of it. "What if the ink's visible to the *malevolent* faeries?"

"Don't you think I've considered that?" he muttered.

A floor later, I asked, "Why did you keep the fact that I can see it from your . . . *brethren*?"

"I didn't want Gregor to hunt you down and take you to Neverra to make you read it."

His words stilled my feet and drew my eyebrows toward each other. "And Cruz? Why did you keep it from him? Aren't you as tight as brothers?"

He worked his jaw from side to side. "He's been keeping secrets."

"So you've decided to keep some of your own?"

His silence echoed against every dusty brick and rusted piece of metal.

"Do you really expect me to believe you kept my ability to yourself for my protection?"

"I don't expect you to believe anything."

I started moving again. "Do I owe you for your *kindness*?" I made sure he understood I didn't consider his act kind in any way. "Wait. I do, don't I? And let me guess . . . you're going to force me to read the book once you get it back? That'll be one hell of a power play. Am I getting warmer?"

"I've been nothing but kind to you, and this is how you repay me?" Actual hurt blistered his tone. "By insinuating it was self-serving? I don't fucking care about power, Catori, and there is *nothing* I need from you that I can't get somewhere else. Nothing." Ace bobbed on the other side of the railing and then he was gone.

As I squinted into the night for his glow-in-the-dark face to make sure he was well and truly gone, my boot caught on a jutting piece of metal. I stumbled into the metal ramp.

A sharp clank, followed by a grating snap shredded the silence.

In horror, I registered where the sound had come from—my hand, still wrapped around the ramp, no longer met any resistance.

My body tipped, and then I flailed sideways, plunging into the void.

35

THE TRADE

I released the railing, but it was too late.

Mom's face flashed in front of my eyes, clearer than in any memory.

And then Dad's.

My grandparents'.

Blake's.

Cass's.

Kajika's.

Bee's.

Mr. Hamilton's—*of all people.*

The graveyard.

The yellow door.

Ace's.

Unlike the others, the faerie's face wasn't a figment of my imagination.

My heart swooped, along with my body, and the ground stopped growing wide and ominous. The images of my loved ones stopped revolving through my mind like a dizzying carousel.

My fingers, which had clamped down on fistfuls of fine navy wool, shook, spasmed. "You—you caught me. W-Why?" My voice was all shaky breath. "You'd have been rid of me. You'd have been rid of the brand."

The muscles in his forearm writhed against the backs of my stockinged thighs. "Couldn't do that to your father."

I untangled my fingers from his jacket, caught the hem of my dress, and held it down as he sailed us lower.

He landed in a crouch, and I righted myself, jerking away from my savior. My knees behaved like maladjusted springs and threatened to tip me off-kilter, but somehow, I managed to keep my balance.

My leather jacket rustled softly as I wrapped my arms around myself. "I'm sorry."

"For what?"

"Always thinking the worst of you."

"Most people do."

I rolled my lips together. I'd always prided myself on not being a sheep, and yet here I was behaving like one.

Something clanked nearby.

I raked the alley with my gaze, expecting the feline version of Cerberus to leap out of the shadows and hiss at me some more. I'd deserve it.

High-pitched laughter trickled through the darkness as a group of women clip-clopped past the alley in outfits that looked better suited for a cabaret act than a night out on the town.

Here I was, judging people again. I needed to stop.

"How does one thank a faerie prince—who has need for nothing—for saving one's life?" I murmured.

"You could go home, Cat. You could stop looking for the printing plates of Holly's book."

"You know?"

"Cass told me, but I would've guessed. I mean, why else would you be going through archives in a printshop?"

"And here I thought I was stealth personified."

His mouth curved with a gentle smile.

"If I find those metal plates, I can print a new book. More than one. You could even replace the one your sister gave the *forma* before Gregor notices."

His smile vanished. "He might already know it's gone. Besides, let's say you manage to print a new edition, how will you cloak the ink? Are you going to *influence* it to disappear?"

"Maybe."

"Be serious."

"I *am* serious. But if you don't care for my offer, then by all means, flit back to Neverra empty-handed and incur Gregor's wrath. What do I care?"

"I don't *flit*."

I rolled my eyes.

Ace clenched his jaw as though irritated I'd belittled his flying. When he spoke next, though, I understood his strained expression had nothing to do with my quip. "What's in that book?"

"Words."

"Besides words."

"A diagram." The truth would perhaps cost me my life if it got out, but I felt like I owed him that much. "I assume it's the burial schematics Cruz spoke about the night he claimed his *gajoï*."

"Describe it to me."

"A circle with lines or rectangles or something."

"Was it lines or rectangles?" His voice was loud and sharp.

"You're scaring me. Why is that important?"

"What else did you see?" he asked without pause.

"I didn't have time to see anything else, Ace. I didn't think I would lose the book, so I didn't rush to read it from cover to cover. And don't ask me how I saw what I saw because I have no clue. I just remember looking at a page, and this sort of holographic image popped out."

"You saw it because Holly used Unseelie magic," he murmured.

"And what? I can see Unseelie magic now?"

"Where do you think hunter powers come from?"

202

Like the strawberry shaved ice I'd slurp down in the heat of summer, his words froze me from the inside out.

"Hunter magic *is* Unseelie magic. You didn't think the Great Spirit was a real deity?"

"Wh-what?"

"Your Great Spirit was an actual spirit. One that managed to get through a portal and lodge itself inside a human. That human was Negongwa."

My fingers crawled up to my face and covered my gaping mouth. "Oh my God," I breathed.

"Which God would that be?"

"Why didn't you tell me this before?"

His eyes tightened on my face. "If hunters know they have allies on Neverra, they may try to climb through a portal."

"I didn't ask why you didn't tell *them*; I asked why you didn't tell *me*."

"You said you wanted to stay human. I was respecting your wish by not ruining all of your beliefs." He rubbed his nape. "It might not seem like it, but I have scruples."

My lips tingled as though to remind me that Ace Wood didn't have *that* many scruples. "Indeed. Hard to believe after the stunt you pulled on the roof."

"It was effective."

"It was also rash and unwelcome."

His gaze strayed to the mouth of the alley. I waited for him to apologize but his lips remained sealed shut.

"Do faerie royals believe themselves above apologies?"

His gaze slammed back into mine, as violent as his earlier kiss. "I don't apologize for actions I don't regret."

My heart caught in a web of confusion. What did that mean? That he'd *wanted* to kiss me?

"It got the job done, and promptly, at that."

The job. My stomach hardened. Why the hell had my mind

203

skipped to the possibility that it had been prompted by some subliminal desire?

"I'll forgive you for being an asshole just this once because you saved me from dying, but if you ever pull a stunt like that on me again, mark my words, I will smack more than your pecs."

His lips rose into a wolfish grin. "Cute threat."

"You won't find it cute once I jam my knee between your legs."

He kept smiling, because, of course, he thought me completely unlikely to follow through with my threat.

"Anyway . . ." I smoothed down the material of my nude dress, tugging at the short hem, drawing his gaze down to my legs. "I need to get back to the restaurant. To make sure Cass hasn't fled with the older gentleman." I turned and started walking when footfalls resonated behind me.

I glanced over my shoulder, finding Ace picking lint off his jacket's lapels as he strode after me.

"What are you doing?" I pivoted but kept moving backward.

"Walking."

"I can see that. I meant, *why*?"

"Careful, there's a lamppost behind you."

I whirled. There was no lamppost.

"Tricked you," he said, his voice lighter.

"Yeah. Your specialty."

His lips bent into a smirk. "I know you asked me to leave, but I saved you—an Unseelie, no less—so you owe me a drink."

I waited for my stomach to cramp; it didn't. "I don't owe you anything."

"You do."

"I don't feel anything."

"Because I haven't claimed my *gajoï* yet. Wait for it . . . Wait for it . . ."

No way in hell did I want to feel an inkling of that pain again. "Fine."

"Besides, the maître d' will be expecting his babysitting stipend. *And* I need to pay for dinner before he tries to charge Cassidy."

"I can pay for my own food."

"I doubt your student allowance will cover that insanely expensive bottle of wine."

"How expensive?"

"Four digits."

"Seriously?"

"My sister appreciates nice wine."

His consideration glanced against my heart, making it slow-twirl. "Should've drunk more of it."

A chuckle slipped from his throat, low and deep. Although it was just a sound, I swore I could feel it wrap around my skin.

"You're a good brother," I said after some time. "I don't know many who'd do what you did."

"You mean, link himself to an irritable, exasperating, and feisty woman with lethal blood? Yeah, I should really get a trophy for that, but I don't think my shelves could hold up any more."

I shook my head, trying to iron my amusement. "You're so pompous."

"It's my second best quality."

"What's your first?"

"It involves less clothing."

I blinked at him, and my boot hit a seam in the pavement. Ace curled an arm around my waist and locked me at his side, keeping my body from going *splat*.

"Have I unsettled you, Miss Price?" He grinned down at me, eyes as luminous as his skin.

Damn, Ace was handsome.

Two girls passed us, and unsurprisingly, both their gazes devoured the faerie prince.

I was still glued to his side. And his arm was still around me. I liked how solid and warm it was.

That arm had caught me more than once.

Saved me.

Shit. He was toying with me.

"Stop using *captis* on me," I blurted out.

His muscles went tight and his grin flickered like our electricity during harsh storms. "I'll try my best, but it's tough to contain all that magnetism."

He must not have tried his best, because I could still feel him everywhere.

Granted, he still held my waist, but I felt more than his arm.

An arm didn't harden your stomach or warm your blood.

Then again, the male was made of fire.

I pulled away, complaining that he was keeping me too warm. After shrugging off my jacket, I walked the rest of the way to the club, our bodies parallel but not touching.

And yet, I *still* felt him everywhere.

206

36

THE FIND

The following morning, after a tumultuous sleep during which Cass talked gibberish nonstop, I gulped down gallons of coffee and aspirin. I was hugging my friend goodbye in the hotel lobby, when she patted my shoulder and told me she'd swung another day off.

I jolted backward. "Really?"

"Really."

"And you want to spend it with me in a musty basement?"

"Couldn't think of a funner way to spend my day off."

I bet she could think of many, but like hell would I try to deter her. "Best. Sidekick. Ever."

She beamed.

Armed with renewed hope, I set sail for Forest Print.

By lunchtime, Cass and I had combed through another three rows of boxes.

By three o'clock, we had two rows left.

"Can you imagine if it's in the last box we find?" Cass asked.

I was beginning to lose hope that we'd find it at all. Slightly deflated, I latched on to another box. My right arm was still sore, but the stab wound had *finally* stopped oozing.

I dragged the box off the shelf, removed the lid, and rifled through the contents until I located the title page plate: *Capture*. That got me thinking about *captis*, which got me thinking about Ace, which got me thinking about last night.

About the brand transference.

The kiss.

My near-death experience.

The kiss ... *again*.

His arm wrapped around my waist.

After I'd stepped away from him, our conversation had consisted mostly of platitudes and awkward silences. After mentioning how relieved I was to see Cass—a couple dozen times —I'd asked him what he'd wanted to drink.

Did I worry he'd order another insanely bottle of wine? I did. After all, the drink was supposed to be my treat. In the end, he asked for water. After I fetched him a glass from the bar, he said he had some stuff to do on Neverra. He shot down the water and gave me a stiff goodnight nod, which I'd returned—just as stiffly.

And then while Cass had continued dancing and making out with the older guy, I'd sat at the bar nursing my own glass of water and came to the conclusion that the dark magic and near-death experience had muddled my senses. Gratefulness induced fuzzy feelings, blurring the line between reason and emotion.

"Um, Cat?"

"Yeah?" I fit the lid back over my box before slotting it back onto the shelf.

"Is wytchen tree spelled with a 'Y'?"

I whirled toward her. "Yes."

"Then I deserve an extra-big hug and an extra-large latte."

I dashed over to her and kneeled by the box, fingers flying across the sheets of etched metal. "You found it! I can't believe you found it!"

"Yeah. Needles in haystacks have nothing on me."

I took out a sheet of metal and ran my fingers over the

grooves. Old ink flaked off. I rubbed my fingertips against my palm, streaking my skin purple. I kept rubbing but the stain remained.

Cass squinted at my hands. "What are you doing?"

"Trying to get the ink off." I turned my hands palm-up to display the dark smudges.

"Um, what ink?"

"The one on my . . ." I flicked my gaze downward to make sure I hadn't hallucinated the stains—I hadn't—then back up toward my friend's deeply concerned face. Awareness that she couldn't see the ink hit me square in the ribs, jolting my heart, setting my revamped brand aglow. "I thought my fingers were stained, but I must've imagined it. It's been a long day."

"A long and fruitful day." She grinned wide. "What now? Do we take the box home?"

"Upstairs." Not only did I need a printout, but I also needed them to use the same magical ink they'd used for Holly.

The box weighed a ton, so we dragged it toward the elevator and brought it to the manager's office, which he'd pointed out yesterday during our extra-long.

"Look at that. You found what you were looking for." He cleared some space on his desk and rose to help us heave the box onto it.

He rummaged inside until he came up with a folder. He pulled a stapled file out, then sat back behind his desk to read it. His eyes grew noticeably wider as he thumbed through the pages.

My stained hands went clammy. "I'd like it printed with the same ink."

"Hmm. I'm afraid that'll prove difficult. You see, the writer sent her own supply of diatomaceous ink."

My joints stiffened. "Diatomaceous?"

"Diatomaceous ink is made with fossilized remains of algae and opal. It turns ink water-resistant."

I blinked once, twice, three times. Ink made with opal. That's how—

"Before anything, though, I'm going to need that proof of kinship," he said. "Can you prove you're related to Ley Lakeewa?"

"Ley?" I croaked. "You mean Holly?"

"No, I mean Ley." He set the file facedown on his desk, then leaned back into his springy desk chair. "You are related to her, right? You mentioned the author was your great-aunt in the email."

I swallowed the thick ball of saliva forming in my throat. "I am."

Why had Holly taken credit for her mother's book?

"Then showing proof should be a breeze."

The metal plates sat inches from my fingertips yet seemed to be slipping away. "But I just want to print a copy for myself. Not to publish it. This isn't for financial gain."

"Instructions are clear. You must prove your kinship first."

My father must have Chatwa's birth certificate somewhere. Since she was a twin, Ley's name would be on there, too. I hoped.

"I'll get it for you. Right now." I stepped out of his office to call my father. When he picked up, I asked, "Dad, do we have Chatwa's birth certificate by any chance?"

"Your mom was a packrat, so odds are a solid maybe."

"Are you at home? Can you check?"

"Yeah." I heard feet shuffling, drawers opening and closing. "What do you need this for?"

"A project I'm working on."

"In Detroit?"

"No. It's an ongoing thing. I'll explain when I get home."

"Okay." He sounded a tad dubious. Couldn't blame him.

"Check the family albums. I remember Grandma Woni loved to glue stuff inside."

"Do we have those? Or does Aylen—Oh no, here they are."

Paper crinkled on Dad's end. "Well, you're in luck. I'm staring at Chatwa's birth certificate. It's a little yellowed but—"

"Does Ley's name appear on it?"

"No. Why would it?"

My excitement came crashing down. I bet there was a great, big, muddy rainbow puddled at my feet. "Because they're twins," I mumbled stupidly.

"Honey, even Siamese twins have their own birth certificates."

I sighed, scraped my hair back. "Can you snap a picture and send it to me?"

"Of course. When are you coming home?"

"Today or tomorrow."

"Okay. I love you. And call me if you need anything else."

"Love you too, Dad."

My phone pinged with my father's text. I downloaded the picture as I headed back inside the office where Cass was flipping through paperbacks with catchy cover designs.

"He's letting me keep all of these." She pointed to a small pile on the desk, eyes sparkling with excitement.

"How cool." I turned toward Mr. Thompson. "I have my great-great-grandmother's birth certificate. She was Ley's twin sister. It doesn't mention Ley's name, but the last name's the same." I handed him my phone, hoping . . . *praying* it would suffice. "I swear it's not for resale. I had a copy of the book, but it was stolen from me. I just want to replace it."

If he turned me down, I didn't know what I would do. Steal the metal plates? File a court order to have them handed to me? Use my hunt—my *Unseelie* magic to convince him?

I felt my body heat up, my brand flare. I shoved my glowing hand into my jeans' back pocket as he handed back my phone.

"It's going to be costly. The leather cover alone was worth over a grand, then. It'll cost more today." He cracked his knuckles. "As for the ink, unless you have some laying around, I'm going to have to phone a supplier, but I can't guarantee they'll have any on hand."

"Okay. That's okay." My heart felt as though as it had hitched a ride on a rollercoaster.

He dialed a number—I supposed his supplier's—and spun in his office chair, stopping when he faced the window. "Hey, Bruce . . . Great, great. Look, I'm looking for diatomaceous ink . . . Yes. For printing . . . Ten ounces should do . . . Two hundred dollars? Let me ask." He spun back toward me, covering the receiver. "Is two hundred dollars okay?"

I nodded so hard my ponytail swung like a clock pendulum.

"Tomorrow morning? That would be great. Thank you. See you tomorrow." He hung up. "You're in luck. He has some."

Hope invaded me.

"So, with the two hundred dollars and the leather cover and the same paper, it comes out to"—he tapped on a fancy calculator with a full keyboard of buttons—"three-thousand-seven-hundred dollars."

"What?" I breathed.

"Without the cover, you could probably get it down to twenty-three hundred. Would you like me to remove the leather cover?"

I pressed my hand to my abdomen. "I—um—No leather cover."

Twenty-three-hundred dollars? I hadn't checked my savings account in a few weeks but I was almost certain I didn't have two grand at my disposal.

I worried my lip. "Could I pay in installments?"

"I'm sorry, but I can't accept installments."

Tears burned my lash line. "Why not?"

"Because of overhead costs and . . ." He kept talking but his voice faded.

I'd had such high, stupid hopes. In the midst of feeling terribly sorry for myself, an idea burst into my mind. I would *influence* him to accept my offer of installments.

"I swear to pay every cent, but in installments." My voice was firm, solid, loud. "Please accept."

He gazed at me in silence for so long that I thought my magic had fissured his stubborn veneer. But then he blinked and looked to the side. "I'm sorry, Miss Price, but I can't afford to have it printed without an upfront deposit of the entire sum."

I swallowed, but my spit couldn't find a path past the rapidly expanding lump. Maybe I didn't have the influence. Maybe back at that biker bar in Ruddington, it had been a fluke.

My knees buckled, and I slumped into the nearest seat. I was being ridiculous. Falling apart over a book. I tsked at myself. Did I really even need it? What exactly was I chasing?

I heard Cass tell him that my mother had died not long ago. Could he really not give me a discount? I closed my eyes and smiled at her sweet attempt.

A hand trapped mine and squeezed gently. I imagined it was Cass, but the fingers were longer, thicker, warmer . . . not feminine.

I flipped my lids up, horrified Mr. Thompson was clutching me. My pulse just barely settled when I saw who held my hand.

37

THE DINNER BARGAIN

"You can charge the full amount to the card," Ace told the owner of Forest Print.

"Of course, Mr. Wood. Right away, Mr. Wood."

"This guy." Cass beamed at Ace. "If you weren't engaged and having a baby, I would seriously make a play for you."

He smiled at her. "I'm flattered."

"Be right back." Mr. Thompson rushed out of his office, fisting a black credit card.

I slowly extricated my fingers from Ace's warm grip. "It's going to take me forever to pay you back."

"I'm not in any hurry."

"Do I owe you a *tokwa* now?" I asked.

He shot me that cocky grin of his.

"A *what*-wah?" Cass asked.

Shoot. I bit my lip, debating how to cover up my slip-up. I decided on the truth, leaving out the magical bit. "A *tokwa*. It's, uh, Gottwa for favor."

"You speak Gottwa, Ace?"

"Catori's been teaching me a couple words."

214

"Uh-huh." She waggled her eyebrows. "That explains all the time you spend together."

My skin overheated at her insinuation.

"As for repayment, you can have dinner with me tonight, and I'll waive your debt."

Cass's lashes reeled up so high I thought her eyeballs would rocket through her bangs and land on my lap.

"I, uh—" I swallowed. "I have to drive Cass home."

"I can take the bus."

"No."

"How about you take Catori's car?" Ace, ever so helpful, offered. "I can drive her back tomorrow. She has to wait for her book to be printed, anyway."

"But it might take days to print," I said. "I'm not going to hang around Detroit—"

"Mr. Thompson seemed quite certain it'd be ready by tomorrow morning."

"Really?" I asked, eyes wide.

Cassidy grabbed her books. "If you prefer I take the bus, Cat—"

"No." I stared squarely at Ace, wondering, not for the first time, what his angle might be. "You can take my car."

The manager returned with Ace's credit card and receipt. Beads of perspiration coated his bald spot as though he'd run to the payment terminal. Even his breathing had hastened. Maybe they kept the accounting department on another floor?

"As soon as I receive the ink, I'll get this printed, and then I'll phone you to arrange pickup. Unless you prefer it be delivered." He rubbed a hand over his sweaty scalp.

"I'll pick it up." I rose from my chair and moved as rigidly as a soldier figurine cast from green plastic.

As Ace thanked the man and exchanged a few last words, I walked out with Cass, who'd stuck half her book haul into my arms. "Is it me, or did the guy seem on edge?"

"He was in the presence of Ace Wood. It's like meeting the prince of England."

Was that it? It didn't sit right, but then again, nothing sat right at that moment.

Especially my upcoming dinner with Ace. Once he caught up to us, I tried bartering it down to a coffee.

"Kitty Cat, we're both spending the night in Detroit, and we both need to eat."

"What I *need* is to check back into my hotel."

"I happen to have a suite with a lot of empty bedrooms."

Cass choked, then proceeded to cough, hugging her books like she'd hugged the man she'd hooked up with last night. Between hacking out her lungs, she said, "Car. Now."

Ace's phone rang. He picked up and paced in front of the brick building while I followed Cass. Maybe I could return to my hotel without him noticing.

I dug my keys out of my bag and beeped open the trunk.

"What the hell is going on between the two of you?" she whisper-hissed, setting down her books.

"Nothing. I swear, nothing."

"He just offered to host you in his suite."

"In one of his *many* bedrooms." I dumped my armload of books beside hers. "Not in *his* bedroom."

"Um, is there really a difference?"

"A big one. Besides, I'm not going to accept." I stuck the keys in her hand. "Stop looking at me like that. I'm not interested in Ace."

Her fingers closed over the keys. "He seems quite interested in you."

Not for the reasons you think. "He's not."

"He just asked you out on a date."

"Dinner. Not a date. Lots of people have dinner together. We're human beings. We need to eat." Well, he wasn't human, but apparently he still needed to eat. "Besides, he's not my type."

"Extraordinarily handsome is everyone's type."

"He's not *that* handsome."

She rolled her eyes.

"Drop it."

"Fine." Her grin turned into a slight frown. "Do you want me to stay? If I leave at four, I can make it back in time for my breakfast shift."

"You're not driving two hundred miles at four o'clock in the morning." I hugged her. "Thank you for asking, though. And thank you for coming with me on this crazy expedition."

"It was the most fun I've had in ages! Seriously. Whenevs, honey."

She handed me her mascara and red lipstick—even though I insisted I wouldn't need either—before hightailing it out of Detroit.

If only I could've left with her . . .

I glanced toward the building. Ace was still prowling the sidewalk, barking into his phone. I could slip away. As long as my pulse stayed steady, he couldn't find me. *Yep*, solid dinner-flaking scenario.

When his back was to me, I started walking—fast. Really fast. But then, when I turned the corner, my stomach cramped. Violently. Which made my pulse zing and the 'W' blaze.

A whole slew of bad words scrolled through my mind. I spat a few out. Didn't lessen the cramping. The only thing that did, was when I stopped fleeing.

Ace swaggered up to me. "I should probably take offense that you're trying to evade dinner with *moi*."

"I wasn't trying to escape. I was—I was looking for a shop. I need a clean outfit."

He smirked. "I love shopping for women's clothes. Especially underwear."

"I'm *never* buying underwear with you."

"Commando works for me, too."

"Any blue moons rising tonight?"

He chuckled. "I chose a fancy restaurant, so you need a fancy dress, and those don't come cheap."

"Can't you make one appear with dust?"

"I could, but you can see through dust, and so can I, so I'm not sure how comfortable you'd be wearing it."

"Ugh."

I went into three stores with Ace. It was nerve-racking—shopping with a guy—but all the attention he received turned out to be somewhat amusing.

"You should tone down that *captis* of yours," I whispered after we left the last shop.

I'd found a really pretty dress, which I'd paid for myself because I didn't want to owe the faerie anything more than I already did.

"I have a secret for you. I'm not using any."

I rolled my eyes. "Right."

When we reached the five-star hotel Ace had booked a suite at, I insisted on getting my own room. One that wasn't in his suite.

"What are you scared of, Kitty Cat?"

My cheeks prickled. "Not scared. I just like my privacy."

Thankfully, he dropped it after that. He rode the elevator with me till the third floor. "Be ready at eight."

After the sliding doors closed, I stared at my reflection in them. Why did Ace Wood want to have dinner with *me*? Surely, he could find a thousand willing companions. Someone he didn't need to compel.

I contemplated returning to the lobby and checking in somewhere else, but one, the hotel had swiped my credit card, and two, my stomach began to spasm.

Ace Wood had cornered me.

No, that wasn't true.

I'd marched into that corner myself.

38

THE NON-DATE

After phoning my father to tell him I would be back in the morning, I soaked in my giant marble tub with bubbles all the way up to my elbows. I spent close to an hour, adding hot water whenever the temperature dropped below tepid.

I held up my fingertips, that were no longer stained with ink, and observed the way they'd pleated. I'd always found the way our bodies adapted to our habitat fascinating. When I'd read that fingertips pruned to give hands more traction in a slippery environment, biology had officially become my favorite subject.

As I wondered whether the humans who lived on Neverra had had to adapt to their habitat, I grabbed a handful of scented bubbles. They slithered down my wrist, popping along the way. The soap smelled masculine, all at once spicy and heady. *Patchouli and black peppercorns.*

I took a picture of the label and sent it to Aylen for inspiration. She sent me a bunch of heart emojis back that made me smile, but a glimpse at my phone's clock dimmed that smile.

7:38 PM.

Ace would be at my door in twenty minutes. If I could've

219

slipped under the foam and stayed there all night, I would've, but one, I had a wound that needed to stay dry, and two, I didn't particularly want to experience stomach cramps again.

Why was I so nervous about dinner with Ace, anyway? It wouldn't be the first time we'd sit at a table together. And it wasn't the first time we'd be alone—well, as alone as two people could be in a restaurant. Plus, I was almost a hunter, which made me an almost-enemy.

I was making a boulder out of a molehill—or whatever the expression was. Unfortunately *that* made me think of the Unseelies who lived in the—*what had he called it again?*—*hareni.*

Sighing, I pried myself out of the bath and dried off, and then I rubbed the divine-smelling lotion onto my legs. I eyed Cass's mascara and lipstick, which I'd dropped on the marble sink top along with a disposable toothbrush and comb.

Just because I didn't *want* to go to dinner with Ace didn't mean I wanted to look unkempt, so I applied both.

And then I blow-dried my hair stick-straight—which took way longer without a brush—and slid on the red dress. It was really bright. Like, stoplight-bright. I should probably have gone with a more demure color. Too late. I was about to put on my boots, not having any other shoes, when the doorbell buzzed.

I pulled the door wide, my stomach performing all types of weird contortions at the sight of Ace.

Between his sky-blue shirt, which he wore unbuttoned underneath a pearl-gray dinner jacket, and the hallway spotlight that cast a golden sheen over his slicked-back hair, he looked . . .

He looked . . .

He's a faerie.

An engaged *faerie.*

With a thick swallow, I spun away from him, returning to the plush armchair in the corner next to which I'd left my boots.

"Wait," he said.

I glanced over my shoulder at him, then at the red shoebox in his hand. "I had some time to kill and happened to walk in front of a store that sold nice shoes."

"And you happened to know my size?"

"I'm observant. Plus, you can't wear *that* dress with *those* boots."

"Are all faeries as fashion savvy as you are, Mr. Wood?"

"Just—here." He tossed the box on the armchair a tad harder than necessary.

Biting down on my lip, I opened the box and parted the silk paper. Inside sat a pair of shoes that seemed carved out of gold. I stroked the mirrored leather, then the tall heel. Beautiful, but not for me. I'd resemble a beanstalk in these.

I slid the lid back on top. "I can't accept these."

"You can. Besides, they had a *no returns* policy."

I eyed the designer logo, highly doubting the store wouldn't take them back.

"You liked them. I could see it in your eyes."

"Didn't know you could read people."

"Not people, Cat. You. I can read you."

That drummed up my pulse, which in turn, warmed my cheeks.

Ace took in my blush, but instead of picking fun at it, he blew out a breath and said, "Please wear them."

I was going to use the excuse of not wanting to owe him another favor, but instead, I went with the truth. "I'm already tall. I really don't need any extra inches."

He frowned. "Is that why you won't accept my gift?"

"You're a guy. You don't have to worry about height."

"Supermodels are tall."

"They're supermodels. They've got the looks to go with the height."

"What exactly do you think you look like, Catori?"

"Like Shaquille O'Neal and Sacagawea had a baby."

"Not sure who Sacagawea is."

"A Native who helped Lewis and Clark during their Louisiana expedition."

"Good to know, but my question was rhetorical."

My blush deepened. I wasn't sure why since it wasn't a compliment. Unless it was?

"Wear the heels. If anyone dares make fun of you, I'll burn their dinner to a crisp."

"Fine." I dropped onto the ochre velvet chair and slid on the red-soled shoes which fit perfectly. "What's it going to cost me?"

"Presents aren't bargains."

I whipped my gaze back to his. "How come printing the book wasn't considered a present then?"

"Because you insisted on paying me back, so it became a favor."

I folded my arms. "So if I tell you I won't pay you back, then I don't need to go to dinner with you?"

A smile twitched at the corner of his mouth. "Too late to change your mind."

I grumbled, "One day, I'm going to become a pro at faerie bargains."

"I have a century on you," he said, as I finally rose. "That's a lot of catching up to do."

I was eye-level with Ace, except his eyes weren't on mine; they were on the shoes. "If you liked them so much, why didn't you get them in your size?"

He chuckled. And then he asked, more seriously, "Can you walk in them?"

I stepped forward. "Apparently I can. How far's the restaurant?"

"Just upstairs."

My mouth went dry. "Upstairs?"

"Relax, Kitty Cat. It's not in my room. It's on the hotel's rooftop. They have an award-winning Asian restaurant."

He swept open my bedroom door. I grabbed my key card and phone, then traipsed past him, trying to make my strides fluid. It was hard work but a glimpse in the hallway mirror reassured me I was doing okay.

"They're really pretty, Ace. Thank you."

"I think the last hunter to thank a faerie so much was Taeewa when Jacobiah saved his life."

"He didn't exactly save him," I remarked, as we entered the elevator.

"He brought him back from the dead."

"But he killed him first."

"And brought him back afterward," Ace insisted. "And then he kept him hidden from faeries. Protecting someone is a form of saving."

"So lying to Gregor was you trying to save me?" I had my back pressed against a mirrored panel.

His lips formed a hard line. "Lying to Gregor was me apologizing for duping you."

The air was so thick and hot in the closed metal box that sweat slicked my palms and magnified the spicy scent of Ace's cologne. It was *everywhere*, leather and ginger mixed with cloves. I was pretty sure I would smell like him all throughout dinner now.

The elevator pinged, and it felt as though I were being released from a maximum-security prison. I walked out ahead of Ace into the air-conditioned restaurant whose walls were lacquered black and adorned with terracotta earthenware. High-backed chairs covered in midnight-blue velvet were arranged around dining tables as black as the walls.

A hostess clad in a mandarin-collared dress escorted us to our seats. She was so mesmerized by Ace that she didn't pull out my chair. She didn't even look my way.

"Demonstrating how it works?" I asked, once she'd left.

"How what works?"

"*Captis.*"

He made a low sound in the back of his throat. "Kitty Cat, if I used *captis* on anyone in this room, they'd be riding me right now. Is that really what you want to see before you eat?"

I didn't even want to see that *after* I ate.

A waiter dressed in a sapphire silk tunic appeared next to our table with a pitcher of water. As he poured some into our glasses, he asked what we wanted to drink. I asked for champagne; Ace asked for Japanese whiskey, no ice. The waiter backed away, melting into the dimly-lit room.

"Why me, Ace?"

He leaned back in his chair. "Why you, what?"

"Don't you have a million better people to have dinner with?"

His dark eyebrows shifted. "Believe it or not, when you don't use brute force, I actually enjoy your company."

I toyed with the napkin on my lap.

"Cass told me you wanted to become a doctor." He tipped his head.

"Did she, now . . .?" I wondered who was the busiest-body in Rowan—Cass or Mr. Hamilton?

"Why medicine?"

"When I was seven, my grandfather started to develop chronic pain in his spine. He'd get this tingling, which would turn into numbness. His muscles would seize up. In a matter of months, he could barely walk or lift a teapot without help.

"Grandma Woni and Mom tried to cure him with Gottwa decoctions that smelled like old socks." I wrinkled my nose as I remembered dipping my lips into my grandpa's cup. "Some days, he seemed better, had more mobility—and everyone was convinced the brewed medicine was helping. Some days, his pain got so bad that he'd sleep in the living room armchair to avoid being moved. I'd sit on his lap those days and hold books out to him so that he could read to me. Not that he really needed books. He always had a story."

I smiled, remembering my grandfather's kind, wrinkled face,

the smell of Vetiver and pipe on his skin, the calluses on his sturdy hands.

"And then one day, his ankle broke. My parents finally took him to the hospital. He was diagnosed with stage three bone cancer. I didn't really know what it meant. I mean, I knew cancer was not something you wanted to have, but my parents tried to protect me by telling me he'd be okay. That he'd be coming home soon."

The waiter deposited our drinks in front of us. He asked if we were ready to order, but Ace waved him away.

I watched the bubbles snake up the sides of my glass and pop at the surface, listened to them fizz. "He never came home. I was angry with my parents that day. Because they'd lied. Because they'd treated him with *tea* instead of chemotherapy." I twirled the stem between my fingers. "I don't know if chemo would've saved him, but it might've prolonged his life. Anyway, from that day on, I decided I wanted to learn how to save people."

I looked up at Ace.

"Before she died, Holly told me that faeries have healing powers, that the best doctors have faerie blood. Another reason I would never choose hunter, Ace. I'm not saying magic heals better than actual knowledge, but I'll take any advantage I can get."

"Unfortunately, our magic can't heal everything." His gaze traveled over my bare shoulder, dipping down to the flesh-colored Band-Aid I'd traded for the white gauze and sterile compress. "How's your arm?"

"Better."

He lifted his glass and held it in front of me. "To your dreams coming true."

I clinked my glass against his. After taking a sip, I asked, "So what do you dream about, Ace Wood?"

He reclined again in the high-backed chair, interlacing his long fingers around his whiskey glass. "I dream that we can learn to live in peace on Neverra. That the Seelie, Unseelie, and *calidum* work together instead of against each other. That my little sister finds her voice. That my father listens to me instead of Gregor and Lyoh. That hunters never kill another faerie. That, one day, I will be free to leave Neverra for good."

"Is it really such a bad place to live?"

"It's not bad, but it's not run the way it should be. We live in archaic times where everything, every relationship is calculated. Where free speech is repressed. You need to make the right friends. If you make the wrong ones, you're reprimanded and punished."

"Do you have a lot of friends?"

"Besides Cruz, I have two, but I'm told they're not the *right* friends."

"Who tells you this?"

"Father, Mother, Gregor, my *right* 'friends' . . ."

"Do you still see your *wrong* friends?"

He put his drink down and leaned his forearms on the table. "Am I sitting across from you right now?"

"Yes."

"Do you think I let people dictate what I do?"

"Don't they punish you?"

"Oh, yes."

"How?"

"I won't run you through all of my punishments, but my latest one is marrying my father's concubine and assuming the paternity of their child."

I knocked over my glass of champagne. It didn't break, but the contents spilled out and trickled onto Ace's lap. "Sorry. Oh my God, I'm so sorry."

"Feeling pretty sorry for myself, too." I didn't think he meant getting his gray jeans soaked.

The waiter stepped out of the darkness again, dishtowel in hand. He wiped the table clean, then handed Ace a fresh napkin. "We'll take two tasting menus and two more of the same." Ace pointed to our drinks. "You eat everything, right?"

I nodded. The waiter receded again into the darkness.

"Why are so many human girls allergic to everything?" he asked.

"They watch their weight."

"Do you watch your weight?"

"No. I should, though. I forget to eat way too often."

"How does one forget to eat?"

"One lives over a lively graveyard in a highly-animated town. One has many things to worry about, like surviving all her visitors."

Ace laughed, and the sound was terrifyingly mesmerizing.

So much so that I had to physically shake myself out of the hypnotic daze it put me under. "I was wondering about something I learned in Holly's book—I should say Ley's. Apparently it was Holly's mother who wrote— Why are you frowning?"

"Holly *is* Ley. She just changed her name when she returned to Rowan. Would've been suspicious if she hadn't."

"What?" I yelped.

"You didn't find their resemblance odd?"

The only picture of Ley I had was the one on my nightstand. She was young in it. I'd only known Holly as an old woman.

"But Ley died in—" When had she died? "She's buried in our graveyard, next to Chatwa." The memory of their matching scars came back to me, and I clapped my hand in front of my mouth. "Holy crap . . . Holly was *Ley*?"

Why was I so surprised? I was having dinner with a century-old faerie who looked to be in his mid-twenties. I'd moved water with my mind. At this point, nothing should've shocked me.

Ace looked amused.

"Why didn't you tell me?" I hissed.

"You never asked."

"How *could* I have asked?"

"You could've said, 'Are Holly and Ley the same person?'"

"You know what I mean."

"Didn't think it would matter."

Technically, it didn't. Although I could've asked her about

Chatwa and Taeewa. Had she known him or had he died before she was born?

"What were you about to ask me about Holly's book?" Ace's voice tugged me out of my head.

What *had* I wanted to ask him?

It took me a minute of thorough digging before it came back to me. "I learned that the first portal your people opened was in the Bella Point Lighthouse. Why Michigan? Why not London or Area 51, or somewhere more exciting?"

"When the first *astium* was built and spelled to allow us to travel, it carried us to this state. We learned only much later how to program GPS coordinates into the *astiums*."

I was about to ask him more about these *astiums* when the waiter brought out the appetizers plated on the most delicate ceramic dishes. A glistening fan of sliced fish was dotted with thick sauce and slivered shiso. On another plate sat a deep-fried rice ball topped with spicy tuna tataki. And from a martini glass poked a skewered, glazed shrimp drenched in a vinegary sauce.

With my chopsticks, I pinched a wedge of fish, smeared it in the sauce, then placed it on my tongue, where it dissolved.

I must've groaned with pleasure because Ace's mouth curved into a knowing smile. "Good?"

"Unbelievable."

He tried one, then nodded.

"Even for you?" I asked.

He frowned. "What do you mean, even for me?"

"You've been around a long time and have a limitless amount of money. You must eat delicious food all the time."

"Believe it or not, I'm still uncovering delectable things." There was something in his tone that made the blood beat against my veins. Which was silly since we were discussing food and nothing else.

I grabbed a skewered shrimp and plopped it into my mouth. Flavor exploded against my palate, momentarily obliterating my sudden unease. After I swallowed, though, the nervousness crept back in, making me wish I were sitting underneath an air-conditioning vent.

"Are you all right?" His deep voice swept over my skin . . .

Under it.

He must've been using *captis*. That was the only logical explanation for how flustered I was becoming. I was about to tell him to stop, but what if—what if he wasn't using any?

"Show me how *captis* works?" I blurted out. "On me. Show me."

He cocked an eyebrow. "Are you certain?"

"Yes." My pulse struck my neck at a chaotic rhythm.

No muscles in his face moved, only his eyes shifted. And then something warm and velvety basted my skin, trickled down my jaw, my neck, slid between my breasts, over them. My nipples hardened.

I wanted to claw at the silk that constrained my breasts, set them free. His lips parted, and for a second, I thought he was going to lean over, drag the fabric off with his teeth, and swirl his tongue over my sensitive flesh.

He was looking at them.

He wanted them.

Wanted me.

No! He doesn't want me. I blinked, momentarily startled by the thought that contradicted everything I was feeling.

My knee knocked against his under the table. It was only a knee, but it created a series of explosions up my thighs. Had he felt it too?

I watched his handsome face, watched his perfect lips part with a wet slide. I dipped my hand beneath the table and grazed his knee, then raked my nails up his rock hard thigh, all the while keeping my gaze locked on his.

His pupils pulsated as my fingers inched higher. Just before I could glide my knuckles over him, he jerked away, chair legs scraping.

My hand tumbled off his lap.

A soft gasp escaped me.

What the hell did I just do?

Flushing, I returned my fingers to my napkin and stared at the bursting champagne bubbles.

Two things I was sure of: one, he had *never* used *captis* on me before; two, I was in trouble.

39

HATE AND LOVE

" I 'm sorry, Cat."

  I wrung the napkin on my lap, tracing the lines of the 'W' that blazed against the black ink of my tattoo. "Why are you sorry? You didn't do anything I didn't ask for." I didn't look up for fear that Ace would spot the anguish devouring me.

Whatever he'd kindled still stirred in my core, still slithered in my veins, diffusing venomous desire.

"I'm sorry I didn't stop sooner," he murmured.

"You mean, before I made a complete fool of myself?"

"You didn't make a fool of yourself."

My hair fell around my face, curtaining off my blazing cheeks. "I stroked your leg."

"Most women would've been on their knees underneath the table. *You* resisted me."

I was pretty certain my skin tone matched my dress. "I didn't feel very resistant."

He scooted his chair back underneath the small table and leaned forward. "Why did you want me to use it on you?"

There my insides went again, turning to mush from his husky timbre.

I licked my lips nervously. "I-I . . . wanted to see if it would feel the same as Borgo and Cruz's *captis*." I spoke my lie so quickly that the words collided into each other.

"And?"

I shifted in my seat, focusing on the soft music dripping from the speakers, willing the tendrils of air-conditioning to cool my fever. "It was the same." *Lie. Lie. Lie.*

One of his eyebrows hiked up. "Really?"

I cleared my throat, glancing up through the long black strands that smelled like the soap I'd used . . . like Ace. "Why is that surprising?"

The table was so narrow that his face hovered inches from mine. "Because *captis* is like a fingerprint. No two faeries possess the same. And it certainly doesn't affect all humans the same way. The end result is uniform, though—we awaken lust or love, depending on what we're after—but the control, the force, the progression, the precision, it's all very different. So if this felt the same as what Borgo and Cruz did to you, then either I'm losing my touch, or you're lying."

One of his hands disappeared underneath the table, lightly cupped my knee. I jerked, adrenaline spiking through me. He glided his hot fingers upward, drawing the silk hem of my dress higher, bunching it in his fist, pursuing his languid assault on my sensitive skin with the heel of his hand.

"And . . ." His voice caressed my forehead like a feather. "As soon as the faerie stops using it . . ."

I could feel the shape of his exhales and the slow pull of his inhales. I lifted my face infinitesimally higher, unconsciously—or perhaps, consciously—aligning our mouths.

". . . like I've stopped . . ."

I jerked my head back.

He hadn't stopped. He was toying with me, seeing how far he could push me.

"The effect. Wears. Off."

I cuffed the hand that had begun to trace the edge of my black thong and stared hard at him. Emotion whirred inside me—anger, hatred, fear, desire, embarrassment; they were all there, whipping me as though I weren't already down.

My eyes heated in time with my hand, in time with Ace's palm that I'd flattened against my thigh to keep it off more intimate regions of my body.

Shame was winning, chafing my tenderized ego. I closed my eyes, and a tear trickled out.

He thumbed it away with his free hand, then twisted the shackled one until his palm faced up. Instead of pulling away, his fingers slotted through my shaky ones. "Cat, why are you crying?"

"I'm mortified," I croaked.

He tucked a lock of hair behind my ear. "Why?"

"Because I'm so pathetically weak."

"Because you can't resist *captis*? I've never seen anyone who could. And like I said, you resisted me. I've never had anyone push back that hard."

"You're just saying that to make me feel better."

"No, I'm not." He cupped my jaw. "Look at me."

Reluctantly, I did.

"Cat, last night, you asked me to stop using *captis*. I'd never used it on you. I would never have dared to." A gentle smile played at the corners of his mouth but never settled. "The fact that you felt something gave me hope that, perhaps, my attraction wasn't entirely one-sided. That perhaps you didn't hate that kiss on the rooftop. That perhaps, you didn't hate *me*."

His thumb stroked the side of my index finger from base to tip, and although it was only my hand he caressed, his gentle touch resonated throughout the rest of my body.

"In retrospect, I shouldn't have acted so . . . impulsively. I shouldn't have kissed you without your consent, but—shit, Cat—I can't think straight when I'm around you."

The heat of the hand cradling my jaw dried the salt tracks on my cheeks and the emotion clumping my lashes.

"I'm aware that's not an excuse."

My throat felt too raw to say anything. I wasn't even sure what to say. I could hardly think straight around Ace, too.

"Please say something, Cat."

"I shouldn't—we shouldn't—"

A vein pulsed at his temple. "Shouldn't what?"

"Fall for each other."

"Too late, Kitty Cat."

I unscrewed my head from his palm, because his proximity was confusing me, and because I desperately needed space to get my thoughts in order. My pulling away made his jaw grind and the divide between his lips narrow.

"Ace, I can't fall for you."

A beat of silence shook the air in the room.

"Why the hell not? Because I'm not a hunter?" His brittle tone squeezed the muscle between my ribs.

"Of course not. Because you have a fiancée."

"It's a sham engagement, Cat."

"Perhaps, but I'd become the other woman in the eyes of the world."

"Who the fuck cares about what the world thinks?" he growled.

I did. Unless he could end his engagement, everyone around us would see me as a homewrecker, and after my stint with Cruz, I didn't want that. Not even if it wasn't true.

When Ace parted his mouth to protest or growl some more, I hushed him with a finger because I hadn't gotten to the crux of why he and I shouldn't be together. "Public opinion isn't our greatest issue, though."

His thumb stopped moving along my index finger. "What—is?" He barely separated his teeth around those two words.

"Our greatest issue is that you fundamentally abhor a significant part of who I am." I expected him to recoil and toss my hand away now that I'd reminded him that I was *gingawi*.

Instead, he drew my hand into his lap, his grip firming. "I don't."

"You said so yourself, Ace. You said that a faerie loving a huntress is the vilest thing in the world."

"When?"

"The day Borgo took his life. You said that his love for Ishtu was an abomination. I listen, Ace. And I learn. Slowly. But I learn. So I can tell you, with absolute, unwavering certainty, that we are the most perfectly wrong people for each other. That we'd end up hurting each other way more than we'd end up loving each other."

His lips flattened.

"I dare you to tell me I'm wrong," I said.

He released my hand and then scooted his legs away from mine. "You've obviously made up your mind about me." He signaled the waiter, his movement jerky. "Could you bring us the rest of the meal, or are all your chefs on break?"

The waiter scurried away.

"Don't take it out on him," I said.

"I'll take it out on whoever the fuck I want to take it out on." His temper flared like a child's. He was over a century old, had been with way more women than I'd ever care to imagine, might have been rejected by some along the way—although I doubted it—and yet his ego ached.

"You gravitate toward the wrong people, Ace," I reminded him. "I'm sparing you one more distasteful connection."

"Stop throwing everything I ever said to you in my face!" He shook his head, and a lock of gelled hair fell into his eyes. He shoved it back. "We've both said hurtful things to each other. You accused me of murder, for fuck's sake. How do you think that made me feel? It pissed me off so much I stayed on Neverra. But I forgave you, Cat, because I knew you spoke out of fear, and nothing I'd done till that point had inspired you to trust me."

My stomach knotted. "Look at us, Ace. Stop talking, and look at us. We're already hurting each other."

He glared at me and then he shot to his feet and stormed out of the restaurant.

The waiter arrived a second later with more plates of beautiful food. Nothing enticed me, so I asked for the bill and signed it without looking at the amount, then pushed away from the table and stood on shaky legs.

I rode the elevator back to my floor, my stomach plummeting in time with my mood, in time with the lift. How I wished tonight had never happened. How I wished Ace and I could return to the place we'd reached after he'd stitched up my arm.

It had been a good place.

A safe place.

A place where desire and pain weren't allowed.

Where hearts couldn't get trampled.

40

THE PACK

The next morning, not knowing if Ace would show up at Forest Print and fly me back to Rowan, I packed my belongings and went downstairs to settle the bill.

As I waited for the concierge to pull it up, I asked for the bus schedule. He handed me a foldout, then told me all the charges on my room had already been taken care of. I looked around me, half-expecting to spot Ace seething somewhere in the lobby.

He wasn't.

I left through the revolving doors, my fabric tote bursting. I'd taken the shoes with me since I couldn't return them once I'd worn them. They felt like dead weight inside my bag.

Even though the sheets had been the softest I'd ever lain on and the comforter had been the plushest I'd ever wrapped around my body, I'd slept poorly. I put on my sunglasses and walked to the nearest coffee shop, the air soothing the ache between my temples. I ordered a black coffee. It was bitter and hot and filled my tormented stomach with a little warmth.

I added a cinnamon roll to my order and forced myself to eat it, even though it went down like sweetened cardboard.

When I turned the corner onto the street that ran between the

237

printshop and the river, there was still no sign of Ace. *Yes*, I was still clinging to the hope that he hadn't retreated to Neverra. I hated the way we'd left things last night.

I supposed I could've sent him a text, but what was the point when he hadn't answered the one I'd sent him before going to bed? Sighing, I went inside the building and asked for the manager. His secretary told me to proceed to his office. I knuckled his door.

Mr. Thompson peered up from his computer. "Come in, Miss Price."

His strained expression made me frown. Hopefully it had nothing to do with the book.

"There's been a . . . *complication*."

I froze.

"The man who provided the ink—well, he asked to see the metal plates. To make sure he'd supplied enough. Anyway, I left him alone with the box for two minutes—just the time it took me to get the cash from our safe to pay him, and, uh"—his scalp gleamed —"when I returned with his money, he was gone, and so was the box. I've already reimbursed Mr. Wood's credit card."

The throbbing in my head intensified. "Are you kidding me?"

His eye twitched. "Afraid not."

"Who is this man? This *supplier*?" My voice shook with anger. "I want his phone number."

"I'm not at liberty to give it out."

"You're not at liberty?!" My hand was on fire. My head, too. "You will give me his phone number right away, before I—before I—"

Ice replaced the fire. It expanded inside me. Cooled and burned me. It filled me like nothing had ever filled me before. It—

Hands spun me around. "Catori, don't make a scene."

I jerked out of my stupor. Blinked. Blue eyes held mine steady. "Ace?" I croaked.

"Calm down," he murmured.

"He *lost* my book!"

"I heard."

I tried to even my breathing, but I was too furious to calm down. Twice now. Twice I'd lost my book, and this time felt no different than the first one.

"I will try my best to get it back—" the man started.

"I bet you will," I bit out.

"Catori!" Ace's voice was sharp. "Let's go."

"Not without the man's phone number. I *want* his phone number."

"I have it. Mr. Thompson was kind enough to give it to me."

The 'W' burned furiously on my hand. *Kind enough?* Was he kidding me?

Ace dragged me out of the office, out of the building, down one street and then up another. We must've walked an entire mile before I managed to rip my arm free of his grasp.

"Give me the phone number, Ace!"

"No."

I jerked back. "What do you mean, *no?*"

"Do you actually think someone's going to answer?"

I balked at his condescending tone.

"The box never left his building, Cat."

"It didn't?"

"No. I had people keep watch last night."

"Faeries?"

"Maybe. Does it matter?"

"Did you tell them what they were watching out for?" I asked frostily.

"I was vague. Didn't you think it was too convenient that his mysterious supplier had opal ink in stock?"

What I *had* thought was that he was nervous.

I took long calming breaths. I didn't feel much calmer, but I also didn't feel like creating a tidal wave to flatten the brick building. "Now what?"

"Now my men will pick him up, and then they'll recover the box and bring it to us."

My chest was rising and falling slower. "Why didn't you tell me this last night? Or this morning?"

"Because I wasn't sure." He shot his gaze to an old couple passing by. "And because I was angry with you."

"Because I said no?"

"I've never been turned down, Cat. Never." His gaze stuck to the gold shoes peeking from the top of my bag.

"I said no because you and me, we're a terrible match. You are— well, you're you, and I'm me."

His eyes met mine again, and he smiled.

"Why are you smiling?" I asked.

"Because of your sound reasoning." He leaned toward me.

I didn't lean away. *No, no, no. Stick to your guns, Catori.*

When our faces were a hairsbreadth from each other, when all it would take was for me to crane my neck just an inch more, I blurted out, "I'm more attracted to Kajika than I am to you."

Ace's breath burst against my cold nose. He didn't move away. He didn't move at all. He would hate me now. But that was best. Liking me would screw up his life and get him hurt. I may not have been a huntress, but I had the gene and the memory of what had been done to Borgo when his affair was uncovered.

Perhaps the king wouldn't maim his own son, but . . . but what if I was wrong?

"Thank you for all you've done, but I need to go back to Rowan. Kajika's waiting for me." I stared at the lapel of his shirt. "I'll take the bus."

A cruel and cold silence stretched between us.

"What about your book?" he asked, his voice toneless.

"I don't care anymore."

"You should care."

"Why *should* I care about something that's brought me nothing but trouble?"

He pressed his wrist in front of my face. A luminescent symbol appeared on his skin. A perfect circle slashed with five irregular-sized lines. "Because if this is what you saw in it, then your world is about to get really screwed up!"

My heart jolted.

"Is this what you saw, Catori?" he barked.

"Don't yell."

"Is. This. What. You. Fucking. Saw. In. Ley's. Book?" Each word was a punch. Some landed on my heart; others hit my stomach and skull.

I stared at the symbol, kneading my temples that felt like a vat of stew, so filled were they with lumpy thoughts. "I don't remember."

"You don't remember, or you don't want to tell me?"

"I don't remember," I said, matching his caustic tone. "What is it, anyway?"

He was breathing heavily. "It's the key to the portals. If the *forma* have it, then you're going to have a hell of a lot more unwelcome visitors in Rowan."

"Can't they already get through portals? Didn't an Unseelie lodge itself inside Negongwa?"

"My grandfather owed a *gajoï* to an Unseelie," he said. "She saved my grandmother during labor, saved his infant son. She claimed her *gajoï* years later. She asked to be given access to a portal. She never returned from Earth, and then this tribe suddenly knew about us, knew how to kill us. And we understood what she'd done. She took Negongwa's life form. And then she infected others with her dark blood."

Two months ago, if someone had told me this story, I would've told them to quit using drugs, but that was two months ago. My life hadn't spiraled out of control yet. My existence was still normal then. I was still just a daughter, a college student, a citizen of a small and extremely boring town.

"If this is what you saw, then"—worry edged his voice, edged his features—"then you'll get your wish."

"What wish is that?"

241

"Of being rid of me for good."

My heart thumped. "I don't—" I swallowed. "I don't want to be rid of you."

He stared so hard at me that I feared he'd see that each beat of my heart belonged to him and not to Kajika.

So I added, "I'd like us to be friends. Allies."

A harsh snort erupted from him. "Not interested in friendship, Kitty Cat. Besides, we'll have to seal the portals, and who knows if we'll be ever able to open them again."

I teetered on the knife's-edge of tossing caution to the wind and confessing my lie—but Borgo's punishment flashed like a car siren inside my head. "Leave them open. The world is already full of evil people. Plus, that way, you'll be rid of them on Neverra."

His gaze raked over mine at dizzying speed.

I knew what he was looking for, so I looked away.

I wouldn't let him see how deeply I wanted him to stay.

41

THE GATHERING

Even though Ace offered to fly me home, I insisted on taking the bus back to Rowan. I needed to put some distance between us before I did or said something that would create more chaos than Holly's stupid book.

Nevertheless, I accepted his offer to walk me to the bus station. We'd both been so ravaged by our thoughts that we'd kept quiet the entire way. Well, until I stepped onto the bus and the doors were about to close.

Then he said, "Might just be burial schematics, Cat." He was referring to the circle I'd seen.

The worry trimming his features didn't do much to reassure me.

During most of the ride home, I tried to conjure the memory of the hologram, but with no luck. I remembered the circle perfectly, but I couldn't remember if I'd seen five lines or more, or had it been rectangles? I gently tapped my head against the headrest over and over, wishing it would knock the image back into my mind.

It didn't.

My thoughts returned to Ace, to the portal, to the book, to deceitful Mr. Thompson. I hadn't thought things could get worse than losing my mother and best friend and watching two faeries combust into ashes, but apparently things could always get worse.

The way Ace had described the Unseelie was petrifying.

They commandeered bodies.

I went still.

What if an Unseelie hijacked me?

I typed this out in a text, which I hesitated to send to Ace, but then curiosity—or was it fear?—won, and I pressed send.

ACE: No. You're part Seelie. They can't enter Seelie bodies.

ME: You're sure?

ACE: Yes.

ME: Could they get into my dad's body?

ACE: They could.

My fingers froze, and then they trembled.

New words appeared on my wobbly screen.

ACE: Lily's been braving the wind chime to check up on him. She'll stay until you get back. Then she'll have to come home.

I read and reread his words.

ACE: Cat?

ME: Yes?

ACE: Just checking you were still there.

ME: I'm still here.

ACE: I'm heading back to Neverra now, so I'll be out of reach. Cell connection doesn't work up there.

ME: You already told me that.

ACE: I'm sorry I tried to push myself on you. Don't remember me like that, okay?

A breath snagged in my throat.

ME: Why would you say that? Remember you? Are you planning on never coming back?

No dots lit up to indicate he was typing a message.

ME: Ace???

Still no answer.

244

The words began to tremble on my screen, and then my hand burned. I traced the W, willed it to bring him to me.

I'd tell him the truth and that I lied about Kajika.

I'd tell him that I was afraid he'd get physically hurt, and then I'd let him kiss me.

Or *I'd* kiss *him*.

ME: Don't you dare leave me here alone!!

My gaze ping-ponged between my screen and my glowing hand for the next several minutes. Soon, my anticipation mutated into fear.

Why wasn't he responding?

Why wasn't he soaring parallel to the bus?

ME: Ace?

I wrote a thousand other words, a thousand confessions as the trees blurred past my window in a smear of green and the blue sky dimmed to gray. I never sent any of them.

When we passed the last exit before Rowan, I called my dad but he didn't answer. I called Bee's to find out if he was there. I landed on Bee, herself, who told me she hadn't seen hide nor hair of him.

I tried his phone again, but it went straight to voicemail. Why didn't people ever pick up when it was urgent yet always took the call when nothing mattered?

When the bus pulled into Rowan, I rushed down the aisle before the few travelers could get up and almost tripped down the steps. I was on Morgan Street, just around the corner from the police station where I'd met Ace for the first time. God, I'd hated him back then. He'd been so damn smug.

"Where are you?" I whispered to the sky.

My faerie prince didn't magically drop from the heavens.

"Cat?"

I looked up.

Jimmy was standing in front of the station, keys jangling in his hand. "You okay?"

I nodded, even though I was anything but okay.

"Cass dropped your car off at your house," he said.

"She texted me that."

"I was just locking up. Want a lift? I'm heading your way."

"I'd love one."

"How was Detroit? Did my sister behave?"

"Cass? Behave?" I said with a smile. "What a question."

He chuckled. "Why'd you think I became a cop?"

"So you could arrest her?"

He grinned, which made his large forehead crinkle. "To make sure that if she ever ends up behind bars, I have the keys to her cell."

I laughed. It felt good to laugh.

As he led me toward the precinct parking lot, my stomach flipped because my mind had just latched onto something he'd said. "Why were you heading my way?"

He unlocked his vintage tan BMW, then pressed a button by his windshield to unlock my side. He'd saved that car from the impound lot and worked on it relentlessly with Blake. I still remember the day they'd finally gotten the engine to rumble.

They'd pranced around the car chanting, "We did it. Yeah, we did it." Cass had recorded them and made a GIF that racked up trillions of views.

As he settled behind the wheel, the leather squeaked beneath his neatly-pressed uniform. "I need to stop by Holly's old place."

I sank into the passenger seat, heart on the very edge of derailing. "You do? Why?"

"Because I had hikers come by the station to report a tall, young man with black hair and tattoos teaching a bunch of people how to shoot arrows. I'm supposing from the description that they were talking about Kajika. I need to tell him he can't go around using public grounds as an archery-training facility. Not only is it illegal, but it's also crazy dangerous. Can you imagine if he hits someone?"

How many hunters had he and Gwen made in my absence? "Actually, I'll come with you."

He glanced at me as he pulled out of the lot. "You sure? These confrontations can get a bit rowdy sometimes."

"I'm sure. Can we stop by my place first, though? Dad's not answering his cell phone. I just want him to know I'm home."

"Absolutely."

We drove up Morgan Street, then turned right toward home.

When we passed Holly's fields, I squinted to see past Jimmy's gangly body. "When you say a bunch, how many are we talking?"

"The hikers mentioned a dozen or so."

I stared at him in horror. Had Kajika woken up his family? Had he been foraging through my backyard while I was gone?

The second Jimmy parked in front of the house, I flung my door wide open and leaped out, taking in the rowan tree circle. The earth was undisturbed. At least, it looked that way.

I bounded up the porch steps. "Dad!"

"In the kitchen," he called back.

I crossed the living room in a hurry but came to an abrupt halt in the doorjamb. Lily was sitting at the little wooden table having dinner with my father. Ace had mentioned she'd be keeping an eye on him, but eating a meal with him?

I must've gaped a really long time, because Dad said, "Lily stopped by for some advice about her wedding dress."

"*Oh.*" I inhaled and exhaled but couldn't seem to slow my heart rate.

Lily's gaze dropped to the glowing 'W' on my hand.

"Did you give her some?" I wheezed.

Dad cracked a grin. "Not *my* advice, Cat. *Your* advice."

I gaped at the blonde faerie.

"Don't look so rattled. You love fashion, and you *love* giving advice."

I must've made a face because Dad laughed.

"Dad, Jimmy's out front," I said.

Dad paled. "Are you in trouble?"

247

"No. He just gave me a ride home since Cass brought my car back."

The blood returned to my father's face and a smile to his lips.

"He needed a pen. You think you can bring him one? I desperately need to use the bathroom." What I desperately needed was to talk with Lily in private.

"Sure." Dad folded his napkin, grabbed a pen from the drawer that contained all the things, and strode out to Jimmy, giving me, I estimated, two point four seconds alone with Ace's sister.

"Can you stay with my father one more hour?"

Her frown deepened.

"I need to go see Kajika."

She gave me a slow, disbelieving headshake. Did she think I was going to see him for a booty call?

"He brought people home to Rowan. A lot of people, apparently. Did you hear about that?"

She confirmed her awareness of the hunter gathering with a nod, then lifted her cell phone and typed: **I can stay but not long. Ace wants me home as soon as possible.**

My heart stopped. Or at least, that was how it felt. "Because—because he's planning on sealing the"—I was about to say portals but decided to use the Faeli word in case Dad was on his way back—"*astiums*?"

Not sure yet. He's exploring other possibilities.

I turned to leave but then turned back. "Lily, is there anything that affects Unseelies—besides dust—the same way iron affects you?"

Vinegar. Lemon juice. Anything acidic. I made your Dad some salad with a hefty dose of both. It should keep him safe for a couple hours.

I committed this to memory then murmured, "Thank you, Lily." Since one *thank you* didn't seem adequate for all she'd done for my father, I added two more.

Least I can do after—her thumb paused over her screen—**I gave away your book.**

She held her phone up to me a moment and then she deleted every line of text she'd written, beginning with the word 'book.'

If only she were able to delete all she'd done, too.

42

THE GREENHOUSE

In front of the farmhouse, there was music, a handful of pitched dome tents, and a stone-lined pit roaring with fire. An entire headless animal was skewered over the fire, a lamb or a pig—it was too charred to guess what it had been. Sweaty soft drinks were arranged on the large tree stump Holly had used as a picnic table during the harvest months.

Eyes sparked suspiciously as Jimmy and I got out of the car. Some of the hunters rose from the rugs they'd laid out by the fire. The ones who didn't stand swiveled around to face us.

I scanned all the faces, looking in vain for a familiar one. Then someone stepped out of the shadows, someone I recognized.

Gwenelda's hair was braided into an intricate rope decorated with small blue feathers. Had it not been for her white T-shirt and jeans, she would've looked like she'd stepped out of Holly's book. On her feet, I recognized Mom's favorite leather and shealing boots. It pained me to see Gwen wearing them even though *I* had given them to her.

I forced my eyes back upward, to the suede choker woven around her neck, to her square jaw, the full lips I'd never seen arch

250

into a smile, the straight nose, and the slanted black eyes that looked as though they could split a person open.

"Hi, folks." Jimmy flashed them his badge. "Mrs. Geemiwa." He nodded toward Gwenelda, then leaned over to me and whispered, "The Woods lied about her being the wife of the dead medical examiner. She's totally unrelated to him."

Gwenelda didn't look at Jimmy, didn't return his nod. She speared me with her gaze. I barely dared move, much less breathe. She was a short woman yet commanded as much attention as a titan.

"Catori, you have come." That strange voice of hers sounded olden, as though her vocal cords had aged during the two hundred years she'd spent below ground.

A man stood beside her, wheat-blond hair shorn close to his scalp, light eyes incandescent in the darkness. He wore army fatigues. Had he served our country or scored a uniform at Goodwill? From the breadth of muscle in his chest alone, I suspected he'd fought in some war, and now he was fighting in another.

When he took a step toward us, Gwenelda raised her palm to hold him back.

"You're back," I said. There were a million other things I would rather have said, but not in front of an audience.

"This is my home," she said.

Was she speaking about Holly's farmhouse or Rowan?

A gust of wind blew the embers of the fire our way. They fizzed in the air like buzzing fireflies.

"Don't mean to interrupt your barbecue, but I got a complaint about unruly behavior." Jimmy rubbed his eyes.

Gwenelda thrust her jaw forward. "Unruly behavior, Officer?"

"'Parently Kajika was teaching some of your friends here"—he sniffed loudly—"archery."

"And it is illegal?" she asked.

"On private property, it isn't, but on public property, yes." He blinked repeatedly, nose and eyes running. "Kajika was practicing on public grounds."

"I am terribly sorry. He must not have realized he had stepped across the invisible border. I will speak to him when he returns and make sure he does not repeat this terrible mistake."

When I caught Jimmy sponge the moisture from his face on his sleeve, I whispered, "You okay?"

"I think I'm having an allergic reaction to something." He sneezed. "Probably just pollen."

I shot my gaze back over to the crackling pit. The flames were pale. I bet they were burning rowan wood, and that Jimmy, although just a tad bit faerie, was having an allergic reaction to it.

"Thank you. You be careful now with those flames. We don't want no fires spreading to our forest," he said.

"The fire never remains unattended," she promised him.

He started to turn when he squinted at the roast. "Did you, um, shoot this animal, Mrs. Geemiwa? Hunting is illegal in this part of the state."

"We have bought this beast from the store. Cuskoo."

"Cuskoo?" Jimmy asked.

"Costco," clarified the man beside Gwenelda.

"Would you like to stay for dinner, Officer? We have been blessed with a most bountiful supper."

The ex-soldier blinked at Gwenelda, seemingly displeased about having a law enforcer join him for dinner. Unless it was because he'd sensed Jimmy's faerie blood? Could the new hunters sense fae? It wasn't as though Jimmy glowed. At least, not to me. Then again, he had a minute amount of faerie blood, and the lesser the amount, the lesser the glow.

I wondered what eating meat cooked over rowan wood fire would do to Cass's brother. Would it poison him, or just make him sick, or did the magic not penetrate food?

"That's kind of you, ma'am, but my mother's waiting for me for dinner. Have a pleasant evening now, and please, no more training with bows and arrows. We've had enough deaths around here to last us a decade." He rubbed his face on his sleeve again. Even his large forehead was coated with sweat. He started toward his car but stopped when he didn't see me follow. "Cat, you coming?"

"I need to talk to Gwenelda. I'll walk home, Jimmy. Thanks for the lift."

"I can wait—"

"Go. I'll be fine. Right, Gwen?"

"No harm will come to you, Catori," the huntress said.

Jimmy got back into his car and idled a couple minutes, as though giving me time to change my mind. Even though the crowd around me looked about as friendly as a pack of wolves, I stayed.

Once his car rumbled away, Gwenelda approached me.

Her new clan whipped arrows and bows from their backs and pointed them at me.

"Lower your weapons," she said. "Catori is one of us."

Some frowned; some hissed.

I was most definitely not *one of them* but like hell I'd tell them that. I preferred not to end up impaled like their roast.

She stopped a few feet away from me. Far enough that she didn't have to bend her neck at a sharp angle to look up but close enough that I could see the brown and yellow dots in the blue feathers. "Have you come to join us, child?"

Child. I had to remind myself that she only *looked* twenty-nine. That, in fact, she was two hundred twenty-nine. "Can we talk in private, Gwen?"

She gestured to the semi-circle of taut-bodied hunters behind her. "They are friends."

"They might be *your* friends but they're not mine."

"What is she, Gwenelda?" the army thug asked.

He'd moved closer to us. Too close. I noted a swirly tattoo peeking from the V-neck T-shirt he wore underneath his unbuttoned camo jacket. Had he already confiscated a faerie's dust or had he visited the ink parlor?

"She is family, Tom," Gwen reassured him.

"She doesn't read like you. She reads—"

Gwenelda lifted her hand, and he stopped talking. What did I read like? A faerie?

"I will walk with you, Catori, but I must remain close to my clan in case the *golwinim* return. They have been making regular visits to our land."

"That might be because you've created an army and killed two of their people," I said.

Gwen's eyes gleamed in the darkness. "They attacked first, Catori. They wielded their *gassen*. We had to defend ourselves."

"By killing them?"

"We did what we had to do. Have you come to criticize our ways, or have you come to speak in earnest?"

"I've come to speak."

"Then set aside your scorn."

I gritted my teeth and fell into step beside the huntress. We walked away from the camp, toward Holly's greenhouse that was foggy with trapped steam. "Where's Kajika?"

"Resting," she said.

The feathers wound in her hair fluttered. When we'd go on walks through the forest, and I'd find a feather, Mom would braid my hair and spear it in. I'd believed they were the greatest treasures and had started a collection. I filled a giant cookie tin with these delicate, multicolored possessions, which I would sort through regularly. I hadn't touched that tin in years.

"Who lit the rowan wood fire in Holly's room? You or Kajika?"

"I did, Catori. Kajika had nothing to do with her death." Was she protecting him by taking the blame, or was she telling the truth? "I have no qualms about my actions since I simply abided by her wishes."

"Were they really her wishes?"

"Yes." Her voice didn't falter; her expression didn't waver.

Carrying out a long-winded debate about whether it was

murder or assisted suicide seemed pointless. I didn't trust Gwenelda and doubted I ever would.

"I wish you'd told me she wanted to die. I would've liked to speak to her before."

"You were away, and when you returned, Aylen unearthed the grave where my mother lay. There was never a proper time to tell you."

"If you didn't feel guilty, why did you leave?"

"I left because I needed to grieve. It is hard to lose a mother."

I ground my teeth. "No kidding."

"I am deeply sorry I took yours away." Her eyes gleamed with sympathy. I knew it wasn't technically her fault, but the fact remained that she was here and my mother wasn't. "I heard the faeries stole the book Holly wrote about our family."

"They did, but it's no longer in their possession."

She stopped walking. Anticipation honed her features into sharp, stiff angles. "They returned it?"

"Not exactly."

"Then who possesses it now?"

Respecting Ace's wish to keep the Unseelie a secret from the hunters, I asked, "Why did you make so many hunters, Gwen?"

She wanted an answer, not a question, but until I received answers to *my* questions, she would have to wait. "The first was an accident. I did not mean to make one. I sliced my palm open on broken glass, and the woman who stopped my bleeding had a small wound on her finger. Our bloods mixed.

"The *golwinim* hunted me down, lashed out at me for creating a hunter, threatened to raze our species if I did not stop. It was only then that I understood what my blood had done. As soon as I understood my mistake, I returned to find her."

"But then you thought it wasn't such a dire mistake and decided to make more?"

"We are too few. And in this way, we did not have to sacrifice human lives to awaken our family."

"Because turning innocent people into prey sounded more humane to you? Gwen, these people aren't weapons."

"I did not force any of them to join us. I spoke honestly. I gave them a choice."

My eyes bulged. "So you've been going around, blabbing about magic and faeries, and people actually believed you?"

"I explained my family was being attacked. I asked who would be willing to help me defend them."

"Did you explain why they were being attacked and what defending them entailed?"

"Yes. I wiped the minds of those who decided not to participate. There was no coercion involved. All of those present came willingly. Only Alice, the woman from the bar, was told afterward. I regret what happened to her. She was unhappy to have been transformed and acted wildly. She killed a faerie by mistake. I imagine you have heard?"

I nodded.

"It took Kajika days to make her forgive us; days of consoling her. And now, she has."

Gwenelda placed her hand on my wrist, wrapped her fingers around it softly. "You have hurt my brother greatly, Catori. He has not been willing to tell me what happened, but I can sense his melancholy, and it pains me. What occurred the afternoon he returned to Rowan?"

I was about to answer her when something thumped loudly against the hazy glass of the greenhouse. At first, I thought it was a bird, but when I looked in the direction of the noise, I realized it was no bird; it was a body part.

A bare bottom that extended into a narrow waist and a bare back.

43

THE GIRL

Gwenelda started walking again. "Come."

She tugged on my wrist to get me to move.

To get me to stop looking.

I did neither.

Blonde hair slid against the glass, fluttering around a long, feminine neck, in the crook of which a second head materialized, this one topped with black hair.

The girl's body struck the glass again.

And again.

And again.

"Please, Catori, do not watch," Gwenelda said, still trying to uproot me. But there was no uprooting me.

Goosebumps rained down over my skin when the man raised his face and his tiger eyes bumped into mine. His forehead and bare shoulders glistened with sweat.

Instead of stopping or moving away from the glass, Kajika stared straight at me and pounded into the blonde whose loud moans seeped through the glass panes.

"Catori," Gwenelda said sharply.

I finally squeezed my eyes shut, heart thumping, cheeks flooding with heat. I shouldn't have gawked at the spectacle. I should've listened to Gwenelda and walked away.

When I felt I had myself under control, I opened my eyes. "He seems to have found a way to get rid of his pain."

Gwen grimaced. "It is still you he loves."

"No, Gwen, the woman he loves was never me. I just look like her."

"It was not just your resemblance that attracted him to you."

The land was soaked in starlight, every blade of grass perfectly outlined, every crooked tree branch sketched out to perfection. "Right. It was also because of the boy who lives inside his mind."

"If that were the case, then I would be attracted to your father, and I am not."

I wrinkled my nose. "Thank the Great Spirit."

The sound of breaking glass shook the night. Several hunters rounded the farmhouse at dizzying speed, stopping just short of the greenhouse. The door had shattered when Kajika had flung it open. The glass lay in twinkling shards amid the ochre grass.

He stormed toward us, still bare chested and barefoot. At least he'd put his jeans back on. Anger rolled off him and flavored the air until the entire property crackled with it. When he reached us, he was breathing hard, his chest rising and falling in bursts.

"Didn't mean to interrupt," I said.

"What are you doing here?"

"I just returned from Detroit and thought I would come by to check up on you."

The rapid tempo of his breathing didn't diminish. If anything, it seemed to escalate. The blonde whose buttocks I was now intimately familiar with walked up behind him. I recognized her from the picture Ace had shown me the day I'd had tea with the three faeries at Bee's. She wrapped her hand around his bicep.

"Leave!" he barked.

Gladly. I turned.

"Not you, Catori," he said, shrugging off the blonde.

"I'll come back tomorrow." I kept walking. "When you're less busy."

"Stay!" he growled.

I stopped halfway down the grassy slope. "My father's waiting for me at home."

Kajika stalked toward me, long legs moving fast. "Please, stay." There was a thickness in his tone that made me pause. It was almost as though he was about to cry.

"I really do need to go."

"You abandoned me," he murmured.

"I went to Detroit to look for—"

"In the woods, you chose them over me. You defended Borgo." His shoulders were tight, yet they quivered. "You do not know what that did to me."

"You're still here, but Borgo isn't, so I think his hurt trumped yours."

Kajika flinched. "He took the most precious thing I had away from me, Catori. He took Ishtu. He took her memory."

"How exactly did he do that? He didn't kill her."

"She was mine!" He made a low, keening sound in the back of his throat. "Her body was not hers to give away."

I blinked. "I thought she was spying for your tribe. I thought—"

"You believed I would have let her lie with a faerie?"

"That's what you *said*."

"Because I was indignant and appalled. Not only did my *aabiti* forsake our marriage cot, but she forsook it to be with one of them."

"So she really did betray you?"

He stared down at his empty hands, balled his fingers into fists. "I deserved your pity. Not Borgo."

I stared at him in pained silence.

"I longed for you to step away from him and come to me . . .

come with me." His raspy voice collapsed over me like raindrops. "But you chose him. You chose them."

I was still at a loss for words.

"I thought that what I felt for you, you felt for me. I thought"—his voice cracked—"that you cared about me."

"I do care about you," I said.

Kajika stared hard at me. "Then why did you wait days to come and see me?"

I stared at the hunter's chiseled face, at his wide, hooded eyes, at the swirls of ink on his bare chest. A patch of skin that had formerly been inked was bare.

I remembered him telling me that he'd confiscated Borgo's dust the day Ishtu had died. The faerie had finally gotten it back.

"Why do you have to care about everyone, Catori?"

"I don't care about *everyone*."

He shot me a heartbreaking smile. "You do." He raised a hand to my face, cupped my cheek.

When I remembered that he'd cupped another type of cheek only a moment ago, I stepped back and shuddered. "Don't touch me. You didn't even wash your hands." I rubbed my face with my sleeve. I'd need to soak my cheek in Lysol.

His hand, which hung in the air, settled back limply at his side. "I am sorry."

I wondered if he meant about touching me or screwing the new huntress. "You're allowed to blow off steam however you want, with whomever you want."

He lowered his eyes to the ground, raked his hand through his silky black locks.

"Kajika, I mean it." I tilted my head to the side, trying to capture his gaze. "It's okay."

His eyes plowed into mine. "I do not want it to be *okay* with you," he growled, and then he spun around and tore up the slope so fast his figure blurred.

Forgiveness and indifference hadn't been what he was after.

He'd wanted rage and jealousy, but I'd felt none. In truth, I was grateful the curvy blonde had brought him comfort, and hopeful she could break his unhealthy fixation for me, the girl who resembled the long-lost mate who'd abandoned him in life, and then again in death.

44

THE LETTER

S o lost in thought about Kajika and Ace, the walk home went by in a blur. It could've taken me fifteen minutes, just as easily as it could've taken me an hour. I had no notion of time.

I trudged past the forever-open cemetery gates, down the long drive hemmed in by headstones, hoping Lily would still be there, not only for Dad's protection, but also for my sanity.

She dropped in front of me like a string puppet.

I slapped a palm over my heart that had dropped in time with the princess's moonlit skin.

I was just leaving, she typed on her phone. **But I wanted to say goodbye. In case**

The absent period at the end of her sentence felt more ominous than an ellipsis. "Don't close the portals. Tell Ace not to close them!"

She levitated without nodding, without acknowledging my entreaty. When she rocketed into the dark sky, I screamed her name so loud that Dad rushed out of the house.

"What happened?" His gaze skipped over the graveyard like a hopping stone.

"Lily forgot s-something. I was just trying t-to call her back."

I didn't know if it was my stuttering or my stooped shoulders, but Dad dashed over to me and pulled me to him, resting his chin on the top of my head. "What's going on, Cat? I know something's wrong. What is it?"

My eyelids felt hot and gummy. I squeezed them tight to keep the tears at bay. How much could one person cry? "Don't worry, Dad. It's just girl stuff."

"Is it about a boy?"

"Yeah."

Dad pressed me away, held me at arm's length. "Did he hurt you?"

I opened my eyes wide, praying they didn't look too wet. "I hurt him."

Him was both Kajika and Ace. After all, in different ways, I'd hurt them both.

Instead of letting me go, Dad hugged me again and stroked my back. I smiled against his chest; filled myself with his sweet warmth and steady heartbeats. I'd just confessed to hurting someone, and yet he kept loving me.

Maybe closing the portals was a blessing in disguise. After all, wouldn't humans be safer?

I shuddered, selfishly loathing the solution.

I should've hidden the book better.

Burned it.

Buried it!

Maybe it was just burial schematics. Would I ever find out or would this secret stay locked up on Neverra along with the people . . . the person I'd started caring about?

I tried calling Ace after parting ways with Dad for the night.

He didn't answer. I pressed my face against my pillow. He'd held it so briefly, yet it smelled like him, and his scent calmed my effervescent nerves. Calmed them so much I fell into a deep, dreamless sleep.

When I awoke, pink morning light fell across my rumpled sheets, over my bare legs and bunched T-shirt. I tugged it down, flipped onto my stomach, and tried going back to sleep, but I was wide awake.

I got out of bed, stepped into a hot shower, then pulled on a loose gray skull-and-bones T-shirt and a pair of tight black jeans. I brushed out all the knots in my hair and braided it, but the braid made me think of Gwenelda, so I let my hair unravel. I dabbed concealer on my under-eye circles before heading downstairs.

I'd forgotten about dinner last night. There was no way my stomach would forget about breakfast.

I hunted through the fridge for something to eat and came up with a loaf of country bread, cold butter, and jam. I toasted the bread, then spread butter and jam over the slice. I ate standing up, gaze skimming the countertop.

When I saw the bottle of vinegar, I thought of what Lily had told me. I made two more butter-and-jam toasts, squeezed a lemon into warm water, and placed everything on a platter I brought upstairs.

"Good morning," I said softly, nudging Dad's bedroom door open with my shoulder.

He yawned and stretched out. "I had the strangest dream."

The last strange dream he'd had involved a woman who looked like both Mom and Gwenelda pushing me on a swing toward a guy who resembled both Blake and Kajika. It had been eerily disquieting. Almost as disquieting as the dream I'd had of my mutating brand.

"Not sure I want to hear it," I said.

After Dad sat up, I set the platter on his lap and went to open his curtains.

"What a way to wake up. I haven't had breakfast in bed since"— his voice caught—"since your mother died." He stared at the toast I'd cut into neat triangles, swallowing hard. "Speaking of your mom, there was something I wanted to give you. He reached into his nightstand and pulled out a small velvet box.

I took the box from him and opened it. In melancholic silence, I stared at the braided yellow gold embedded with tiny, twinkling rubies—Mom's engagement ring. "I thought you'd buried her with it."

"No." He smiled. "She would never have forgiven me if I hadn't saved it for you."

I tried it on. It fit the middle finger of my right hand, so that's where I kept it, next to Ace's brand and the inked reminder of who I was before faeries arrived in my small town and hunters rose from their graves.

I held my hand up to the light streaming through the window. The rubies gleamed like droplets of blood.

"Nova was in my dream. And so were you."

I guessed I would hear about the dream whether I wanted to or not. I lowered my hand and took a seat on the foot of Dad's bed, tucking my legs underneath me.

"You were swimming in Lake Michigan, and your skin . . . it sparkled. I swear, it looked like you were gold-plated. I was standing at the back of a boat, desperately trying to fish you out, sure you'd drown, but your mother was telling me to let you be, that you were perfectly safe, that water was your element. Weird, right?" Dad raked his hands through his messy blond hair, then picked up one of the toasts and chomped on it.

I'd heard weirder, but yeah, gilded skin was definitely strange.

I spied Mom's dream dictionary on the built-in shelf over the headboard, which she'd once referred to as her shrine; only her favorite books made that shelf. The worn spine was wedged between much-loved copies of *Tuck Everlasting* and *Big Little Lies*.

I was about to pull it out when a larger, squarer book haphazardly piled atop the neat row of Dad's nonfiction hardcovers caught my attention—a family album. "Is that where you found Chatwa's birth certificate?"

Dad turned around, almost knocking over the mug with the hot lemon water. He steadied it just in time. "Yes. I've been meaning to show you something I found inside."

With his free hand, he snatched the album and propped it on the comforter between us. He opened it to the last page, to a folded sheet of vellum.

"I think your mother stuck it in there recently because I don't remember ever seeing it. Maybe Holly gave it to her?"

I picked up the piece of paper and read it.

January, 1938

Abiwoojin,

I miss you dearly. Often, I sit by the mist and watch the horizon, and when it silvers with stars, I think of Rowan. I think of the nights we spent on the beach as girls gazing up at the constellations, wondering if we would spot a pahan shooting across the sky.

I am a gateway away, yet the distance feels unconquerable, even though the pahans managed to conquer it.

I know you despise them, despise me, but I have not abandoned you. I have not chosen them over you. I could never choose them over you. You are my twin, my sister, my blood and bones, my heart.

Shame sometimes consumes me that I live in the baseetogan. I feel undeserving of our ancestors' sacrifice, disrespectful to have razed my bloodline, and yet, when I look around me, the Isle feels like home.

It is a wondrous place, not unlike our birthplace. It is much smaller and built high instead of wide, with a ribbon of mist that rises and falls. The colors are strange here, and the tongue and customs take some getting used to, but pahans, especially bazash, are friendly. I have learned so much from them.

I have compiled these stories in a book for you. It is not just a book, though. You will understand when you see it.

I have returned to Rowan now and would love to visit and meet your little girl, who is no longer so little. Your daughter is beautiful, abiwoojin. She looks very much like you with her mane of black hair and obsidian eyes.

I was pregnant with a child once, too. A daughter.

Your sister always,
Ley

I BLINKED BACK tears at the emotion lining each word.

"I had the *exact* same reaction. I'm supposing *abiwoojin* means 'sister,' or something like that. It was clearly a letter to Chatwa. But I had no clue what *pahans* and *baseetogan* mean. I did several Google searches, but nothing came up, so I called Aylen and she translated them!"

Excitement thrummed over my father's face while dread pulsed through me.

"*Pahan* means 'faerie' and *baseetogan* is the place they supposedly live." Dad grinned. "Woni told me Ley was a kooky one, but writing about faeries? That's a whole different level of kookiness."

The blood drained from my face. I shot my gaze back down to the letter so Dad wouldn't sense my trepidation.

"You okay?"

Of course he'd sensed it. "Yeah. It's *totally* crazy." I forced my gaze back to his, forced my lips to bend into a smile.

Two possibilities ran through my mind. The first was, I could come clean with him. Tell him Ley was not irrational. But then what?

The second possibility was to keep him in the dark, hoping the dark would be a safe place. So that's what I did. "That's probably why Chatwa and Ley fought. Because she was insane."

"That was my conclusion, too!" He lifted the mug to his mouth, took a sip, and grimaced. "What's this?"

"Lemon water. It's good for you."

"Good for you definitely does not mean good."

267

"Dad, drink it. Please. Every morning from now on."

"Yes, Dr. Price."

"Every morning, okay?"

"Fine. But you'll have to make it for me because I'll probably forget." He drank more and then set it back on the platter. "Oh, and did you notice the date?"

"*Nineteen thirty-eight*," I read, then shot my gaze back over to my father. "The year Chatwa died!"

"I think she probably wrote it because she was in shock or something. I wonder if Chatwa ever got to read it."

I wondered about something else entirely. I wondered if the book was in some ways linked to Chatwa's death.

45

THE ATTACK

I'd grabbed my bag to head over to Bee's to see how she was doing when our doorbell rang. It was just a doorbell, but it sounded ominous. Perhaps because each time it had rung in the past few weeks, it was to announce a death.

After checking through the peephole, I drew the door open. Kajika stood on the other side, his hair wet from a shower, his face pale and bruised by lack of sleep and an ugly punch.

"Did you get into a fight?" I asked.

"I went to the fighting ring. We needed some money, and I needed to *blow off some steam* as you called it."

"Did you win?"

A single corner of his mouth lifted. "I never lose."

I returned his smile. "The other guy must look pretty awful then."

"Is this not a good time to visit?"

"I was about to head out to visit Bee."

Disappointment marred his already ragged features.

"But it can wait a couple minutes. You want to come inside?"

He took a step past the threshold, but then his eyes watered, and he retreated onto the porch.

"What is it?" I asked.

"Something inside. It is hurting my eyes."

I sniffed the air. It smelled faintly like vinegar. Had Lily sprinkled some throughout the house? "Why don't we take a walk?" I said, grabbing my keys off the hook by the front door and joining him outside. "It's nice out."

He looked up at the bright blue sky, squinting when his eyes met the unobstructed sun. When he brought his gaze back down to my face, he asked, "Why did you go to Detroit, Catori?"

"Because I found the place where Holly got the book Stella stole from me printed. I wanted to have it reprinted so I could read it."

His puckered forehead told me that was not the answer he'd expected.

"What did you think I was doing there?" I asked, starting down the gravel path that snaked through the cemetery.

"I heard talk you were with Ace Wood."

"You *heard talk*?"

"Cassidy. I asked her where you were."

"And she said I was doing *what* with Ace Wood, exactly?"

"She just said you were in Detroit with him, and he was going to drop you back off in Rowan soon."

At least, Cass hadn't inadvertently spread any rumors. "Ace *was* there. He found out we were looking for the book."

"The one you told me about? The one where you saw a drawing of me and the strange diagram?"

"Yeah." I tucked a flyaway strand of hair behind my ear. "That's the one."

"Did Ace attempt to stop you from printing it?"

"No. He came to help. Anyway, the man who owned the printshop pretended it was stolen, so I never got a copy, but Ace said the box never left the building so it couldn't have been stolen."

Kajika grunted.

"What?"

"How did Ace know the box did not leave the building?"

"He had people watching. He thought the guy was suspicious."

He grunted again.

This time, I narrowed my eyes at the hunter. "What?"

"How naïve are you, Catori? When are you going to wake up and realize that faeries are not your friends? That you cannot trust them?"

I froze as though he'd slapped me.

Kajika pivoted toward me. "Your box *was* undoubtedly stolen. And my guess would be *by* the faeries."

I wanted to tell him he had it all wrong.

"Why would a faerie help you print a book that contains harmful secrets about them?"

"Because it was stolen from them, too," I said, before measuring the risk of confessing this.

Kajika tipped his head to the side. "Who has the book now?"

I looked down at the grass poking around my Stan Smiths. "They don't know," I mumbled.

"Don't lie to me," he said in a gentle voice. "Please. I am not your enemy. I never will be your enemy."

"As long as I don't become a faerie, you mean?"

He gestured to my tattooed hand. "Have you changed your mind about staying human?"

"No."

"Then I will *never* be your enemy. I solemnly swear this. May the Great Spirit hear my vow."

The Great Spirit? What a great spirit it was.

"Now tell me, who has the book?"

Telling him meant crushing his beliefs, and I didn't feel like hurting Kajika. "Other faeries. Bad ones."

He examined my face, probably to detect if I was lying. "They are all bad."

"These are badder."

"May these faeries hope to never encounter me," he said, with a caustic smile.

Except these faeries already had . . .

The smile whizzed off his face. Had I spoken out loud?

He scanned the woods belting the cemetery at dizzying speed.

When his eyes locked on something, he shoved me to the ground so hard I didn't even have time to break my fall. The back of my scalp struck the ground first, momentarily knocking me blind.

I was trying to prop myself onto my elbows when Kajika roared, "Stay down!"

I didn't have time to flatten myself to the ground when the first rowan wood arrow struck me.

46

HUNTER BLOOD

Kajika threw himself over me and ground his teeth as the arrows rained down on his back.

I was too startled to move, too stunned to scream, too shocked to breathe. I held still. Perfectly still. The only thing that moved on my body was the feathery tail of the arrow stuck inside my shoulder. It shivered in the warm air.

"Stop!" Kajika growled.

I thought he meant staring at the arrow so I squeezed my eyes shut. And then I started to tremble. Even my teeth chattered. I felt incredibly cold and incredibly flimsy.

Kajika had been right—I was not strong enough to defend myself.

Not quick enough.

Not astute enough.

He'd sensed the hunters; I hadn't. How was I supposed to survive with such poor instincts?

I searched within me for the dormant power that had manifested the last time my skin had been pierced by an arrow, but it must've been in hiding, because I came up empty-handed.

273

Long fingers stroked my cheek. "Catori, are you okay?" The hunter's voice was soft now. As soft as his touch. "Catori?"

I opened my eyes and croaked, "They shot me."

"I know. I am sorry. I will make whoever did this pay, but first I need to get the arrow out of you."

The forest was quiet. The grass motionless. The air still.

"Are they gone?" I whispered.

"They are gone." He knelt and wrapped one hand around the embedded arrow, then placed his other hand against my collarbone. "They believe you a faerie. I tried to explain but they said they sensed something—"

Without warning, without a countdown, Kajika ripped the arrow from my flesh. A shrill, inhuman howl rose from my throat and saturated the air.

"Forgive me, Catori," he said. "It is out now. It did not splinter."

I hadn't even thought about splinters. I spun onto my side and threw up the toast and water from breakfast. I felt like I was throwing up an organ.

Monochromatic dots danced before my eyes. My pulse jackhammered in my veins. My hand burned.

Kajika grabbed it. I balled my fingers into a fist and tried to pull it back against me, but I was empty of strength.

"Why did the mark on your hand grow?" he asked.

I didn't answer him; didn't want to answer him. It didn't concern him.

Cold sweat beaded over my forehead, mixed with the tears that had sprung from my eyes and dampened my hairline.

"It hurts," I whimpered. "It burns."

"It is because of your faerie side."

I gritted my teeth as the fiery sensation penetrated deeper, took over my entire shoulder. Borgo's arrow had grazed my skin in comparison. "Can you make the pain go away?"

"I do not have any herbs or balms, but Gwenelda has some in the farmhouse."

"I'm not going back there. I'm never going back there," I whimpered.

"There is one other solution, but I am not sure if it will work."

"Anything, Kajika. Anything to stop the—" I ground my teeth together as the agonizing ache spread down my arm and cramped my chest.

Kajika ripped my blood-soaked collar, then grabbed one of the arrows in the grass and slashed his palm with it. He stuck his bleeding hand against my pulsating shoulder.

I stared in horror at his solution. "Are you making me—making me a ... a—"

"I am trying to heal you with my blood, Catori. That is all I am doing."

"B-But ..."

"But it might turn you? Holly said there needed to be a blue moon, and the next one is not rising for another few weeks, so you need not worry about becoming one of us."

I gaped at him in horror. What if he was wrong? What if hunter blood hitting my veins was enough to change me?

I didn't want to be a hunter. I didn't want to be part of a tribe of people who shot others because they were different.

Nursing my arm against my chest, I flung Kajika's hand aside and rose to my feet. "If this makes me a huntress, Kajika, I won't take part in your fight. I'll—I'll—" I was so angry my thoughts were getting jammed up. "I'll—"

What would I do? Force Gwen's new tribe out of Rowan? Drink vinegar straight from the bottle to poison my Unseelie side?

Would that even work?

"Your wound is healed," he said calmly.

Blanching, I stared down at my shoulder. Had I healed because ... because ...? I couldn't finish my thought.

Rubbing his bloody palms over his jeans, Kajika stood.

And then he reached backward, bending both his arms, and

plucked handfuls of arrows from his back. In my pain and fury, I'd forgotten he'd used his body to shield mine.

I stared at him open-mouthed.

He tossed another handful of white sticks on the ground. How many archers had been hiding in the dense foliage? How many arrows had they fired?

"I will go have a word with my clan. I will find the culprits and punish them according to our laws. Before I go, though, before I chastise them, I want to know why your mark has changed."

I owed him that much I supposed, but how would he react? Would he rethink punishing his people? Would he encourage them to open fire on me again?

"Why does it now look like a 'W', Catori?"

I sighed. "Because Cruz passed my mark on to Ace."

He frowned. "That is impossible."

"They found a way."

"What way?"

"Lily didn't want me to be linked to her fiancé and—"

"How did they do it?" Kajika's voice carried over the headstones, over the gravel, over the tall gates of our property.

I was so tempted to tell him it was dark magic, Unseelie magic, hunter magic, but if I opened that can of worms, so many more invertebrate revelations would wriggle out. Starting with the fact that hunters were simply a type of faerie—made with blood instead of fire—not a type of human.

"They performed a spell."

"You let them use faerie magic on you?" he hissed.

"Yes. Just like I let *you* use hunter magic on me."

"How dare you compare me to them! How dare you." He shook his head as he backed away from me, black strands flapping around his forehead like raven feathers.

I folded my arms in front of me. My body trembled again, but this time not from fear or physical pain. It trembled from nerves, from his reproach, from dejection.

After Kajika had vanished from view, I searched the woods for gleaming eyes or shining arrow tips. I saw neither but knew that meant nothing. I wiped the salt off my cheeks and looked up at the sky, wishing my brand had conjured up my keeper.

I pondered what Kajika had said—that the faeries stole the metal plates.

Had Ace simply acted distressed upon hearing the news of the theft?

Had his concern for me been a performance?

That thought hurt way more than the arrow that had speared my arm.

47
THE HOSPITAL

Kajika's blood had healed both my wounds. There was still a slight discoloration, but my skin had knitted back together without puckering or hardening. I should've felt relieved, but pure hunter blood was inside me, and God only knew what it would do.

I reassured myself that there needed to be a blue moon for my body to transform. That was what Holly—*Ley*—had said. Still, it irked me.

Carefully, I collected all the bloodied arrows from the grass and stuffed them in the dumpster behind our house. I tossed my tattered T-shirt in there too, then walked back toward the house in my bra. Once safely tucked away in my bathroom, I pulled off all my clothes and took a shower. Dried blood ran over my skin in pink rivulets and vanished down the drain. I scrubbed my face clean and washed my hair. I felt cleaner, but not calmer.

Each time I closed my eyes, I saw arrows fall from the sky, heard them whizz past my ears. I pictured Kajika's grief-stricken face and felt warm blood ooze out of me.

On the outside, I looked like the same Catori who'd woken up this morning—with one less wound.

On the inside, the wounds were everywhere. I was scarred and bitter and frightened.

I finally cut the water and dried myself, arms shaking. I was cold. So very cold.

After drying my hair, I pulled on a thick black sweater and black leggings and called Cass.

I wanted a friend.

If only I could tell that friend everything.

"Are you at Bee's?" I asked after she answered.

She sniffled. "No."

"Are you crying?" My angst faded when I heard more sobs. "What's going on?"

"Grams. She just died." Cass hiccupped. "I didn't get to say goodbye, Cat. I got here too late."

Astra was gone? Could this day get any worse? "Are you all by yourself?"

"No, Faith is here. And Mom and Jimmy are on their way."

"Where is *here*?"

"Mercy Hospital."

"I'm getting in my car right now."

"Okay," she answered in a small voice.

I drove like a madwoman, completely disrespecting the speed limit. Astra was a faerie, so she'd disintegrate when the fire went out in her veins. How soon would that be?

I needed to get there before that happened, or Cass and Faith would have one hell of a rude awakening.

Maybe Etta would get there first. Maybe she'd have time to get her mother out of the hospital bed before it happened.

Did she even know what she was?

Would Stella come home for this?

Could she come home or had the portals been locked?

Thankfully, it was not rush hour and no traffic cops were prowling the roads. I took the ramp toward Mullegon way too fast and almost veered off the shoulder of the freeway. I needed to slow down if I didn't want to end up like Astra. I weaved through the town at a more leisurely pace. Still, I was driving faster than I should.

When I saw the enormous white cube that housed the hospital, I jerked my steering wheel to the right and gunned my car into the parking lot. I swerved into the first free spot and ran into the hospital.

"Astra Sakar. Which room is she in?" I asked one of the nurses at the reception.

"Fifth floor. Room 503. Are you family?"

"Yes," I said sprinting toward the bank of elevators.

As I took one to the fifth floor, it dawned on me that barely an hour before, I'd been shot, and now I was in the hospital for an entirely different reason. I must've been tapping my foot because two people were staring at my shoe. I glued my sole to the vinyl flooring and syphoned in a couple calming breaths.

When the doors opened, I shot past them and followed the sign toward room 503.

Five people stood inside, crowded around the medical bed, and two had flaming red hair.

48

DEATH

I went inside the crowded hospital room on taut legs, eyes riveted to Stella. The only plus side of seeing her was that it meant the portals hadn't been sealed.

"Hey." Cass gave me a one-armed hug.

For a moment, I set my anger aside to focus on her. I squeezed her tight and murmured how sorry I was. After she released me, I extended my condolences to Etta and Jimmy, and then to Faith, who was sitting in a chair opposite the others. She clutched her grandmother's hand in hers as though holding on to her would keep her from truly leaving. I'd learned the hard way it didn't work like that.

I half-expected Faith to ask what I was doing there, but she didn't. I suspected there was too much pain inside her to allow for malice. Finally, I turned toward Stella. Her usually impeccable complexion was splotchy, and her eyes were as wide as the over-sized gold buttons on her cream cardigan.

I folded my arms in front of me and said through gritted teeth, "You came back."

She blinked rapidly, then glanced around her to see if the

others had heard my comment. If they had, no one was paying attention to us.

I tipped my head toward the hallway.

She flinched. What did she think? That I'd let her theft slide because her mother had died? If I didn't corner Stella, she might slip right back into Neverra.

"I'm not asking." I kept my voice low, but Etta heard me.

She watched as her sister and I left the room.

After I shut the door, I asked, "How could you do that to me?"

"My mother just died, Catori."

"I'm truly sorry for your loss, but this is the first time I've seen you since you stole my book," I hissed. "Why did you do it?"

She dropped her voice. "That book could've gotten the hunters inside Neverra. I was protecting my people."

So Holly's book *was* a key to the portals. "You weren't after the burial schematics," I said more than asked.

"The burial schematics might've been inside, but that was never the issue."

"So waking Negongwa and getting him to annul his regulation on your dust was a cover-up?"

A tight smile squeezed onto her lips. "Gregor and I thought it best not to alert the boys to the real reason. After all, they're neither smart, nor dependable."

I flexed my jaw.

"Everything all right out here?" Etta had opened the door a crack to stick her head through.

"Yes!" both Stella and I said at the same time.

From the shrillness of our voices, I doubted Etta would believe us.

"I should probably call Derek," Etta said. "To tell him to prepare a plot."

"Mom didn't want to be buried," Stella said in a flinty voice.

"She didn't?" Etta raised a brown eyebrow.

Where Stella had amber hair, Etta's hair was as brown as Cass's. Although a lot of her hair had turned gray recently.

"Mom wanted to be cremated."

I watched Etta. Waited for a spark of comprehension. Only wide-eyed surprise registered. Did Etta not know what her mother had been? Did she not know what *she* was?

"But why don't you call him to help you with the flower arrangements? We can hold the wake at the bakery. Mom would've liked that."

"Okay," she said. Then, "Are you coming back inside?"

"In a minute," Stella answered. "Can you close the door?"

Etta slipped back inside, and the door snicked shut. Two nurses walked past us. I caught wisps of conversation about what one of them should wear on a date. How I wished I could be discussing outfits for dates.

"She doesn't know, does she?" I asked.

"No. It was Mom's wish not to say anything."

"Then how did you find out?"

"I met a man who explained everything to me."

"Faith's father?"

She nodded.

"Who is it?"

"It doesn't matter who it is."

I supposed it didn't. "Why didn't you ever tell Faith about her heritage?"

"I was respecting my mother's wishes."

"Why didn't Astra want anyone to know?"

"Because she hated the Isle. She never told me why, but she said that if I ever spoke to the others about it, she would wake the hunters and get Holly to give them her book so they could raze Neverra."

"So that's how you knew about the book!"

Stella pressed her mouth shut, breathing only through her nose.

283

"Are you going to tell Faith now?" I asked.

"After she has her baby, I'll tell her."

The tension in my jaw slackened. Faith was *pregnant*?

Stella tilted her head to the side. "You didn't know, did you? I guess people don't feel comfortable confiding in you, Catori."

I ignored her jab. "Faith and I have never been close."

"Look, not that I'm not enjoying our little chit-chat, but I have a family to go back to. I have preparations to make—"

"My book plates disappeared."

"I heard."

Of course she had.

I suddenly hated myself for wondering if Ace had a hand in their disappearance. "Give them back to me, or I'll tell everyone in that room what they are and what you did."

She took a step toward me. Her musky perfume was so strong it burned my nostrils. "Little girl, don't threaten me."

I shook my head, rage swelling within me. "You stole from me. Twice. You stole from me twice!"

She backhanded me so hard my face flew to the side and my cheek burned. "Don't you ever speak to me like that!"

I raised my palm to nurse my stinging cheek while Stella inspected her hand as though checking for a chipped nail.

My pulse jackhammered through my veins, sent more fury thrashing through my veins. Or was it magic?

"Get out of here, Catori. This is *my* family, not yours. Get out of this hospital before I really lose my temper."

"I never understood why Faith didn't want you around, but now I do. You're an awful mother, Stella. An awful human being." Before I could react, she raised her palm and dust shot out of it. It sparkled as it flew across the small divide between us.

I jammed my mouth closed, flung my forearm against my nose, and lurched backward, but her dust managed to sneak in.

I tasted it on my tongue. The rancid mouthful glided down my throat—tart and bitter, like a skunk's spray, like warm garbage, like rotten eggs. My tongue ballooned inside my mouth—or was it her dust that was expanding?

Eyes wild, I sputtered and reached out toward a wall, knocking into it. I couldn't breathe. I yanked my hand off my nose and inhaled, but no air breached my flaring nostrils.

I gasped for breath, but it was like trying to suck air out of water. My lids drooped, but I forced them up. There was a flurry of movement around me. Someone dressed in blue scrubs; more than one person dressed in blue.

And then Stella was there, crouching in front of me.

"Don't know what happened," she was telling the nurses, brown eyes shimmering with hatred.

Fight back, my mind screamed. *Fight back!* I grappled for some remnant of energy, some thread of power, some morsel of fresh air, but there was only smoke.

Acrid . . . putrid . . . smoke.

If only I'd pocketed one of the rowan wood arrows.

I would've pierced Stella's black heart with it.

If only—

Her face was so close to mine. Too close. I clawed in slow motion at the air to push her away. It must've worked because suddenly her face was no longer there. No longer in front of mine.

I blinked sluggishly, my lids feeling like sandpaper over my eyes. When I managed to focus, I found Cass kneeling over me, puffy eyes darting through her bangs. Her mouth was making a sound, but I couldn't hear what she was saying.

Stella's dust felt like a noose; a rough noose made of smoke and venom. My lids slid shut again, and again I dragged them up.

The hallway had turned paler. The blue scrubs, gray. Cass's bangs, black.

My chest cramped, and pain, worse than a claimed *gajoï*, erupted in my heart. It felt as though a rabid animal were clawing its way out of me, shredding me from the inside out, tearing up my organs, ripping out my veins.

I wanted to scream. Maybe I did. I had no clue. I'd stopped hearing real sound. All I could hear was the sluggish thump of my pulpy heart.

Everything twirled around me, spun. Up became down, and down became up. My body was being moved. Something sharp jabbed my throat. In some distant recess of my mind, I deduced they must have intubated me.

Silly them.

Magic was stronger than any human tool.

Defeated, I closed my eyes and waited, counting the seconds in my mind.

How much time could a brain function without oxygen?

Three? Four? Five minutes?

How much time had gone by already?

How much time did I have left?

49

THE REFLECTION

It was the taste that faded first.

Like dew evaporating from a petal, the foul tang of Stella's dust receded. And then the swelling lessened. My lungs no longer felt like inflatable buoys; my tongue no longer felt as though it had taken over my mouth; my gums no longer felt like they were about to eject my teeth.

Had I died?

If I had, then why did my throat feel as though it were on fire?

Something beeped.

I expected the afterlife to be a silent void, but either I had been mistaken, or I hadn't made it there.

Something beeped again. This time, I slammed my lids up. Above me, there was a dusky gray ceiling. Paint smeared over a plastic casing. Inside the casing, long buzzing fluorescents.

"Cat? Cat?" someone said excitedly. The voice squeaked again, piercing my dazed eardrums, echoing around me, as jarring as percussions.

Two faces hovered over mine.

Both familiar.

Both strained.

Both had blue eyes.

"Cass?" The whispered word made my throat ache wildly.

Memories of earlier returned. They'd sliced my throat open to insert a breathing tube. I raised my hand to touch my throat, expecting to feel a plastic tube. I only felt skin and a slow pulse.

The heart monitor strapped to my finger emitted a loud, long beep. I lowered my hand.

Had a human tool managed to save me?

I looked at the other concerned face.

At the deep grooves between the dark brows.

At the shadows swimming over the bright blue irises.

Shadows that seeped into the sharp jaw and compressed lips.

"Oh my God, you gave us such a scare!" Cass said. "I can't believe you just started choking out there!"

Was that the story? That I'd simply started choking? "Where—Stella?" I whispered.

"She ran to get Ace. Not sure why she thought he could do anything. No offence, Ace," Cass said.

"None taken." Ace's voice was low and rough, a perfect match to his expression.

The anger pulsing from him told me Stella had most definitely not gone to him for help. He'd probably come because of the mark on my hand. It must've lit up at some point. I tried to remember, but instead of events, I recalled only smells and tastes, so I banished the memory deep.

"I'll go get Derek. He's been so crazy worried I sent him down to have tea with Mom and Jimmy in the cafeteria." Cass started to leave but doubled-back and planted a huge kiss on my cheek. "Don't ever do that to me again!" she said, eyes misty but bright.

I nodded.

When the door closed, I fixed my gaze on Ace. "Where—is—Stella?" This time my words were a little clearer.

The tendons in his bare forearms roiled even though he hadn't moved. "Stella's back on Neverra."

So she was still alive . . . I never thought I'd be disappointed to find out someone was still alive.

The heart monitor didn't beep for a couple of long seconds. When it did, the resonance felt like a fire alarm against my sensitive eardrums. "She tried—to—kill me."

"I know." His jaw set into a hard line. I couldn't tell if he was angry or concerned.

"What?" I asked, trying to see past the shadows that populated his eyes, but they were too dense and fluctuating too fast.

He lowered his gaze to the crinkly bedspread. "What did you do while I was gone?"

I felt my forehead crease. For the life of me, I couldn't understand his question. I wanted to ask what he meant, but my bedroom door opened, and then people were rushing in, and two large palms were cradling my face, and a mouth was crushing the frown on my forehead.

Dad.

He ran his hands through my hair, pushing it off my forehead, behind my ears, patting it down. "Oh, baby, you're all right. You're all right." Tears ran down his alabaster cheeks.

I raised my fingers to wipe some away. I couldn't catch them all, though.

He laid his big head against my shoulder and sobbed, wetting my hospital gown.

I stroked his back with the hand that was not attached to the heart monitor. "I'm okay, Daddy," I croaked.

He sobbed even louder.

I kept stroking his hunched back until he finally calmed down. When he pulled away, he again grabbed my face between his hands, and again he kissed my forehead. "You're not allowed to leave me, you understand?"

I smiled. "I'm not going—anywhere." I took a long breath of air. It had never tasted so fresh or sweet. "Can we—go home now?"

He sighed. It resonated in his chest and through the room. "Not yet, honey. The doctors want to run tests on you to understand why your throat closed up."

I looked at Ace, silently willed him to come up with a solution to have me discharged. Instead of helping, he turned toward the window. It was dark out, and the lights of Mullegon glimmered like Stella's dust.

"Ace offered to spend the night, so you're not alone," Dad said.

I watched the reflection of the faerie's face in the glass. His eyes were so tight that they appeared bracketed with wrinkles, wrinkles that had yet to score his youthful face.

"I don't need—anyone to stay," I said, even though I didn't want to be alone. What if Stella returned?

Dad's gaze flicked to Ace. He must've picked up on the faerie's tension, because he said, "Actually, I can stay."

"No, Derek, you need to go home and rest," Etta said.

"I'll rest when I'm dead," Dad volleyed back.

Cass pressed the bangs out of her puffy eyes. "Please don't talk about dying."

Ace finally turned away from the window. "Mr. Price, I promise to watch over your daughter until you come back. Like I told you, I rarely sleep at night anyway."

Dad thumbed his ear. "What do *you* want, Catori?"

My poor father looked so depleted that I said, "Ace can—stay."

He sighed. "Okay. But call me if you change your mind, or if you need anything."

"A change of clothes would be—nice." I wondered where mine had gone. Not that I wanted to wear them again. I dreaded that they'd smell like Stella's dust.

Dad nodded. "Yes. I'll grab something. Maybe Cass can help me do that."

I smiled. "Good idea." I was a little worried what sort of outfit my father would bring me. Plus I didn't really want him rooting through my underwear drawer.

"Glad you're all right, Cat." Jimmy wrung a baseball cap

between his fingers. He screwed it on his head, and it swallowed a few inches of forehead.

I smiled. "Thanks, Jimmy."

He nodded. Smiled back. Nodded to Ace. When he got no reaction from the faerie, his smile fell and he turned to leave, his mother in tow.

"Bye, sweetie." She waved at me from the doorway.

Dad kissed the tip of my nose before following Etta and Jimmy out.

Cass was the last to go. She wished me a good night and warned me not to do anything stupid while she was gone—like choke on my own saliva again.

"Love you, too," I murmured, before she closed the door.

The steady beeping of the heart monitor and the buzzing lights were the only sounds in the room for a long time.

"What's with—the attitude?" I finally asked, throat still raw.

Ace's gaze, which had been on everything but my face, ground into mine, and then it dipped to my throat.

I touched my neck. Was there a hole? I didn't even feel a bandage. "What?"

"Did a blue moon rise in the twenty-four hours I was gone?"

My fingers froze mid-exploration. "A blue—" I sat up, and the jerky movement unclipped my heart monitor, which went positively haywire.

Ace punched it. His fist cracked the screen. The beeping stopped. I was expecting a nurse to trundle in, but no one came. His knuckles crackled like dry leather, then smoothed back instantly.

The blood drained from my face.

Had I become a hunter?

Had Kajika's blood obliterated my faerie side?

I took inventory of how I felt. Battered. Tired. As though I'd gone a couple rounds in the fighting ring with Kajika. I did not feel particularly strong. Nor did I feel particularly different.

"Why did you ask—about a blue moon?"

"Look at yourself!"

I frowned. If there'd been something different about me, wouldn't my father, Cass, and the others have mentioned it? "There's no mirror."

He exhaled a rough breath. "In the window. Look at yourself in the window."

I got out of bed on shaky legs. Like a foal defying gravity, I inched over to the window. Ace trailed me with his gaze, but didn't offer support.

His arms were still folded, his jaw still set.

A foot away from the dark glass, I raised my gaze to my reflection.

And then I gasped.

50

THE NEW TATTOO

Around my neck stretched an intricate arabesque, with whorls and spikes and smooth curves. It wound almost all the way to my top vertebra and pulsed like Kajika's tattoos. It took my addled brain a second to comprehend where it had come from.

"I confiscated Stella's dust?"

"You're the huntress. You tell me." Ace's voice was searing.

I shivered. The room felt like an icebox.

I touched the tattoo, felt it beat underneath my fingertips like a pulse. It was alive. I expected it to choke me, to breach my skin and leak into my larynx all over again.

Trembling, I lifted my face, pivoted my head from side to side. I looked for the hole I remembered feeling, but all I saw was the tattoo. "How come Dad and the others didn't say anything?"

"I dusted your neck so they'd see a bandage."

Reflexively, I shut my mouth. Tried not to breathe.

"Relax. I'm not planning on finishing Stella's botched attempt at murdering you. Even though I probably should."

Hurt filled places in me that no longer hurt. "Why would you say that?" I whispered.

293

"Why did you choose them, Cat?"

His somber timbre drew goosebumps from my skin.

"I didn't choose them," I murmured.

"Then how come you have a fucking tattoo around your neck?" he roared.

I recoiled from his raised voice. "Don't yell at me."

He squeezed the bridge of his nose between his thumb and forefinger, and just breathed. "You know, I *almost* killed her. Almost. But then you were dying, and I didn't want to let you out of my sight, and she escaped." He breathed long and hard. "I would've gone after her, but I was expecting your human body to fail. I was expecting to have to call you back. Little did I know, your body was no longer human. Little did I know, your blood was so full of iron it would magnetize Stella's dust."

I turned to face him. His face wobbled. "The new hunters—they attacked me this morning. You would've known this if you'd come back, but you didn't come back for me." Tears glided freely down my cheeks. "Kajika was there, though. He saved me." I spoke slowly, with great difficulty, but at least, I spoke. "One of their arrows hit me. He pulled it out, then used his blood to heal me. I told him not to, but I was too weak to push him away. So I don't know what the hell's happening inside me right now." I blotted the tears with the sleeves of my hospital gown. "Why don't *you* tell me, Ace? *Am I* a huntress?"

"You healed and confiscated a power."

I hung my head and lowered my voice to a mere whisper to ask the defining question. "But do I smell like them?"

His lingering silence coupled with his curled lip told me that I did.

How could this have happened to me? I wiped my cheeks. I thought I'd have a choice, but Holly had lied. She'd lied about everything!

I turned back toward the window and studied the strange tattoo wreathing my neck. "Why are you still here, Ace?" I swallowed hard, and the dust underneath my skin shifted in its new tracks.

Ace stood behind me. Our gazes locked in the blackened glass. His face grew closer to mine. "You don't smell like them."

My heart missed a beat. "I don't?"

He shook his head.

Could Kajika's blood *not* have transformed me?

He lowered his gaze to the inches of linoleum separating my bare feet from his brown suede shoes. "But you're different, so I don't know if it means anything."

"Is there any way to find out?" Had there been anything fae about me before? "I resuscitated a bird!" I spun toward him. "A long time ago. Apparently that's a faerie quality. Maybe I could try to heal another animal. There must be a vet clinic nearby—"

He raised his gaze back to mine, eyes finally soft. "How about you rest a little first? You did *almost* die."

"Except I didn't. Besides, I *need* to know."

He pulled at the roots of his hair, mussing it up even more than it was already. "Have you ever heard the saying, *ignorance is bliss*? Once you know, it'll change everything."

"More than it has already?"

"Cat, if you're—if you're a huntress, then—then . . ."

"We can't be friends? That's so very nineteenth-century of you." I smiled.

He didn't seem the least bit amused.

"If being in my presence isn't torture, then I don't see why we can't hang out. Borgo and Ishtu were friends." *Sort of.* "Jacobiah and Negongwa were friend*ly*."

"For fuck's sake, Cat, I don't want to be your *friend*."

I pushed a strand of hair behind my ear, but my fingers shook too hard and I missed, and the long lock came rushing back around my face.

"Why did Stella attack you, Cat?"

So that's why he'd stayed . . . to take my statement.

I was so offended I almost didn't answer. "She attacked me because I told her she was an awful person."

"So you didn't threaten to kill her?"

"Have I ever threatened to kill anyone?"

"Me, once or twice."

I glared at him. "I gave you what you wanted, now please leave." My words were cold and flat.

His eyes gleamed as though the fire inside his veins skipped behind his pupils. "You didn't give me what I wanted."

"What else do you want, Ace?" I asked, all at once disheartened and offended. "What other confession or testimony do you need from me?"

"Confession?" he grunted. "I'm here because your brand fucking flickered on my hand tonight, Cat."

Of course. My magical leash.

I bit down so hard on my lower lip that I thought I would draw blood. That would surely make him flee. After all, it was surely now ten times more lethal than it had been when Borgo had used it to commit suicide.

"My brand flared many times since Detroit. You didn't come. Not once."

He growled as though exasperated with *me*. "I've been waiting for the Night of Mist to end. That's why I didn't come. With Cruz and Lily, we've been guarding the portals. There are hundreds of them! I couldn't exactly leave."

"Yet you did."

"Because the brand—it flashed and *fucking* fizzled." His eyes bore into mine. "I thought you'd—I thought you'd died."

"How unfortunate that I didn't, huh?"

"Yeah. Would've made things a hell of a lot less complicated if you had."

I flinched.

"You really have no clue what I want?" His voice had become as rough as sandpaper.

Suddenly, it dawned on me. "You want me to read the book! You managed to get it printed, and now you want me to read it."

"What?"

"The book." I folded my arms in front of my chest. "You found the box with the metal plates that Stella stole and you got it printed, didn't you?"

"What the hell are you talking about?"

"It's a yes or no question."

His jaw ticked and ticked. "I did recover the box, but the metal plates had been melted." His anger transformed into something else—regret? Guilt? "Holly left instructions that if a faerie were to ask for the box, everything inside be destroyed. If I hadn't shown up, you would've gotten your book." His voice was low, begrudging. "I'm sorry I tried to save the day."

Like a block of ice melting, my tight stance thawed and my arms unknotted, plummeting back along my sides. "But Stella said she stole the box—"

"She was probably trying to rile you up."

Boy, had it worked. "Ace, don't blame yourself. If Mr. Thompson knew what you were, then he knew what Cass was."

"*She* doesn't even know what she is. And he's not a hunter, so there's no way he could've sensed her." He walked over to the window, splayed his hands on the sill, and looked out at the dark town.

"What is he then?"

"A friend of your ancestors. A knowledgeable friend. I didn't detect anything magical about him, though." He pressed his lips together, then relaxed them slightly. "I left him in pretty poor shape."

"Will he live?"

Ace turned his head toward me. "Unlike some people may believe, I don't go around killing people."

I didn't say anything, just stared at his unblemished knuckles that belied the punches he'd rained on the printshop manager.

"Are you angry I punished him?" he asked, after a long silence.

I looked back at the reflection of his face in the glass. "No." Another stretch of stillness swept over the small hospital room, over us. I kept my eyes locked on his the entire time. "I *am* a little hurt, though, that you treated me like a traitor earlier."

"Same here." He pressed away from the window and turned back toward me.

"I'm hurt that you don't want to be my friend," I continued.

"Why does that hurt?"

"Because, Ace, believe it or not, I care about you."

"If you cared about me, you'd trust me."

"Like you trust me?" I volleyed back. My breaths came in short, sharp bursts, popping angrily against my palate and tongue. "Now, can you please tell me why you're still here? I'm tired. I'm really tired. And I don't feel like playing any more guessing games."

As though fueled by his emotions, the heat of his skin seemed to have doubled. It blazed in the narrow space between our bodies. Licked my skin.

I shuddered as it replaced the chill.

His eyes absorbed my every twitch, narrowed on my tremulous mouth. He looked pissed off to no end, and for the life of me, I didn't understand why. I'd answered all of his questions. He'd answered all of mine.

What else was there left to fight about?

What else was there to be angry about?

"Ace, what do you want?" I asked gently.

In answer, he seized both sides of my face and brought his lips down on mine. His swift breaths filled my mouth, warmed my tongue, set every inch of skin on my body ablaze.

His scorching fingers traveled down the length of my neck, the curve of my shoulders, wound through my hair, and cupped the back of my head. He coaxed my lips farther apart, touched his tongue to mine. The taste of him, the warmth of him made me dizzy and euphoric. It brought me back to Detroit, to the rooftop restaurant where I'd burned with humiliation.

Now I burned with desire.

Exquisite desire.

I finally kissed him back, matching his hunger, his momentum, his intensity. I kissed him for all the times he'd saved me, and for all the times he'd protected me, for all the times we'd fought, and for all the times we'd made up.

I kissed him because I'd been dreaming of kissing him every second of the day we'd spent apart . . . the day I thought I'd lost him forever.

I was afraid to stop, afraid that if I pulled away, he'd never kiss me again. So I didn't. And he didn't either.

I locked my arms around his neck and pulled him closer to me until our chests were flush, until his heartbeats penetrated mine.

Breathless, we finally broke apart, but neither of us let the other go. My lips felt as though they were on fire. I licked them to make sure they weren't, and then I licked them again because my saliva acted like a welcomed cooling balm.

Ace's eyes roved over them. He didn't talk. One of his hands still tugged and weaved through my long hair; the other simply lingered on my exposed spine, right above the elastic waist of my black panties.

At least, whoever had undressed me hadn't stripped me bare.

"I thought you wanted to kill me," I whispered against his mouth.

His lips curved. "Sometimes, I do." His voice was hoarse. "Most times, though, I just want to take you somewhere private." He tugged on my hair, tipping my head back.

I sucked in air through my teeth, which turned his grin downright cocky.

"And just so you know, I'm not using *captis* on you."

I matched his cocky grin, trailed my fingers lightly over his jaw. When he shivered, I said, "Maybe *I* am, though."

He laughed.

"Why are you laughing?"

He caressed the slope of my neck, his fingertips trailing over the burial place of Stella's dust which thrashed hard, as though begging to be set loose.

I caught Ace's fingers in mine, because he was *still* chuckling.

"It only works on humans." He pressed his lips against the skin at the base of my neck, against my tattoo, and I shuddered right along with it. "But I really wish you *were* using *captis*." He kissed his way up my neck, across my jaw. He stopped against the corner of my lips, letting his mouth hover there. "I would've really liked to have magic to blame for how fast I'm falling for you."

His confession made my already unsteady heart trip over several beats.

Suddenly, a thought struck. "Does it work on hunters?"

"What?"

"Does *captis* work on hunters?"

"No."

"Use it on me."

"What?"

"If it still works, then that'll mean I'm not—it'll mean I haven't changed."

His gaze leveled on my neck, on Stella's trapped dust. "And what if it doesn't?"

"I would hope it wouldn't change anything." I tried to catch his attention, but he was focusing all of it on my new mark.

I suddenly felt his lips on my neck, except his mouth was nowhere near my skin.

His hands were balled at his sides, yet I felt them stroke down my rib cage.

I felt the heat of him, the energy and the strength of him.

I felt pressure and caresses in places he was merely looking at.

I tipped my face toward his and kissed the corners of his immobile mouth, then untucked his shirt, gliding my nails against the hard planes of his stomach.

His breaths hitched.

I did it again, combed my nails around his waist this time, splayed my hands on the base of his spine.

He closed his eyes.

The audacity that had possessed me to undress him broke, but so did the skin of fear which had filmed my heart since Kajika had healed me.

"It worked," I whispered.

He bowed his head, lids coming up.

"I'm not—I haven't—" I started, stopped, full of so many emotions.

He crooked a finger underneath my chin and tilted my face up. "It would've been too late to matter." He kissed me, and I thought my heart was going to burst, not only from his touch, but also from his words. "It's been too late for a long time." He nuzzled the skin behind my ear. Kissed me there. "Feel free to keep undressing me."

I grinned. "Nice try."

As he linked his hands behind my waist and realigned his face with mine, he shot me a brazen grin. Too quickly, though, the teasing curve became fraught.

"What?"

"Nothing."

"Ace, you think all over your face. What is it?"

He inhaled deeply. Exhaled even deeper. "What about Kajika?"

"What about him?"

"When you said goodbye to me back in Detroit—"

"I lied."

His gaze flitted over my face. "You killed me with that lie."

"I killed myself with that lie. I was afraid you'd be punished for taking a liking to the enemy." I stared into the infinite blue depths of his eyes, desperate to believe we could truly be together in spite of all that we were, and all that we were not. "I still am."

"I'm the prince of Neverra, Cat." He nudged my lips apart and pressed a featherlight kiss to them. "I dare anyone to lay a finger on me and keep their hand attached to the rest of their body . . . or their heads."

"Ace," I hissed, wrinkling my nose.

"What?" A brazen smile canted his mouth.

I tried to toss away the image of beheadings. "You're *truly* not scared?"

"Oh, I'm terrified"—he kissed my top lip and then my lower one —"that you'll change your mind."

"I'm serious."

"So am I, Cat. So am I." His neck straightened as his face lifted away from my flushed one. He drew his thumbs across my cheek-bones, then down the frame of my face, before threading his long fingers once again through the black mass of my hair. "I've never had anything to lose before, and *that* is terrifying."

51

THE STARS

News of my "anaphylactic shock" had spread around Rowan like a forest fire. And I'd only been home a couple of hours. At lunch, when I'd glanced at the strawberry on top of my dad's cheesecake, he'd gulped it down at record speed, reminding me of what the doctor had said.

In truth, the man had simply said what I'd influenced him to say—that I'd swiped a strawberry from Astra's tray and had a severe allergic reaction to it. I hadn't been a hundred percent sure it would work, but miraculously, it had.

My silly feat had set my ego and hand aglow.

I'd traced the 'W' and thought of Ace.

Thought of the night we'd spent together.

Thought of his lips. Of his hands. Of his eyes. Of his words. Of the dust he'd left behind to cloak my neck.

Before he'd flown back to Neverra to patrol the portals, I'd insisted he take it back, but he hadn't. He'd reassured me his fire could do just as much damage to an enemy as his dust. I wasn't reassured.

I conjured up our kiss several times during the course of the day in an attempt to accelerate my pulse. I'd watch my hand with bated breath until the 'W' revealed itself in all its glorious splendor. Only then would I relax, because as long as it existed, so did Ace.

But my relief was short-lived. Until the Night of Mist ended, until Ace returned, there would be no true solace.

I checked my watch for the umpteenth time that day—9:05 PM. In fifty-five earthly minutes, dawn would spill over Neverra and put an end to Ace's guarding duty.

During the early hours of the morning, curled up against me on the hospital bed, he'd told me all about the precarious night. Once a Neverrian month, the Unseelie could leave their underground home and the Seelie could act without consequence.

It was a night where everything became permissible. Where fae could desecrate their marriage beds without reproof. Where they could turn their brains to mush by ingesting too much mallow. Where the marsh-dwellers could penetrate the palace and revel alongside the mist-dwellers and the grotto-dwellers.

It sounded wild, and not in a good way.

I hadn't wanted Ace to return even though I understood his need to. Before drifting off, I'd made him swear not to leave without saying goodbye.

I'd awoken to him standing by the window, his broad body outlined in pink and purple light. I watched him in silence for a while, wondering what was going through his mind.

Did he regret what we'd done?

My heart had somersaulted at the possibility, sparking my brand, giving me away.

He'd turned around, a smile straining his haggard face. I didn't spot regret, only exhaustion.

Dad had barreled into the room at that exact moment, barring me and Ace from talking any further about Neverra.

He didn't kiss me in front of Dad—neither of us were ready for that. He'd merely squeezed my fingers, holding them a beat too long for friends, and promised to stop by Rowan later tonight.

That was almost sixteen hours ago, and his absence was driving me mad.

High on adrenaline and nerves, I hadn't been able to do anything besides gnaw the life out of my lip. That I still had a lip was a miracle.

I'd been so wired that after an early dinner with Dad, which included a lot of freshly squeezed lemon juice on his pan-fried fish —I wasn't sure how my body would react to lemon so I avoided it— I dabbed on makeup and curled the ends of my hair. Then I put on my black leather leggings and a sleeveless turtleneck. Yes, Ace's dust still cloaked my neck but I desperately wanted him to take it back.

9:55 PM.

I went over to my window and gazed up at the night sky. Clouds as dense and shiny as steel-wool obscured the moon and the stars. I watched and I waited for a brilliant body to puncture the thick cover. Ten minutes later, no body had dropped from the sky.

I texted Ace. My message went unanswered.

I trundled downstairs where George Jones and Dad were watching a basketball game, chugging down beers as though they were back in high school. "I'm going over to Bee's for a little while."

"Okay, honey. Don't come home too late." His fatherly concern filed away some of my edginess.

I promised him I wouldn't, wished the sheriff a pleasant evening, and then grabbed my keys and drove over to Morgan Street. After parking down the block, I peered up at the sky again. There wasn't even the faintest glimmer of light.

It was the darkest night ever.

When I walked into Bee's, the few diners lingering over drinks and slices of pie peered at me. I fired off brisk waves as I made my way to the bar where Cass was drying glasses.

"Did you manage to rest?" she asked.

"Nope." I climbed onto one of the bar stools and folded one leg over the other. My top leg bobbed feverishly.

She slotted the glass down next to the others on the wooden shelf behind her, then leaned over the bar. "I've been meaning to ask you something." Her expression was so serious that I stopped joggling my knee.

Had she found out about Astra? Whatever had happened to her body? Had Ace managed to get it out of the hospital before it had turned to ash?

"I found something in your sock drawer," she said.

What had I put in my sock drawer?

"A handwritten dictionary. At least, that's what I think it is."

My pulse faltered.

She peeked at me through her long bangs. "What language is Faeli?"

"A vernacular language some Gottwas used." The lie slid right off my tongue, but I peppered it with some truth: "It was spoken by their ancestors, the, um, Faelies."

"Never heard of them," she said.

"They were a neighboring tribe."

She frowned, which sparked my heart rate and my hand. Thankfully it wasn't in Cass's line of sight. I still worried she would spot the brand's glow if she looked hard enough.

"Ace has Native ancestry?"

"Huh?"

"Some of the words he spoke the night we came home from that ultimate fighting match resembled the ones in that dictionary."

I tucked a lock of hair behind my ear. "Probably a coincidence." I fired my gaze toward the door that had just jingled. Disappointment flared behind my breastbone at the sight of old Mr. Hamilton. "Then again, what would I know?"

"I'm pretty sure you know a lot of things about Ace. After all, you guys spend *a lot* of time together. Feel like telling me what's going on between the two of you?"

"Not yet."

Her irises danced with curiosity. "I really want to know."

306

"And I really want to tell you, just not tonight."

She pushed away from the bar to uncork a bottle of prosecco. She filled a tall glass with ice cubes and splashed the golden liquid over it. "If anyone asks, it's sparkling apple juice." She winked at me as she put the bottle back inside the wine fridge. "Where is he, anyway?"

"Working."

"What exactly does the son of the richest man in the universe do?"

"I don't know," I said, because confessing he was protecting faerie portals was out of the question. Plus honestly, I had no clue what his princely duties consisted of.

"So if you guys aren't discussing your lives, what exactly are you doing when you hang out?"

Heat flushed my cheeks. "Stop fishing or I won't tell you a thing, ever." I took a long swallow of my wine, relishing the frosty taste of it.

"Usually, I bore her with my family problems while she drones on about her long-lost relatives."

My gaze bounded upward. "You're back," I said, my voice catching.

Ace smiled.

Whatever heat had filled my face was nothing compared to the one that swarmed through me at the sight of him.

"Told you I would be."

Someone called out Cass's name; I could've kissed that someone.

Actually, the only person I wanted to kiss was sitting on the bar stool next to me.

He was really the last person I should've thought about kissing, though.

"Did—Is it over?" I whispered.

"Until next month, it is."

"Did any—even try?"

He shook his head. "I'm hoping they might not be able to read the book after all. Perhaps it was just your family."

He swiveled my stool so that I faced him. As he pulled his hands away, his fingers grazed my thighs. I half-expected the leather to catch fire because the spot he touched was scorching hot and palpitated with a life of its own, a lot like the frenzied dust around my neck.

Speaking of. "I want you to take your"—I looked around to make sure no one was in hearing range—"dust back."

"And do what with it?"

"Protect yourself."

"I have fire, Cat."

"I know, but you're in a town full of hunters."

"They wouldn't fare too well if I set them ablaze."

"Please, Ace, please take it back. I'll wear scarves, or I'll tell Dad I got a temporary tattoo."

"No."

I narrowed my eyes. "Fine. I'll release it, then."

A muscle leapt in his jaw. "Don't you dare. Not only does Stella not deserve her dust back, but I also don't want you carving up your pretty neck."

I wrinkled my nose. "Is that the only way?"

At his nod, my stomach contracted.

"Done with your wine?" he asked.

The glass was half-full. The thought caught me off guard. I'd never considered anything half-full.

"It's juice," I said for the sake of eavesdroppers. I didn't want Cass to get in trouble for serving me alcohol.

One of his dark eyebrows lifted.

"I'm nineteen," I murmured. "Not allowed to drink yet."

"You're so law abiding, Miss Price."

"You know me," I said.

"I'm starting to, but I'd like to get to know you a little better."

His hand hadn't breached the walls of my chest—after all, the male was no vampire, only a faerie—yet it felt as though his fingers were kneading the great scarlet muscle.

He seized my glass and downed it. "Now you're done. Let's go."

"Where?"

"You'll see." Ace stood and extended his hand.

I didn't take it, still too worried about sparking little fires that would get back to my father, or make the rounds on social media.

"Aw, are you guys leaving already?" Cass had just returned and was wiping her hands on her black waist-apron.

"Terribly sorry, Cassidy, but I need Cat's medical advice on something."

Cass released a very unlady-like snort. "Well if you get bored, come back!"

Nervous as I was, I turned and blew her a kiss.

Once we were outside, away from everyone, Ace laced his fingers through mine and tugged me toward the parking lot behind the inn. And then he wrapped his arms around my waist tightly. "Hook your legs around me."

I blushed. "I can't do th—"

He lifted off the ground, and I found out that I could do just that.

I hooked my arms around his neck and my legs around his waist like a koala, and then I prayed a little. To all my gods.

We soared upward, surrounded by cold air and dark silence. Keeping one arm around his neck, I stuck the other out toward the thick clouds. I'd always dreamt of touching clouds. In my child's imagination, they'd feel like fluffy wool. In reality, they felt like fog, like tiny drops of suspended rain. The dampness coated my skin, but I didn't shiver. Ace's body kept me warm.

Slowly, we glided farther up until we broke through the clouds. Surrounded by miles of stars, Ace stopped moving, and we hovered in silence.

"You take all your girlfriends up here?"

"I've never had a girlfriend."

I looked away from the glimmering night and into his gleaming eyes. "In a century and a half, you've never had a girlfriend?"

"I've never dated anyone long enough to call her my girlfriend."

"What's long enough?"

"A couple days."

My chest locked tight. "Is that all I'll get with you?"

"Depends how good you are in bed."

"Be serious."

"When I get nervous, I say stupid shit."

My heart pounded with hope. "You're nervous right now?"

He gazed down at me through his dark lashes. "Nervous that you'll slip away from me," he said in a low, hoarse voice.

"Better not let go, then."

"I wasn't talking about tonight."

"I wasn't, either," I said, raising my face toward his.

He met me halfway. Bobbing in the inky ocean of stars and silence, Ace kissed me like no one had ever kissed me before, with the most ravenous sweetness and the gentlest hunger.

It was the sort of kiss fairytales were written about.

Except my life wasn't a fairytale, even though it was filled with faeries.

EPILOGUE
ACE

I landed on the palace's stone esplanade and walked the rest of the way to the dining room, striding through the grand hall with its vaulted ceiling and bobbing faelights; past the dais upon which stood the crooked tree my grandfather Maximus had had carved into a throne.

The fibrous, tawny leaves flapped like tiny palms as I breezed past them, in a hurry to wrap up the family gathering, so I could portal back to the girl waiting for me in Rowan.

The girl who was finally mine.

As loud as I wanted to clamor it from the top of every *calimbor* in the kingdom, my nascent relationship needed to remain a secret a while longer, just until I could figure out a way to end my sham engagement without it costing me my life.

I nodded to the *lucionaga* manning the tall golden doors ahead. They swung both open, even though one would've sufficed.

My arrival caused a great stir among my father and his entourage of sycophants who'd all gotten used to my prolonged absences. I loathed the palace I'd grown up in, because it was cold, like the monarch who ruled it, and garish, like the courtiers who populated it.

"Ah, my heir deigns to grace us with his presence." My father sagged against the upholstered armrest of his throne-like chair, which took up one end of the gargantuan table, blue eyes hazed by faerie wine. "We started"—he hiccupped—"without you."

"Naturally." *Skies, give me the strength to endure this shitshow.*

Mother blinked my way, then blinked away, high—as always— on her favorite drug. Although ingesting mallow in small doses was no worse than a glass of wine, snorting the drug frittered away brains.

In my youth, I'd attempted to wean my mother off the stuff by razing her stock of powdered leaves and setting fire to every mallow tree on Neverra. My 'misplaced' concern had earned me lashings that had torn my skin and obliterated my faith in parental affection.

"A toast." Father raised his golden goblet, and his sixty or so minions crammed around the dining table followed suit.

Only my sister didn't raise her glass.

My sister *and* Cruz.

Both squared their shoulders, bracing themselves for whatever fresh invective would roll off the king's tongue.

"To the family that we bear"—I didn't miss the curl of Father's lip as he stared between Lily and me—"and to the one that we choose." His gaze traveled over his guests, an imperious smile stretching his face.

"Touching speech, Father." I traipsed over to the last empty seat —between my sister and my intended—and tucked my heavy chair under the *calimbor* that had been sacrificed so that my grandfather could have a dining table worthy of a king. "Baby's well, Angelina?"

The dark-haired faerie, who was several centuries younger than my father, stroked the swollen abdomen that she forever kept bare so everyone could spot the royal bastard she carried. "Our son is well, Ace."

With a snort, I seized my goblet and drank, hoping that a slight buzz would make this tedious affair slightly less tedious. "A boy, huh?"

313

"Not just a boy." She sat up taller. "The future king."

Delusional and an idiot, just the way my father liked his women. I could only pray my half-brother wouldn't grow into a callous half-wit.

Although I was far from perfect, I was principled and empathetic—qualities my father had tried to beat out of me, the same way he'd tried to beat words out of my sister's throat.

He'd failed at both tasks, which naturally despaired him to no end. Thankfully, he'd never taken his ire out on the woman who'd made it her life's mission to keep Lily and me from rotting on our family tree's branch.

If he'd lifted a finger on Veroli, that gold wreath tangled in his reddish-blond mane would have, at present, graced the top of *my* head.

From across the table, Lyoh Vega narrowed her toxic green eyes on me, posture as rigid as the picket-fence of *lucionaga* guarding the room. "The hunters are keeping you busy, I hear."

"They're a lively bunch. Are you planning a trip to Earth? Kajika mentioned he'd quite enjoy catching up."

Dark smoke coiled off her formfitting black dress as though she were about to puff into her dragon alter ego. "The only thing that savage would enjoy would be planting a bloodied rowan arrow through my heart."

Lily pinched my leg, a plea not to stoke Lyoh's fire.

Fine. I'd behave.

The thought of behaving made my attention swerve toward the *draca's* son. Ever since Lily suggested he and I swap brands, Cruz had become a mix of contemplative and testy. We'd never fought before Catori. Although, could we call it fighting when I'd won?

I lifted the goblet and savored the wine, *and* my win. I was petty like that.

Not to mention, I was still pissed off at him for having hurt my sister who looked upon him as though he was her entire world, while he looked upon her as though she were a mere cog in his.

I never thought I'd suspect Cruz of using Lily and me for personal gain, but I was man enough to admit I'd misjudged people before.

I'd misjudged Cat, after all.

What if I'd misjudged the faerie I'd always considered like a brother?

Over Lily's head, his green eyes met mine. They were guarded and flat, and although they didn't smack of malice, they glinted with something unsettling.

What secrets do you keep, my friend?

ACKNOWLEDGMENTS

Thank you to my Dream Team: Theresea, Vanessa, Katie & Astrid. You are all rock stars! Nothing I write is allowed to see the day without all of you reading it first. You challenge me and console me, correct me and cajole me. You are simply the bestest (and yes, I know this isn't a real word, but it should be).

To Jessica Nelson, you are a fabulous editor. I hope you enjoy correcting my books, because I have a lot more coming your way.

To Tia Bach, thank you for reading through my manuscript and teaching me about pronouns.

To wonderful, amazing Rachel Theus Cass, you complete me, or at least, you complete my sentences. ;P

To my readers, thank you for accompanying me on all my fantastical journeys. Hope you're ready to portal to Neverra... See you on the other side.

To my family, thank you for allowing me time off from my responsibilities and from you. I know disappearing in my writing cave isn't your idea of great mothering, but I believe it does make me a better mother. And a better role model for my girls. Sweethearts, you can have it all.

Adam, I promise that one day, I will write a book with you. And yes, we can include magical watches in our story.

To my husband, I simply love you.

ALSO BY OLIVIA WILDENSTEIN

PARANORMAL ROMANCE

The Lost Clan series

ROSE PETAL GRAVES

ROWAN WOOD LEGENDS

RISING SILVER MIST

RAGING RIVAL HEARTS

RECKLESS CRUEL HEIRS

The Boulder Wolves series

A PACK OF BLOOD AND LIES

A PACK OF VOWS AND TEARS

A PACK OF LOVE AND HATE

A PACK OF STORMS AND STARS

Angels of Elysium series

FEATHER

CELESTIAL

STARLIGHT

The Kingdom of Crows series

HOUSE OF BEATING WINGS

HOUSE OF POUNDING HEARTS

HOUSE OF STRIKING OATHS

The Quatrefoil Chronicles series

OF WICKED BLOOD

OF TAINTED HEART

YA CONTEMPORARY ROMANCE

GHOSTBOY, CHAMELEON & THE DUKE OF GRAFFITI

NOT ANOTHER LOVE SONG

YA ROMANTIC SUSPENSE

Cold Little Games series

COLD LITTLE LIES

COLD LITTLE GAMES

COLD LITTLE HEARTS

ABOUT THE AUTHOR

Olivia is the byproduct of a meet-rude in a Parisian discotheque that turned into an epic love story spanning several decades. Naturally, this shaped the way she viewed romance.

After meeting her own Prince Charming—in a Parisian discotheque of all places—she decided to put fingers to keyboard and craft love stories for a living.

None of her characters have ever met in a Parisian nightclub... as of yet.

WEBSITE
HTTP://OLIVIAWILDENSTEIN.COM

FACEBOOK READER GROUP
OLIVIA'S DARLING READERS